KINGDOMS OF HELL

BY

STEPHANIE HUDSON

Kingdoms of Hell
The Transfusion Saga #7
Copyright © 2020 Stephanie Hudson
Published by Hudson Indie Ink
www.hudsonindieink.com

This book is licensed for your personal enjoyment only.
This book may not be re-sold or given away to other people. If you would like to share this book with another person, please purchase an additional copy for each recipient. If you're reading this book and did not purchase it, or it wasn't purchased for your use only, then please return to your favourite book retailer and purchase your own copy. Thank you for respecting the hard work of this author.
All rights reserved.
This is a work of fiction. Names, characters, places, brands, media, and incidents are either the product of the authors imagination or are used fictitiously. The author acknowledges the trademark status and trademark owners of various products referred to in this work of fiction, which have been used without permission. The publication/use of these trademarks is not authorised, associated with, or sponsored by the trademark owners.
Kingdoms of Hell/Stephanie Hudson – 2nd ed.
ISBN-13 - 978-1-913769-42-0

This is one book that I most definitely had to dedicate to my boys, one being, at this point in time, a redheaded rascal who likes to bite and growl. The other, who has taken on the role of protecting his younger brother from the first day he was born. I can only hope that the love they have for each other will grow into one mirrored in the relationships I write in my books. That together they will always want to look out for their big sister and of course, love their mum and dad.

My dedication to my little Ava bird will always be in the children's book I wrote for you. This one, is for the boys.

I love you my children.

xxx

For Jack and Halen.

WARNING

This book contains explicit sexual content, some graphic language and a highly additive dominate Vampire King.

This book has been written by an UK Author with a mad sense of humour. Which means the following story contains a mixture of Northern English slang, dialect, regional colloquialisms and other quirky spellings that have been intentionally included to make the story and dialogue more realistic for modern day characters.

Thanks for reading x

PROLOGUE

A *Phantom of the Future*
That was what this was now. So, as the beautiful notes of the Phantom of the Opera played, I was forced to look down at what caused it as my own image spun around in my hand. One surrounded by the dying leaves that I had failed to stop from falling from the Tree of Souls.

The words being sang out in my mind, becoming something more than a song we once danced to.

It became a symbolic glimpse into my own future this time. For I had seen how Lucius' life began, and this was now my turn to see how my own ended.

'…in dreams he came, that voice which calls to me and speaks my name…'

"Amelia, I am waiting for you."

And then the glass shatters and the figures of us both slip from my hands. And as they fall to the ground, I know only one thing is certain…

I had failed.

CHAPTER ONE

EVERYTHING

"I stole the soul of an Angel and that of...*A first born Vampire.*" The second the words were spoken I felt my entire world crumbling around me. I couldn't believe what I was hearing! I couldn't believe that all this time he knew what I was, or more like... *what I could have been before he stole it from me!*

"*Hh...h...how...?*" I said as I barely heard the whisper that was stuttered through my utter agony, unable to raise my head from looking at the floor. But this wasn't enough for Lucius.

"Amelia, look at me...*Amelia, please*... please, *fuck*... just look at me," Lucius pleaded as I remained there on the cold broken stone floor feeling as if my entire world had been split open and torn apart. Everything I had given this man! Every single fucking piece of me and yet more he took, even the parts of me I didn't know fucking existed!

He took them all.

"*Please,*" he pleaded and finally I raised my head in time for him to see the heavy tears start to fall. Then he told me,

"I...didn't know...I swear to you, I didn't do this...not intentionally...please, you have to believe..." His broken declaration did little to comfort me, hence why I shouted,

"Believe you...believe you! How could I ever believe a single thing you have to say to me? How...how...tell me, Lucius...*how could I?*" I ended this on a sob of words making him wince at the sound. I then watched as my tears fell to the ground and I frowned the second I saw it hit one of the roots under the broken stone floor, momentarily turning it back to grey from the charred black it had been. What did that mean?

"Hey! Get the fuck away from her!" Lucius shouted, making me look up in time to see him at the shimmering wall between us, now looking beyond furious at the three headed creature at my back.

"But Master, we wouldn't hurt her."

"No not I, not he, not we... for we are the Keepers of Three."

"Mnkn knuhheee." They all said in turn, but Lucius looked less than convinced.

"Amelia, get up and walk towards me, do so quickly," Lucius ordered, clearly not trusting them. But this also had me questioning why. What else was for me to discover? Which was why my gaze turned suspicious before I asked,

"Why?" Lucius flinched back a fraction at the question and I knew in that tiny reaction there was something more.

"Why? Why do you think?!" he snapped making me grit my teeth and stop myself from asking if he was seriously acting this way now because of everything I had just learned. Because the only one in this room who had hurt me had been him, not the Keepers of Three.

He had stolen part of my fucking soul, for fuck sake!

"They haven't hurt me," I told him, barely able to keep from screaming this at him.

"Not yet!" he snapped, making me unable to hold back from throwing some truth his way.

"No, the only one who has hurt me is you and right now, I trust them more than I do you!" I said, lashing out at him, this time making him jerk back as if I had struck him physically.

"Amelia, I can explain, and I will…"

"Well, that will make a nice change!" I bit out sarcastically, only he ignored me as he continued quickly,

"But first you need to fucking listen to me. Now, get up and…"

"No!" I told him cutting him off again and this time he gritted his teeth and snarled,

"Now is not the time to be foolish, girl!"

Naturally at this I'd had enough and he knew it when I picked myself up off the ground, getting back to my feet, then raised my head to look at him dead on. Doing all of this while I asked the Keepers behind me,

"You said that you see, hear and speak of all that the Blood of Kings commands…right?" Lucius scowled at me and said,

"Amelia, what are you up to?" I ignored him and turned to face them, this time repeating my question,

"That's what you said, right?" Each of them nodded before repeating,

"As the Seekers we seek…"

"For all the King's memories as the Keepers we keep."

"Mmmen emek." I ignored Lucius' warning growl and instead took a deep breath, knowing what I now had to do. So, I took a few steps closer towards the Keepers of Three, again having to ignore the growls of disapproval behind me as Lucius' anger grew. Then, after another shuddered breath, I demanded in a stern, determined tone,

"Then show me."

"What?!" Lucius' cry of outrage was again disregarded as

all three heads turned and looked at each other in a questioning way.

"Can you do it...can you... any of you...can you show me?" I asked making Lucius roar in anger,

"NO! DON'T YOU FUCKING DARE!" I looked behind me and nodded to the barrier between us and asked,

"Can he get through it?" He looked beyond murderous and I knew that if he did manage it, the first thing he would do was get rid of his own threat and rip the Keepers apart, meaning they would be joined no more. Which was why I was glad when they told me,

"No, only one may enter."

"For Keepers we seek."

"Monen mnol mmmut mals eeke."

"What did he say?" I asked nodding to the one with a hand permanently in his mouth.

"One soul at a time or the walls won't break." I looked back at Lucius to see him telling me,

"Amelia, don't fucking do this!" I shook my head at him before asking the Keepers of Three,

"So, you can show me?"

"You wish to see?"

"The life of three?"

"Mloood eeemee?" I nodded for them to translate the mumbled answer again.

"The blood of He," they told me and I swallowed hard before telling them,

"Yes, I wish to see."

"AMELIA, NO!" Lucius roared and I sighed before walking over to the barrier to speak with him, knowing that at the very least with what I was about to do, he deserved to know my reasons for it. I saw him release a sigh of relief, one he obviously didn't know yet was premature.

"Good girl, now try walking through the barrier, as I think it will allow you to come back through if I force it," he said looking around the sides of the tunnel's opening as if he was looking for its weakness or something. His false hope made what I needed to do next even harder, despite the mountain of reasons stacked up against him of why I had no choice.

"I am afraid I can't do that, Lucius," I told him, making him tense and I watched as his whole body turned rigid, as if my admission had suddenly made him turn to stone. Then I watched as he clearly struggled to simmer down his anger enough to speak to me, no doubt being cautious with my fragile state of mind.

"Yes, you can, Amelia, and *you will*…now just step through and we will figure this out…*together.*" His emphasis on that last word couldn't be missed and I closed my eyes against the pain of it, telling him,

"It's too late for that."

"No! No it isn't! It's never too late for you to listen to reason and act on it!" he snapped making me open my eyes and look at him, I mean really look at him. And what I found were so many emotions on his face, it was clear to see. Even if they were all merging together as one. His anger, his frustration, the hurt, worry, pain and panic were all there. And whenever he looked past me, a deep hatred for the Keepers, who he no doubt deemed responsible for all that was happening now, was seen in crimson eyes. But what he didn't yet understand was that he was the cause of all of this.

His lies.

His secrets.

His thievery.

"I am acting for my own reasons, Lucius, because you had your chance. You could have told me everything, but you chose not to and now, well that time has passed you by and I'm sorry to say but the result of what happens next is your own doing," I said making him tear his face away from me in a furious and frustrated way.

"How could have I told you, Amelia? When was there a fucking time to tell you something like that!?" he snapped making me force myself to hold on so as the tears wouldn't rise again. Then, as calmly as I could, I told him,

"There was a time, Lucius."

"You would have hated me," was his pained reply and I shook my head, saddened that he thought so.

"Then that is your mistake made, for you should have trusted me," I told him, making him hang his head as if it weighed too much to hold up any longer. But then, they often say the weight of guilt could be too much for some people.

"Then you're right, that was my mistake, but I promise it is not as it seems and if you would just trust me now and walk through here, then I will tell you everything, but please... please, by the Gods, Amelia, just don't fucking do this, don't ask them to show you," he pleaded with me, making me frown before asking him,

"Why? Why is this so important to you if you have nothing left to hide?" The second I asked this I knew, for I saw it in his eyes and I fucking knew! He was still lying to me! I tore myself away from the sight of him, turning my back on him and making him say my name again,

"Amelia, please... fucking Hell, just look at me! You're right, I am keeping something else from you, but you have to trust me, it was only ever done to protect you!"

"Protect me!" I shouted whipping back around to face him, the look of disbelief clear on my face.

"Yes," he answered quickly.

"Protect me from what, the fucking truth!?" I saw Lucius take a deep breath before he admitted on a whisper,

"From yourself." I frowned at him at the same time his answer made me take a jerked step back.

"From myself?" I questioned as if needing it confirmed that this was what he really meant.

"You have to trust me here for I promise you it is not as you believe it to be and if you would just take that one step I will show you that you can trust me… just reach out and give me your hand Sweetheart and let me reward your trust with the truth," he said reaching out his hand for me to take, his fingertips only an inch away from the barrier, one he knew he couldn't touch. As it was clear that what it did to him was far more powerful than what it could do to me, as it hadn't knocked me unconscious.

And in that moment I wished I could have had enough faith in him left to do what he asked.

But I didn't.

So, I couldn't.

Which was why, the moment I realised that my hand was rising, I fisted it and let it drop, telling him,

"I can't, *I'm sorry.*" I saw him close his eyes, as if the pain of what I'd just said became too much to bear.

"You will be sorry if you choose to let them show you, for it won't just be the answers you seek, it will be my entire lifetime since I turned…do you understand what that is, Amelia? Do you understand what it is you are asking for! Are you really prepared for that?" I swallowed hard, knowing what he was really saying…was I prepared to see all those lifetimes of him living without his Chosen One in the world.

After I took a deep breath I answered with certainty,

"I am."

"NO! NO, YOU'RE FUCKING NOT!" he suddenly roared making me wince and step back at the sight of his demon shouting at me. So, I turned quickly, now ignoring his anger and walked back towards the Keepers of Three to the sound of Lucius' temper as he started punching his fists into the tunnel walls. The sound of stone crumbling from his rage was one that echoed throughout the huge open space, becoming a haunting melody to the next step in my destiny. One I felt deep down and in the very core of my soul that I had to take.

But then he started to take on a different approach,

"Amelia, wait, please just wait…just give yourself some more time to think this through, please… I am sorry I shouted at you, I am fucking sorry okay, but just come back to me and we will talk! I will tell you without you walking through, just come back here…*come back to me,*" he pleaded, making it one of the most painful things I had ever had to listen to.

"If you show me, will it damage me in anyway?" I asked the Keepers of Three, now having no choice but to ignore Lucius and all the reasons he was telling me not to do this. The Keepers looked hesitantly over my head at who I supposed they considered was their Master. But then, they also seemed to consider me as such too, which was why eventually they answered me,

"Hurt you it will not."

"For your mind will only witness."

"Motmin mmor."

"He said, and nothing more," they both added making me nod.

"Then I want you to…" I was cut off when Lucius suddenly said,

"Then you don't love me." Just hearing it was like receiving that fucking arrow to my body all over again, only this time it didn't hit my shoulder but instead my fucking heart!

"What did you say?!" I asked in a warning tone as I turned side on to look back at him.

"If you do this, it will mean you don't love me, for in this moment it is all I ask of you...*all I will ever ask of you,"* he replied and I felt the angry hot tears start to surface. Which was why I stormed back over to him and was about to hit out at the barrier, seeing now his arm was at the ready, and I knew what he was doing. He was trying to goad me. To get me so angry that I would lash out enough at him so he could grab me and pull me through. It was then that my anger left me, seeing the lengths he would go to, to stop me. Which was why I told him,

"You know I love you, just as I know you love me... it's why you're so afraid. I see that now. You're just afraid that when I come back through the other side from all I have seen that I won't love you anymore and that, Lucius...well, that is where you have to trust me...trust that I will still love you, no matter what." Again he looked so pained by my words that he couldn't even look at me. Even when I raised my hand up as if I had the power to raise his face to mine without even touching him.

"I love you, Lucius, I always will, no matter what I see...I will love you until the day I die and far beyond it. But now it's time that *you trust me."* He closed his eyes and once more tried to stop me,

"Please, my Khuba, please... *you don't need this."*

"I do. I have to see with my own eyes, only then can I fully trust you again." He snarled,

"You think my love for you needs fucking testing! I searched the ends of the fucking Earth to find you!" I looked back behind me at the tree and said,

"Then I trust you to search beyond it." At this he frowned and snapped,

"What the fuck does that mean?!" I didn't answer him, but instead walked back to the Keepers of Three for the last time and said,

"I am ready."

"What does that mean!?" he shouted again and when I didn't answer him, he must have started to panic as his mind started to piece together my plan,

"NO! You cannot be fucking serious! I swear to you, Amelia, if you do what I think you are planning to do, I will not be held accountable for what I do! For I will unleash my fucking Demon and destroy this fucking place...I will tear it to the fucking ground!" I looked back at him and then looked to the single blood red rose at the very top of the tree, *my soul...* the piece of me he owned.

Then I told him,

"I know you won't, because that would mean you would destroy the piece of me you own, for you were right, you truly do own a piece of my soul, now it's time to keep the part of my heart that I gave to you." Lucius snarled in return, too far gone in his rage for he had tried everything to stop this and he had failed. He knew this when he heard me say,

"Now, show me..." He bellowed in anger after I told the Keepers of Three this single order, making me close my eyes as they nodded and three hands, ones that belonged to each of them, came to my head about to take hold of me.

"NO!" Lucius roared but I was no longer listening.

No, instead I was whispering to the Keepers of the Past.

Lucius' past.

I asked them...

"Show me everything."

CHAPTER TWO

DEATH OF JUDAS

I briefly heard the echoing of destruction behind me as Lucius' demonic fury hit new heights. But then, as soon as the three hands touched my head, everything else in the reality of my world was lost. And what it started with was the most horrific start to a life I could ever imagine, for it started with,

The death of Judas.

The body that hung from the tree was barely recognisable as even being a human body, as it had clearly been tortured. This started with being left to hang still alive in the burning sun for days. His bloodied face hung down, and he was clearly now dead for the others stood around him checking that the deed was done.

The glint of silver sticking out of his torn and bloody mouth, told me exactly what other tortures had taken place. How many pieces of silver had they forced him to swallow, was it thirty as the story was told? It made me want to cry and for all I knew I could have been, because when I looked down at myself all I found was the ghost of a body. I looked more like a distant memory stepping through time and my faint figure of a body had only been granted to me just so my mind felt safer in this place. Because, in reality, I knew I wasn't really here. No, I was still back in the Temple of the Tree of Souls and Lucius was being forced to witness my crime against him.

However, just because I forced myself to watch this, it didn't mean that it was exactly easier on me than him. But then, doing things for love, never was. I was just relieved to see that the dead man hanging didn't look like the Lucius I knew. Although, the most shocking thing was that one of the men who stood nearby, did look like Lucius!

There were two men in robes that stood in front of the dead body along with two more who looked as if they could have been servants of some kind, one of whom held such a startling resemblance to Lucius, it took my breath away.

I frowned, wondering what was happening, was this how his rebirth started, was this to become his new vessel and if so, how? Obviously, my mind bombarded itself with these questions, despite being here now to witness the answers for myself.

"We will cut him open, retrieve the silver we forced him to swallow and buy a field somewhere, maybe south of Mount Sion, before dumping the body there," one of the robed men said. He had a trimmed beard and beady, cruel eyes. Just the sight of him made me question if he was one of the disciples responsible for this as he seemed to be the one making plans on how to get rid of the body.

"Let the people believe he took his own life by placing this in his hand." The same man pulled a sharp weapon from beneath his robe and another flash of an image hit me, as if coming from somewhere else.

It was of Judas, the man who looked nothing like the

Vampire King I knew and loved. As it was only his mind, his memories and that of his soul that had passed on, as he was the same man, just not the same outer shell.

An angry Judas grabbed the spear from a soldier after he had pushed his way through the crowd that had been there to witness the death of Jesus Christ. The sight had me gasping back a startled breath that hitched at the blinding historical moment I was being gifted to witness. A single moment in time that changed the world forevermore. It was a sight no one ever got to see and the significance of this moment most certainly wasn't lost on me, nor would it ever be.

But I knew the story without this scene being added to it. A Roman soldier named Longinus had been ordered to make sure that Jesus was dead. He had taken his weapon and stabbed Jesus in the side too hard which meant that when he removed the spear from Jesus' side, the tip had snapped off, still embedded in his side.

However, the part I hadn't known, was of Judas' angry reaction to this when pushing those aside so he could wrench the spear from its owner before he snapped the pole in rage. This all happened before he was captured by the disciples whom he had classed as his brothers in faith, dragging him away with the crowd cheering them on...the word for traitor of God chanted from their unholy lips.

For God had well and truly,

Forsaken him.

"The broken spear that pierced Jesus, how did you get that, my brother?" the disciple next to him asked, who looked younger with longer, darker hair. He had asked this to the one who seemed to be in charge, and the one who now held the weapon in his hands. His answer came as he nodded towards the now dead Judas and said,

"From our Lord's betrayer." Then he quickly used it to slice open Judas' guts, making me want to gag even though it was just a vision and I knew that I wasn't really there. But it just felt all too real. The crimson coins spilled from within the contents of his stomach and his organs followed them.

Then the furious actions of the disciple ended this by stabbing the remaining spear up into his insides. This was just as the world started to go dark as the hushed words of the younger disciple uttered in fear,

"Look brother, God is angry with what we have done, for the sky darkens just as it did at the crucifixion on the ninth hour that the Son of God died." I looked to see that he was right, a great eclipse started to happen as the sun was overtaken by the moon, only this time it created a blinding crimson ring, bathing the sky in a dark hellish glow and covering the world in a bloody haze. The other man looked to the sky and hissed as the sight burned his eyes, covering his face with his arm.

"Let us leave this place immediately," the young one hissed in fear before he looked back to Judas and nodded in question,

"What about the body?"

"Gather the silver but leave enough for the men we hired to dispose of the body. Like I said, there is a field I know of, once purchased under Judas' name, we will have them dump him there," the bearded one said before I watched as some of the blood money was gathered and half left for what I assumed was the hired clean-up crew, being the two men who had remained close to the horses. Then, once the disciples walked away after first conversing with the other two, no doubt issuing their orders, that was when the image of Lucius appeared once more. Naturally, the sight of him again struck something deep within me, making me take in a quick breath. It was strange, as it was him, but yet it wasn't. As if something was missing, but of course I was right, something was missing,

The right soul.

But he also looked different as his hair wasn't blonde and his eyes weren't their stunning bluish steel grey but instead very dark like his hair. Of course, this made sense seeing as he was first born from an ancient Jewish ancestry.

"I don't like this, look at the sky, what if they were right? What if God is angry at them and therefore punishes us?" The man with the body of Lucius asked, making the other man scoff,

"It is merely an early darkness."

"Early darkness! Are you a fool, brother? Look at the sky, for that is no early darkness, for the sky turned to blood just as those men spilled it upon the ground," the vessel of Lucius said and the moment he said the word 'brother', I could see the slight resemblance, although he was not as handsome and was obviously older than Lucius' early thirties.

"Well, as long as it offers enough light for us to find the payment, that is all that matters to me, now you retrieve the silver first and then get the body down whilst I get our horses," the brother said making Lucius sneer at him, muttering,

"Glad I get the easy job." Then the man I knew would soon become one with Judas' soul reached down and picked out the silver, cursing under his breath as he did so. But it was after he rose to his feet that my utter shock hit me once more when he lifted the battered face of Judas and after brushing back his bloodied matted hair whispered,

"I am sorry, my friend, for I didn't know they planned death for you...life is sacrifice and in death peace is never found for the guilty, for this I am sure to learn one day." I sucked in a startled breath once more, feeling my heart hammering in my chest as the man's confession was heard. It was obvious that he had been a friend of Judas and had betrayed him, unknowingly causing his death. Gods, but how the circle of betrayal and sacrifice was about to come full circle.

I knew this when suddenly the body of Judas started to lift, moving ever so slowly at first making the traitorous friend jerk back a little before shaking his head as if he was seeing things. However, there was no mistaking the sight of the spear being sucked deeper and deeper inside Judas' body until it vanished completely from sight.

"By the Son of God, what is...?!" Lucius said before he looked over to his brother by the horses, who had his back to him. He was about to speak when suddenly a demonic hand burst out of Judas' sliced gaping flesh and in its clawed grasp was the spear. It lunged forward so quickly that Lucius didn't have a chance before it was suddenly being embedded into his gut. This stabbed in so deep that he doubled over the hand that still had hold of the weapon.

Then the sky above started to clear making his brother shout from by the horses,

"See, for there was nothing to fear, it is clearing now." Meanwhile Lucius was reaching out a shaky hand towards him in a desperate attempt to get to him, when he was clearly too far away. A croaked sound trembled from his lips,

"Br...brother." Then the demonic hand withdrew and suddenly the earth opened up beneath him, just as it had done with me when my blood had spilled and seeped into the ground like an offering. Lucius' body disappeared, falling to what I knew was the cavern below, although this time he didn't have anyone to save him from the deadly fall as I had done. And with it, my vision quickly changed and soon I was to understand the strange dreams Lucius told me about when first finding ourselves in the Temple. The dreams he had experienced but didn't know whether or not they had been real. That was because they hadn't belonged to him but to that of his stolen vessel.

The one the Devil himself had chosen.

I knew this for certain because my next image was the sight of the Keepers of Three dragging the half dead man along the floor of the cave and each time they went out of view, my vision of the past changed.

This continued until eventually they came to a portal and it was one that looked to have been summoned on a gigantic stone tablet that stood upright, reminding me of an unbroken version of the Rosetta Stone. It was one that was surrounded by colossal pillars, all carved and decorated with the history of man. This quickly told me that this was what the Temple had looked like before the tree had grown around it, consuming the tablet so only the gateway into Hell remained to this day. As this was the same opening that was glowing crimson inside the Tree of Souls.

And as I continued to watch the Keepers of Three drag Judas' new vessel along the floor, one not broken yet by the roots of time, it didn't take a genius to know where they were heading. This also meant that, with a sickening fascination, I couldn't take my eyes from the sight as they reached the ominous opening. Then, without so much as a single word spoken, they tossed his body inside until it disappeared from view, doing so as though it had been nothing more than disposable garbage.

I was truly sickened by the sight because this may not have yet been the Lucius, I knew being treated this way, but it was still a piece of him. However, I wasn't granted too long to dwell on it as another vision quickly took its place. First a looming darkness filled my senses and a feeling of overwhelming dread filled my non-existent body. As, instead of a continuous flow from one vision to the next, this time it felt more as though something was fighting with me, tugging at my soul, as if I was being pulled in too many directions.

Then suddenly, the only way to describe the feeling was that

I had been plunged into time instead of being guided through it, simply stepping into it like the few times before. Which made me feel as if I was not only unwelcome here but more like... *forbidden.*

Now it was time for my first taste of Hell, as Lucius' soul and new vessel were now in the hands of...

The Devil.

CHAPTER THREE

BY THE DEVIL'S HAND

The sight in front of me quickly left me breathless as my view came into focus because the whole merging into this vision had left me feeling dizzy, even without the entirety of my body being with me. From what I could make out the closest I had been allowed to get to the Hellish scene below was also about as close as I ever wanted to, as right there below me now was none other than the Devil himself!

Looking down it seemed as though I was perched on some kind of small rock ledge high above what must have been Lucifer's throne in Hell. It looked as if it was made from the bones of some enormous winged beast, as its spine curled up at least fifteen feet in the air creating the back of the throne. Its ribs had been pulled back and suspended in the centre of the fan of bones was what looked like a black onyx heart with a huge sword embedded at its frozen core.

Either side of this were the bones of what were once its wings, now swathed in black leathery fabric, like scaled skin.

As if the creature had first been skinned upon its death and this had been used to decorate the throne. Its massive boned legs made up the sides of the throne, with its giant clawed feet displayed at the bottom. Its head, however, wasn't attached to the rest of the skeleton but instead, it was mounted high above on the wall behind. It was obviously a trophy of some kind, maybe some honoured kill of Lucifer's that he felt proud enough to have a throne made from it. Well, from the size of the thing, then it wouldn't have been surprising. As I think anyone would have counted it as a skilful victory, seeing as it looked as if it could have been a demonic dragon of some sort.

And speaking of the Demon that could take claim to that impressive kill, I was now looking down on the large masterful body that filled the throne.

The Devil.

I swear, being faced with the two in such a short space of time, I didn't know which vision had me more breathless, the sight of Jesus dying on the cross or the one that faced me now as Lucifer, King of Kings in Hell, was about to give life to his first son.

My Vampire King.

Lucifer sat with his back to me, lounged out and side on, facing a dark, open archway where the walls seemed to be moving as if they were swarming with some kind of demonic parasites. I couldn't see his face but just his large muscled back clad in black armour that seemed to move with the rest of his body. One moment it was as hard as rock and forming deadly spiked horns and jagged teeth, positioned at his huge shoulders and arms, whilst interlocking plates like scales coated the strong contours of his indestructible looking body. But then, in the next instance, it would all evaporate before clinging to his bare skin like vapour or some spell attached to his very soul. As if a demonic cloud was attracted to his flesh, only managing to stick once he was still enough to do so. That, or it was commanded with a mere thought. This was more likely, as who just stood still in battle?

I watched as he raised his hand, one gloved in demonic plating that didn't move like the rest of his armour but stayed in place as he motioned for something to be brought forward. A shadowed figure below approached his throne from behind, one I couldn't see from where I was situated. But Lucifer didn't even turn his head to look, which told me that the being must have been considered unimportant, as his massive curled horns didn't move an inch. Unsurprisingly, they were impressive in their size and most definitely added to the intimidating figure of a God.

One set of dark red horns looked more ribbed and from what I could see, started from the top of his forehead, with his thick black, reddish hair braided in lines around them in a Viking style. The twists of hair also framed the bases of the smaller horns before they curled back over the top of his head away from a face I couldn't yet see. The other much larger set were matt black and came out from the shaved sides of his head and stretched outwards past his shoulders before they started to curl back in on themselves, with the glowing tips high above the back of his head.

But as I said, they didn't move an inch as the other being approached. No, they simply continued casting dark shadows on the walls and backdrop of crimson material flowing either side of his throne. It was so silky, it looked more like liquid running down the wall...in fact, on greater inspection that was exactly what it was!

A bloody waterfall.

I followed the liquid to the source above and saw two giant gargoyle heads. Both had their snarling mouths held open by thick chains the width of my thighs, attached to stone nostrils and fixed to the jagged rock ceiling above. It also looked as if Lucifer's palace had been carved out of part of the mountain, which instantly made me think of Lucius' German home, Blood Rock.

Gods, but if I hadn't been able to feel the ghost of my body, I would have raised a fist to my mouth.

"My all Masterful Lord, are you sure this is wise?" The voice of a servant said, one that was still hidden in the shadows.

"Are you questioning me, Ba'al Zəbû, because I think you know what becomes of those that do?" Lucifer said in a dangerously serious tone that spoke of nothing but deadly calm. Even I swallowed hard, which was strange, as it was as if my reactions were being mirrored in real time back at the Temple. But then I also had to wonder where I had heard that name before?

"I would never be so bold, Sire," was his reply to this obvious threat.

"Nor so reckless and daring," Lucifer added, and I watched as he tapped a few wicked taloned claws against the boned throne, making a particular sound that had me wondering if the bones had turned to stone upon the death of the creature.

"I merely meant to ask if the obsession with the girl is worth it?" At this, two things happened simultaneously. The first was lightning fast as the shadowed armour suddenly formed a cloak full of demonic clawed hands. These were all reaching out from his back like angry souls trying to grab the one who dared speak of a girl Lucifer obviously felt a strong connection to. At the same time, a low and very threatening sound came from deep within Lucifer's chest and it was by far one of the scariest sounds I had ever heard in my entire life! Even the shadowed figure I could barely see seemed to close in on himself, trying in vain to retreat from his master's wrath.

"You are lucky your senses are intact enough, for if you had spoken her name, one I have forbidden to pass through the lips of all in my Kingdom, then you would have lost your tongue before finding your head nailed to my fucking wall! Now, do not question me again!" he growled, crushing the bone armrest in his fist, until it crumbled into dust.

"Now, bring him to me!" Lucifer shouted out his order, whilst gaining his feet, and I watched utterly horrified as the near naked body of Lucius was being brought forward, after he had first been nailed to a cross so as to experience his own Crucifixion. Well, at the very least it looked like the body of who would soon become Lucius had been dead first, unlike Jesus Christ who hadn't received the same privilege.

"Gods, no." I hissed and the sound entered the past like a shadowed whisper, one Lucifer tensed at, doing so now as if he had heard it for himself. But that was impossible…*wasn't it?*

His shadowed armour vibrated around his flesh slightly as if this was a reaction to hearing me before they then calmed. I held what felt like my breath back in the Temple until I thought it was safe to let it out again, thankful the tense moment had passed. Then I continued to watch in utter horror as demonic minions scurried around the floor as they dragged the upturned cross closer.

They looked like large plucked, featherless chickens with the heads of snarling skinless dogs all snapping tiny rows of sharp teeth at each other. The chains some had in their mouths dripped with thick saliva, slapping on the floor in pools of drool before they were quickly sucked up by even smaller creatures. These were centipede like insects with bodies the size of rats and hundreds of tall legs that stood at least a foot off the ground. They were also about the length of my arm and made a chilling sound as they scuttled across the stone floor.

The movement of the cross stopped and when it did, all the creatures stopped with it, as if frozen by their master's will. The body of Lucius had been flipped upside down on the cross, creating the sign for the antichrist, with his head closer to the ground along with his outstretched arms nailed to the crude wooden structure. Lucifer clapped his hands, obviously delighted with the view or maybe just a way to get the creatures to leave as they all scattered at once, making him feel the need to kick one as it hurried past.

"Piss off cretins, be gone with you now!" he said as they all ran out of sight, especially after seeing their comrade being kicked so hard, he hit the side of the arched wall that Lucius on the cross had just emerged from. The moving darkness covered the dog sized creature in seconds as an unseen swarm devoured him, leaving only his bones as evidence. His bones fell from the wall with a snap, shattering on impact when they hit the ground, telling me that even the walls of this place were deadly!

Like a swarm of fucking, demonic piranhas!

He then walked towards his prize, still keeping his back to me and as the shadowed armour lagged behind, he ended up showing me more muscles than I ever thought possible on a living being! But then again, this was Lucifer we were talking about and he was the God of Hell… and well, right now he looked every inch of it.

"Oh, but how I have waited for one such as he!" Lucifer said as his armour turned now to that of a living cloak, one that shuddered and vibrated in response to its master's pleasure.

"For a man to renounce his faith just on the cusp of being granted eternal life. A life bestowed onto him as an Angel for what was asked of him from the Son of God…ironic then, don't you think, as now he will now become my son…The son of a very different God," Lucifer said making the one named Baʻal Zəbû nod, before agreeing,

"Yes, my masterful Lordship, he is perfect." Lucifer scoffed before saying,

"Not yet he isn't, but he soon will be. For it is time I created my first son, one born directly from the blood of my heart, for it is time to breed new life upon the world" He paused and stepped closer tapping a claw over Lucius' heart before declaring,

"...and you, my boy, will one day be King of all those beneath you!" After this he took hold of the wood at the top where Lucius' feet were nailed to the cross, one over the other. He then yanked hard and the whole crucifix spun, until Lucius was now back to being upright.

"Now it is time to unite your soul with your new vessel and for this birth of new royal blood to be consumed, I will first need your heart to beat once more." After this a bright blinding light erupted from within Lucifer's chest and it flowed out of him and directly into the vessel. I gasped in awe at what I was yet again being made to witness, as Lucifer obviously had the ability to contain Judas' soul within him. This being at the ready until he had a vessel to release it into and the body of the man who had betrayed him Lucifer obviously saw as a fitting choice.

The second it flowed into him, Lucius gulped back a deep and large breath, one as if he had just emerged from drowning in an ocean of blood...

But where had that thought come from?

"Ah, I am so proud, look at the strength of him, for he does not emerge screaming as the others did." I frowned wondering what others Lucifer spoke of...*had he tried this before and failed?*

"Yes, he is strong my, Lord King," the shadowed figure of Baʻal Zəbû said, agreeing with whatever Lucifer would say.

"And he will be handsome too, for once he has my blood inside him how could he not be?" Lucifer said like...well, almost like a proud father. And the Devil was right, as it was the image of Lucius but not quite as I knew him. Almost like a dulled down version, for he wasn't as strikingly handsome as I knew him to be. He didn't yet have the light of sand in his hair or the grey blue in his striking eyes. His skin did not look as if it had been bathed in moonlight and his body was not yet that of a strong and powerful being, with the muscles that spoke of both in abundance.

Not yet anyway.

"Awake now, for you are Judas no more!" Lucifer said with pride again coating his masterful words. Lucius opened his eyes at the command, taking one look at all that was happening. But it was strange, as despite all that faced him now, Lucifer was right, he should have woken up screaming. But instead, it was as if he knew. As if by the last words spoken and forced from his dying lips, he knew this was where his fate would lead him. Meaning that this right now was Judas merely accepting that fate.

His bravery was utterly astounding.

To the point it took my breath away, telling me that even before Lucifer made him into a God in his own right, Judas was both fearless and strong. I knew this when he looked around him, towards his nailed arms before commenting dryly,

"A fitting punishment it would seem." Lucius then looked down at the rest of himself and winced only slightly at the pain of moving when he tugged on the crude hellish nails embedded in his flesh, ones that held him prisoner to the cross. The weight should have torn straight through his flesh but there were multiple nails along his arms also. But the second he breathed new life once more, it was obvious that his heart too was back to pounding in his chest, for his nailed flesh had started to bleed.

"Well, so far I am fucking impressed!" Lucifer said clapping his large hands in enjoyment.

"No, my boy, this isn't punishment, this is your reward,

your gift of a new life I bestow on you unlike any other," Lucifer told him making Lucius look wide-eyed and shocked.

"A gift?" he questioned.

"Yes, for I am the God of Hell and the one you chose over another with the last of your dying breath." Lucius looked thoughtful for a moment, lowering his head as if everything started to make sense within him. Then, before Lucifer could question his actions, Lucius raised his head back up and displayed that deadly and knowing grin he was well known for. As his face said it all, for it was all Lucius and soon to be the demon I knew well.

"Then it looks as though I made the right choice, my Lord God," Lucius said making the Devil laugh, and as he did, he threw his horned head back and awarded me a slight sight of the smaller row of horns down either side of his forehead.

"That you did, my Son. Now it is time to make you a God in your own right, for your own Kingdom awaits," Lucifer told him, making his eyes widen in surprise again, as if he could barely believe this was happening to him.

Lucifer motioned a hand forward and the cloaked figure, the one named Ba'al Zəbû, stepped forward, telling me he was also a sizable being and one with hoofed feet and wings that were mainly covered by the cloak he wore. He carried with him a bowl of golden fire and at its core, the spear with the missing tip sat untouched by a single flame. Then Lucifer's large, clawed hand reached in and grabbed it, making him hiss as it started to burn his skin, sizzling his flesh.

Once in his hand, he laughed at the possible pain before he turned the blade on himself. I could barely see with only his back facing me, but it looked as though he was using it to cut into himself!

After he was done, he roared in what could have been as much triumph as it could have been pleasure, which made everything seem to shudder and shake around him from the force of it.

All but Lucius that was.

No, because he didn't even flinch!

Lucifer dropped the bloody blade back into the bowl of golden flames, one still held by his servant, then he turned back to Lucius who merely asked,

"Will this hurt?" Lucifer's tone seemed intrigued and he answered,

"Yes, it will hurt, enough that you will wish you would die to end the suffering."

I had thought this answer might have finally affected him enough to respond in some fearful way, but I was wrong. As Lucius merely nodded and then replied,

"Good, that way I will know that I am actually alive." Lucifer seemed impressed by his response and commented to himself,

"Then I picked well."

After this he turned his own clawed hand in on himself and when it started to disappear, I combined the sight with the sounds of squelching. This told me the Devil had now dug his hand inside his own chest, the one he had used the spear to cut open, in order to try and reach his own beating heart. The thought alone made me want to vomit. Something I might have done had I been in my body and for all I knew, I was in the Temple currently retching.

After this I gagged again as his heart came into view and I was barely able to make sense of it as he held it in front of him. It was still clearly beating, as black veins and arteries were still attached to the inside of his chest. The heart itself was huge and matched the size of the God of Hell it belonged to.

It was dripping with a mixture of black and crimson lifeblood, one that seemed thicker than normal human blood.

Then I watched as he proceeded to dig a clawed, curled talon deep within one of the heart's chambers, gathering up his own blood straight from the beating source. This told me that what I was witnessing now wasn't exactly something Lucifer would have done more than once. Which meant that Lucius had obviously passed the selection process.

"Now it is time to be reborn, my Son, for with my blood you will be more powerful than all my creatures who walk the Earth…you will be a God and King upon where I must not go. Then one day, you will bring her to me…you will bring me my Queen!" Lucifer shouted before he roared a demonic growl as he dug deeper still, until he had enough blood gathered in his claws. Then he hammered his fist inside Lucius' chest, cracking straight through his ribcage, meaning this was when he finally got,

His screams.

I closed my eyes unable to take in the sight of Lucius' utter agony and torture in what was him being remade from once a man, now into everything Lucifer had claimed him to be.

A God amongst men and a King amongst all Vampires.

Because this was Lucius' beginning.

This was his…

Resurrection.

CHAPTER FOUR

THE LIFE OF A VAMPIRE KING

Tears and screams.
This was what followed, the first was coming from me as I silently sobbed from having to witness the true torture of what the man I loved had had to endure to become what he was. In fact, it affected me on such a deep and disturbing level, that I wasn't sure I would ever get the memory of his screams out of my mind, as it sounded as if Lucius was being ripped apart.

I don't know how long this lasted, as it began to feel more like a test of strength on both our parts. Especially seeing as I was quickly questioning why I was being made to witness so much of Lucius' beginning. Was this my penance for demanding these visions from the Keepers of Three?

Finally, after the screaming agony had finished, I got to witness Lucius' transformation, starting with when he forced his body from the nails that had kept him prisoner on the cross. He growled in anger and tore each arm free first, before using the freedom of his arms to push the rest of his body from where he had been nailed in place. Blood spurted from the holes made before I watched in fascination as they started to close, along with the biggest wound of all, *his chest.* At first it had looked as if it had almost caved in on itself from the impact Lucifer's hand had made when punching through the ribs to get to his heart.

As now I could see his ribcage fusing back together at the breaks where they had snapped, before his flesh, muscle and skin started to knit across the hole. This continued until it was nothing but a large chiselled chest, one significantly more muscled and toned than before. But this wasn't the only transformation his body received, as everything about him started to change. It was as if before he had only been half living and now his new life truly looked touched by that of a God.

His skin looked pale yet in a healthy way, as if the new blood coursing through his body had made it glow slightly. His hair looked the colour of the desert sands touched by the sun, one he would no longer wish to bathe under, as it was the eternal darkness of night that would forever call to his Demon.

His once dark eyes turned to that of molten steel, with the hints of blue flashing brighter as his cunning and quick mind took in everything around him. He looked down at his fist as he clenched it tight before telling the Devil who made him,

"I feel strong, powerful, as if I could kill with barely any strength needed."

"That's because you can, and you will."

"I will?" he asked looking up making Lucifer throw his head back once more, laughing at the question before telling him,

"Yes, my Son, you will and what's more...*you will enjoy it.*" Lucius grinned back up at him and it was one of knowing that sent chills down my spine, reminding me just how brutal and vicious Lucius was at heart, despite the love he held for me.

"But first, I bestow on you your last gift, a reminder if you will," Lucifer said before he clicked his fingers, making his hand ignite and become engulfed in crimson fire. Then, with his flaming hand, he placed a fingertip to Lucius' temple and the second he did, Lucius fell back against the bloody cross.

The impact of the Devil's touch was quickly explained the moment I saw that same crimson fire being absorbed into his skin and start lighting up his veins as the demonic power coursed through his body. An extreme power that would obviously take some getting used to as the moment he gripped the wooden beam at his back, it suddenly burst into flames. Lucius stepped away from the now burning cross and looked at what he had done with both shock and excitement.

"I feel...*incredible!*" Lucius said surprising himself again when this last word came out as a deep growl, but nothing more shocking than when the demonic wings suddenly erupted from his back. In what then seemed like a natural reaction, they stretched out, displaying a huge wingspan of stretched black skin in between finger like bones. These were spiked with razor tips and in a similar shape to that belonging to a bat.

Two massive horns had grown from near his shoulders at his back, spanning at least six feet long each side and they narrowed out into deadly points. They were also black with deep ridges along the top that gave them the appearance of a demonic spine. The underbelly of them was where his wings began, with the leathery skin attached there before the first of the boned fingers sectioned off the rest of each wing. The thick bone curved giving them their shape and function, with the last finger curling out past the front of his body near his feet with the longest and most deadliest claw of all.

Down the centre of his spine was what looked like exposed

black bone covered in between with a fine black fur that looked surprisingly soft to touch. What followed after the discovery of his wings, was the transformation of his entire human body as it changed into that of his Demon. A form I had only seen once at the top of his silent winter garden. Even now, it still was a terrifying sight to behold and Lucius rose up to his now taller height before he looked down at his demonic hands before they both clenched into fists. Then he pounded one to his chest like some wild alpha before he threw his head back and let go of a deafening roar as his Demon was finally set free for the first time.

He looked unstoppable.

Lucifer raised his hands to the side as if marvelling at the sight of his creation just as Ba'al Zəbû cowered back at the sight of such power. For Lucius started to grow, his mighty leathery wings stretching out as he threw his arms back, his chest went forward and the full extent of his power burst through him, as this time his demonic roar cracked the walls and shook the ground.

He looked more like the Devil King in front of him than anything else, which was when I realised that was precisely what his demon side was...

The Devil in his soul.

"Now for the reminder of exactly how you came to be," Lucifer said before quickly grabbing him by one of his horns and spinning him around. Then, with the back of his wings now facing Lucifer, he applied the pressure needed to force his new creation to his knees. Lucius went down on one knee at the same time Lucifer reached back behind him until he located the spear once more, one that again burned him the second he touched it.

"Now it is up to the Fates to make you a true God!" he roared before raising the weapon high and powering it down in between his wings, stabbing Lucius down the centre of his back. The spear ended up implanted beneath his exposed bone, making him fall forward to both knees. Then I watched in astonishment as the full length of the blade delved deeper underneath his flesh, embedding itself and fusing the metal with the spine of his demon until hidden safely between his wings. Lucius remained on his knees, panting and shaking his head trying to dispel the obvious painful effects of what Lucifer had just done.

"Now you are Judas no longer, for it is only right for a father to bestow upon you a new name, for yours will no longer represent the betrayer of God, one the memory of your human life will forever hold. But instead it will represent the light that now burns within your soul, for you are the Light of the Seventh…so from this day forward, your name shall be…*Lucius Septimus.*"

I gasped just as the vision changed to that of him waking ten feet away from the tree he had been hung from, under the blood moon. And this time there was no tugging feeling gnawing at my soul as if the edges of my consciousness were being jerked in all directions. But then, the moment Lucius rose to his feet, I could see for myself the utter rage in him was not the same as it had been today.

No, this was the fresh newborn son created by the Devil and the anger that was coursing through his veins had a direct link to Hell. I knew that the moment I barely recognised the terrifying demonic killer glint in his blood-red eyes. The first thing he did was lift a hand to his face before he engulfed it in Hellish flame just as Lucifer had done when calling forth his Demon for the first time. After this he walked directly to the tree of his death and with what looked like barely any effort, he tore the thickest branch from the rest, letting it fall to the blood soaked earth. The scorched and burning bark sizzled in the liquid as he looked down at it in pure rage. This was because it had been the branch he had been hung from and one that was a cruel reminder thanks to the bloodied nose that was still attached.

Although where his previously broken body had gone, I had no clue.

After this he picked up the branch, one that quickly became engulfed in flames he created. He stood still for a moment as he watched his own human blood burn away from it before throwing it with such force, it scattered in the dirt at least thirty feet behind him. I could barely see it still burning in the distance against the night sky and then with a flick of his wrist, the entire tree went up in a mass of flames. I sucked in a shuddered breath, watching now as he calmly walked away from the site of his death, happy no doubt in the knowledge of it now burning to ash behind him.

But little did he know at the time it would only continue to grow back for as long as he lived.

Just like the Tree of Souls.

The sight of him walking away quickly gave way to the next vision, one that started to play out differently than before. It became an almost flicker book of destruction, blood and gore as Lucius' reign of terror flowed throughout the world of Vampires. It was almost like standing on the very edge of time so you were not a part of it but just close enough to watch as it sped forward, slowing enough to only catch glimpses of its motion. Almost like looking out of a car window and going from a hundred miles an hour of blurred landscape to just slow enough to catch sight of a single aspect of the world you travelled through.

And his world was a bloody and brutal one!

Because his new deadly rule swept through each continent until every last Vampire he found was either kneeling at his feet and being fed by his wrist or they were in bloody pieces scattered around him. Either way the choice became clear, accept the Devil's claim or die. Needless to say, most chose to kneel and those that believed themselves stronger, soon realised they were wrong…in the 'eternally dead' sense.

I didn't quite know how long this took him, as he travelled the world with the limitations set against him. But as I watched him on one ship after another, I knew that this had most likely taken him a long time to accomplish. And in truth, it was terrifying to watch the raw, untamed strength and rage inside him that merged into one. The way his presence would sweep through the land like a plague among his people, making them cower in dark and shadowed corners trying to escape the choice forced upon them. Some would even band together, thinking to bring him down in greater numbers.

But again, *they were wrong.*

Nothing and no one could stop him. Not the biggest, not the oldest and not the ones with what they foolishly believed was enough skill in fighting.

Lucius was a machine.

A cold blooded, methodical killer. He was the threat that always followed through and he was the nightmare to those that believed they had created the name. And then, when the last of the entire race was brought to heel, Lucius found himself yearning for something more. Some sort of direction or his own master to follow, for it soon became apparent that his desire to be a king hadn't been born with him in his new life.

Which was why he ended up sat on a sand dune with a

stunning golden city glittering under the full moonlight in the distance. The blood coating his hands and face clear to see and looking almost like black ink bathing his pale skin under the star blanketed night sky. A servant was cowering behind him as Lucius asked,

"What city is that?"

"Ctesiphon, My Lord," his servant answered in a fearful tone, bowing as he spoke even though Lucius still had his back to him. Of course, I had heard of the name and not just because I was a historian by profession but for more personal reasons. I heard the name spoken in great fondness by my father. I had grown up listening to the stories of the most fearsome warriors on horseback that were skilled in defeating the Romans time and time again. This done with their unique battle tactics with little more than a bow and an endless supply of arrows provided by a caravan of servants with supplies. They were also expert riders on horseback with a skilful aim at both firing an arrow forward and back behind them as their horses rode away.

But their skill in war wasn't the only thing the Persians were well known for, as it was also where the word paradise was born. Persians were known as the world's greatest landscapers, having the most exquisite gardens, this thanks to their extensive knowledge and collection of plants and also their underground viaduct system that fed water straight down from the mountains and into their cities.

Now, what brought Lucius here at this moment in time I didn't know, as the visions leading up to this point moved by too quickly to understand why. Why I now found him staring directly at the city that I would have given anything to experience, just once. Which was why I also knew that here, through the vision of his memories, was as close as I was ever going to get.

This was also when I realised what the Keepers were showing me, as so far it had been slowed down at every single turning point in Lucius' life. The things that happened to him pathed the course for not only his future but for the future of all of those around him. Setting the way and planting bloody footsteps for the Fates plans to take place for us all. Which of course, was the next fated journey that had obviously led him to,

My father.

"And who is its King?" Lucius asked.

"That would be Arsaces of Parthia, the King of Kings to the human world." At this Lucius straightened a little and turned to look over his shoulder at his servant, I could then see his fangs flash in the light before he asked,

"And in *my world*, who is he in that one?" The servant bowed low obviously used to Lucius' dark rage, yet still not knowing when it would appear.

"He is also known as the King of Kings, my Lord, for he is the first ruler and known as the overlord of all Supernatural beings." Lucius hummed and looked back towards the city.

"Is he now?" he mused obviously deep in thought, now with a strange glint in his eyes as he looked intrigued.

"If…if I may be so bold, Master."

"Speak!" Lucius snapped waving an impatient hand in the air.

"He is known as the most powerful being on Earth and his armies above and below are both vast, so it would not be wise to…"

"Above and below?" Lucius' question cut him off.

"It is what makes him so powerful, for he is the first and only one of his kind," the servant replied, obviously holding himself tense as if at any minute this conversation would end in him losing his head.

"And that is?!" Lucius asked, clearly getting irritated at having to wait for the information he wanted.

"He is both Angel and Demon, my Lord, born from both royal bloodlines of the highest-ranking Angel and Demon. In fact, I believe his father is Lucifer's most trusted confidant and is a Prince in Hell," the servant told him, and I couldn't help but smile as I thought about my unconventional grandparents who, for obvious reasons, were not together.

"And that would be?" Lucius enquired with more calm now.

"His father is Asmodeus, the Prince of Lust, My Lord." At this Lucius reacted, telling me that he had heard of my grandfather, who was in fact said to be Lucifer's closest friend.

"Now that is interesting," Lucius replied, more to himself.

"Sire?" his servant asked after Lucius nodded to himself, now looking more than pleased. Then he gained his feet, dusted off the sand from his dark clothes and said,

"Then I have found what I have been looking for."

"How, my Lord?" he asked, but Lucius ignored this and instead gave him one last order,

"You may go, I have no more use for you, and you are free of my service. Go and live life as you please, for I am done ruling over it," Lucius stated and before he could hear the servant's utter gasp of shock, he released his huge demonic wings and was up in the air in seconds, now travelling towards the city with speed.

This fading image of Lucius disappearing out of sight after taking to the night sky, signified the end of one vision before another swiftly took its place. But this time it became more like a series of quick events that included a glimpse of not only his past life, but also that of my father. To see him now as a Persian king was a sight I would never forget and nor would I ever want to.

It was a startling sight to behold and to see him sat in those ancient times on his glorious throne…well, simply put, he was magnificent.

But in regard to Lucius, as time was spun quickly in front of me it also became clear that he became more than just my father's right-hand, but they became comrades as well. Brothers at arms that fought side by side in many battles together. And this wasn't all, as a new series of visions portrayed Lucius as something other than simply good in a fight. No, instead of him swinging a sword on the battlefield, visions of him stalking the city streets at night showcased another acquired skill of his. This was when my father had sent him on missions, that mainly included stealth, cunning, speed and the deadly hand of an assassin.

However, over time it also became clear that Lucius' aversion to sunlight faded somewhat, even if it was something he obviously kept quiet about. As there were times that I would see him on that same sand dune, once more looking out over the city, alone and deep in thought as he watched the sun setting for the night.

But during these times, there was always one expression on his face…*longing.* In fact, out of everything that I had seen so far, if there was one time I could have paused and stepped right into, then it would have been in that exact moment. I would have sat down beside him, taken his hand in mine and watched the sun setting with him, before ending the night asking him what it was he was thinking about.

The question soon lingered in my mind even as time continued to play out. As for his other aversions, silver was one he always stayed away from and I was unsure if it was just the reminder that made it this way or did it actually have the power to burn or even weaken him? Again, this was yet another question I ended up having no choice but to add to all the rest, especially as time continued to span through the ages.

Questions like, why did I see him on a rooftop with my uncle Vincent, stalking someone who looked like my Aunty Ari from a different time? Especially if the oil lamps, cobbled streets of London and period dress were anything to go by.

But then, something even more shocking was watching as Lucius walked out of a bunker that I recognised as being Führerbunker, wearing a German SS uniform. This had been where Hitler had famously shot himself and where Eva Braun, his wife of less than forty hours, took cyanide. However, when Lucius calmly put the gun that was still in his hand back into the holster on his uniform and got into an old black car, I had to question those once believed historical facts.

Especially as Lucius was now clearly stealing Hitler's armoured Mercedes Grosser and from the looks of things, he was doing this just after shooting the Führer himself!

Gods, but there just seemed like an endless amount of questions I would need to ask once this was all over and I would have dwelled longer on each of them had the next vision not started to take hold of my mind. Because this was soon the point when I found myself witnessing modern day as it finally came around, meaning that even more questions took precedence than those before.

Dangerous questions that arose the second I saw the other most important person enter Lucius' life.

That being, of course…

My mother.

CHAPTER FIVE

A HAND ON LITTLE KEIRA GIRL

I sucked in a harsh, ragged breath, for I knew these were the years that would be the hardest to witness. But I was soon dumbfounded, as the first time seeing her wasn't when I thought it would have been. It hadn't been when he had ordered Pip and Adam to kidnap her like the stories I had heard. Or even before this, when she had first arrived at Afterlife, as it made sense that he would spy on her before making his move. No, instead it had been when my mother was only a child, shocking me that he had known of her so many years before the point in time he had first made himself known to her.

At a guess she looked about seven years old and was currently stood in line for some kid's ride at what looked like a travelling fairground. Lucius was just standing at the edge of it all silently watching, with his arms folded and a mean looking black Lamborghini Diablo at his back. But then, as the passenger side door went up, I gritted my teeth as I recognised bitch face emerging.

"The witch will be here soon," she said after pulling down

the hem of her tight red dress that had ridden up when getting out of the low car. Big, blonde hair and heavy makeup made her look like a whore and I would have sniggered at the bitchy thoughts had she not tried to curl herself against Lucius' side. I was at least glad to see that he didn't reciprocate the affection, but just remained as he was. It made me realise that even all those years ago, she had been dreaming, thinking that she meant anything to him and just seeing his cold treatment of her, then it was little wonder why she hated me so much.

"Who is this little rodent anyway for you to be so interested?" Lucius reacted slightly to this, shrugging her off his shoulder before telling her in a hard tone,

"Just call it a Pet project of mine, one whose memory you will not hold with you past this day." As he said this he raised a hand to her face and I tensed thinking that it might have been in a tender gesture but the second I saw her eyes glaze over I knew that he was actually stealing her memories and controlling her mind.

"Yes, my Lord."

"Good, now get your ass back in the car!" he snapped after dropping his hand, one I noticed was not covered in a glove and was just like his other; pale, large and strong. Layla seemed to snap out of the trance he had put her in and huffed in a spoilt way before doing as he ordered. After this he went back to watching my mother as a child as she giggled and threw her hands up in the air. She was currently sat inside the first car of the rollercoaster, its head a huge fire-breathing dragon. It also looked like she was next to her older sister, my aunty Libby, as her bright red curls were easy to spot anywhere.

But like Lucius, I couldn't seem to take my eyes off her. She looked so happy and carefree, just as any child should be. Which made me question when it was in her life that she started to see Demons and Angels, just like I did. It didn't look as though it could have been now, as I doubted she would have looked quite as joyful as she did.

Of course, I had been born with this gift, but the difference was that I had grown up seeing them and viewing them as people I cared deeply for and called family. But my mother didn't have this, for she grew up in the human world, meaning that the rest of it had to be utterly terrifying for her. I honestly couldn't imagine it!

The next person to enter the vision of the past was who I quickly recognised as Lucius' witch, Nesteemia. This was when I started to have a bad feeling about this and shot a panicked look towards my mother who was now just getting off the ride and walking back to my grandparents.

"You found her, my Lord," Nesteemia asked as she approached, looking every bit the gypsy witch.

"I have," he replied in a cool tone that gave nothing away.

"What would you have me do?" Nesteemia asked looking wary and unsure.

"Start the process," was Lucius' unfeeling reply, making me flinch at the sound. He just sounded so heartless.

"You're sure about this?" she asked, obviously not agreeing with his decision. Lucius didn't react other than to say,

"The girl's fate was sealed the moment she was born for him. Might as well get her used to the life, for she cannot escape it now," he replied making Nesteemia nod in understanding, bowing her head in respect as Lucius turned around and opened the driver's side door. His witch started to walk towards the fairground, the only human in her sights being that of my mother.

"And, Nesta…"

"Yes, my Lord?" The witch stopped and looked back over her shoulder at him, waiting to hear what he had to say. Lucius then looked one more time at my mother, who looked now to be trying to drag her sister over to a sweet stall.

"Let her enjoy the day at least, for come her seventh birthday... *it will be one of her last,*" he said before folding himself inside his 90's supercar and making it the only evidence for me to witness that even during this time,

Lucius had a heart.

After this time sped up, creating a montage of times when he would be watching her. But as the years of my mother's life flashed by, it seemed that this stalking was more in a protective way. Because not once during this time did he ever cross a line. He never watched her from the foot of her bed or creep in the shadows as she undressed. It was never anything like that and he gave her as much distance as he deemed necessary, not once coming close enough that she ever saw him.

But then came the first time that the rule of distance kept between them was shattered and I felt my whole body tense at the sight. However, it had nothing to do with jealously or anything like that, but more to do with the horror of the situation that forced him to break that rule. I knew the moment he entered a hospital, walked down a corridor and entered one of the rooms, exactly what this was going to be. It was why a sob was caught in my throat the second I was made to endure the sight of my poor mother as I had never seen her before...

Utterly Broken.

I thought back to the horrific experience she had obviously been forced to live through and the fresh bandages on her arms made me want to cry. They were stained slightly as the fresh wounds still wept with blood and her face was so pained it was as though she could still feel the injuries being inflicted. I felt sickened by what had been done to her, knowing that with her being there, that it must have only just happened.

But where had her protector in the dark been during this time?

Another question to add to the many, I guess. Lucius stood in the corner of the room and with his hands balled into fists by his sides, I knew of the rage he felt at seeing her this way. He walked to her bedside seeing as it was safe to do so with her being asleep and gently brushed back a piece of her hair. Then he looked at the monitor at her bedside for her vitals as they spiked by his touch. However, she didn't stir, so he continued to lean down and laid a kiss on her forehead doing so now with a vow,

"I failed to get to you in time, but have no fear my little Keira girl, he will pay for what he did to you, by my hand or that of your King." After this he watched as she started to moan in her sleep, so before he left, he adjusted her medication and she quickly fell back into a state of unconsciousness with the extra drugs in her system. After this he left with only one promise issued,

"Soon, little Chosen One, *soon.*" I swallowed hard and hated the jealousy that seeped inside me, like a coiled snake hissing its poison. I knew this was irrational as it was years before I had even been born, but the sight of such would still haunt me, because I found myself questioning every word in that statement made. Did he think her to be his Chosen One or named her such because he knew she belonged to my father?

Something I hoped to discover when time sped up once more.

Although, I had to say I was at least thankful that the time Lucius spent with my mother was quick and brief, but I wondered if this was because I could hear myself utter the moment she came into view,

"Oh no, not this."

Had the Keepers of Three wanted to spare me the

heartache? Because I was pretty sure this had been classed as an important time in Lucius' life. But then I was the one clearly running this show and they were the ones obliging me with this vision fest. So, as it sped through time, showing brief moments at Blood Rock I was at least thankful it happened quickly. However, there were times, like when he danced with my mother in the same place he had danced with me, I had no choice but to grit my teeth and bear it.

It was the same when seeing things like the altercation he had with the likes of Layla, which must have been when he banished her. The many times he seemed to save my mother's life, one ending in a battle scene. It was in what looked like a crumbling temple and it especially caught my attention as it seemed to be when Lucius changed from just a Vampire to something more...

Something gifted this time from Heaven.

But again, it happened so fast that I didn't get chance to see all of it, only the moment his wings broke out of their demonic mould and into that of a flaming phoenix for the first time. Then time shot forward again, to an even stranger one of my mother, who looked to be trapped in a giant birdcage.

I shook my head as a blurred image of them both together in some sort of bell tower had me questioning what they had been doing as all I saw was the mere hint of naked flesh? I quickly decided that I didn't want to fucking know and was nearly on the cusp of shouting out for the Keepers of Three to stop it all.

As I couldn't stand it any longer!

But when I finally did shout out, it wasn't for it to end like I thought it would have been. No, instead it was for the vision to slow down so I could see the next event that changed Lucius' life forever!

"Wait!" I demanded, because suddenly Lucius was back in Hell and looked as if he had just been fighting in some demonic battle on the edge of being forced into the belly of a volcano. Huge waves of lava splashed up against the sides of the flat rock a few others were stood on, but they were shadows as my vision focused on only one man.

The platform seemed to be getting smaller as the whole thing shook, with giant pieces of it breaking off at the sides and crashing into the river of molten death below. Blurred figures of people started moving backwards the second the lava rose up and burst over the sides. Even I thought that this was it, they were all done for as only those who had wings had a chance of surviving this. But then something started to happen, as the molten rock started to form into shapes.

It started to flow over itself instead of its continued journey forward, now creating giant uneven black bricks on top of each other like a pyramid. And as it built up higher, the flowing magma defied gravity by following it, now running up the sides of what was beginning to look like something built by the Aztecs. Then, when the flow of lava reached the top of the pyramid, it disappeared in what I assumed was a way inside. And speaking of a way inside, high up the structure, the last part to form was an arched doorway. It was one created by cooled lava that formed a crust of black rock and was decorated with a strange keystone. It looked like the angry face of a God, that had no choice but to drop open its mouth, despite the obvious rage at being forced to do so.

"Duty calls," Lucius said before giving way to his demon side, one that yet again had changed. Because now it looked exactly like the one I had seen that night when he had saved me from the Hellhounds. Something had happened to him yet again that had changed him into this, and it made me question what. What had I purposely been forced to miss in the visions that led to this point?

Well, I was about to witness at least one more event in

Lucius' life that answered a question...what had happened to his hand? One that Lucius looked down at now after first flying up to the arched doorway. Then he fisted it before bringing it to his lips and biting into it, more viciously than I had seen him do before. It was as if he needed a greater amount of blood to flow.

"Gods, no!" I found myself shouting out, despite it being a plea unheard in this time, as Lucius then held himself rigid as he plunged his hand into the open mouth, obviously needing to feed it his tainted blood. It then became the second time I heard Lucius' screams and I knew why the second the mouth locked down around his arm, before the sickening crunch of bone and flesh could be heard.

Lucius staggered back the second it released him and lost consciousness just as he went tumbling over the edge of the pyramid. His wings caused his body to spiral down a little as they vibrated in the air, cradling only half of his body as they were unused in his descent. It happened so quickly, in the time it took me to suck in a panicked breath his body had landed, doing so hard enough that it cracked the stone beneath him as a cloud of dust rose before settling. And as it did, it revealed the unconscious form of Lucius, in a mass of twisted demonic wings and a pool of his own blood.

That, and a piece of him that had been completely severed.
His hand.

I felt myself crying, whispering his name in a different time,
"Oh, Lucius." However, by the time it made it past my lips, the vision was no more. Instead, his days that followed merged into weeks, months and then into years. It skipped through them with haste and brief moments were getting even harder to make out. Like a quick bus journey, which was gone in a second where he had looked to be sat next to my mother. Then the fast forwarded destruction of some college library. After which came the battle of the start of what was known to us all as the

Blood of the Infinity Wars. But by this point I could make out nothing but a blur of a past life lived through that clearly was not my right to witness.

Was this because time could still be affected in some way if I had? After all, to know of the past would undoubtedly affect the future and clearly the Fates had some sort of plan for me. But speaking of my future, now it was time for the entirety of it to be explained, as I had finally arrived at the one memory that could answer the biggest question of all.

"Oh Gods, this is it," I muttered the second I knew which part it had slowed right down to. The time that I had wanted to see the most and the sole reason I had asked the Keeper of Three to show me everything.

As it was none other than the day Lucius had stolen two pieces of my soul. He had stolen the Angel in me and that of the first natural born Vampire.

But most importantly, now it was time to find out not only how but mainly…

Why?

CHAPTER SIX

A HUNGRY SOUL

The start of my fate began looking more like a celebration than what I would have expected someone stealing your soul would have been like. Although, what had I been expecting, Lucius hiding in the shadows of a child's nursery like the child catcher in Chitty Chitty Bang Bang? He wasn't some thief in the night waiting to strike with an oversized soul catching net over his shoulder.

It all started when suddenly my visions had come to a soundless halt, stopping at what looked to be a party. And it didn't take me long to discover what it was for, as now I was looking around the walls of Afterlife. Walls, that certainly hadn't changed much, despite the decorations that now adorned the stone. And this claim also included the people now standing within them...

My family.

But like I said, the only difference now was the room had been decorated within an inch of its life and the culprit soon went skipping by with green and blue hair. Aunty Pip was carrying a massive bunch of baby pink balloons and she had drawn pictures in black marker on them all. Some were just smiling baby faces but others looked like a warning sign. This consisted of a crudely drawn condom with a circle around it and a line across. Underneath were the words,

'No condoms were harmed during the making of this baby!'

Needless to say, as she passed, some people just shook their heads and others sniggered after first looking towards the baby making pair…
My parents.
Gods, but they looked so happy! My mother was utterly beaming down at the baby in her arms, which was obviously me. My father was positioned behind her, with his arm around her shoulders, tucking her close as he nearly always did. He, too, was beaming down at the sight of me as a baby but whenever he glanced back at my mother, the emotion was one that was easy to see…*Pride.*

The drawing room, where the celebration was being held, was overflowing with gifts, decorations and party food. Which from the rainbow of colours, it looked as if Aunty Pip had been in charge of it all. Even my human grandparents were there, looking nearly thirty years younger than I ever would have remembered seeing them.

The room was a mix of both supernatural and human life congregating together, with only one side knowing the other side of the family as being different. This included my Aunty Libby and Uncle Frank, with my cousin Ella running riot in between everyone's legs. Even to this day my Aunty Libby had no idea of what her sister had become or what life she had married into. This would have also included Ella too, had it not been for me sneaking into Jared's fight club and her following me that night when I was sixteen.

Gods, but just looking at her now and she had been such a cute kid, and it was no surprise that she had turned into such a beauty, considering how beautiful her mother was. Jared Cerberus most certainly had his hands full there, that was for damn sure. Because he may have been King of the Hellbeasts, but there was no claiming her spirit and expecting to rule over it.

I took in the rest of the room and it looked as though everyone was there, minus the Hellbeast himself. But the rest of the Kings were there, looking as handsome and as striking as always. Along with the timeless beauty that was my Aunty Sophia and the mad beauty in Aunty Pip, who was dressed like a kid's Bunny Rabbit. It also had a flap at her butt that whenever it popped open it showed a little naked bum, one that Adam continued to rebutton for her, making her giggle as she wiggled making the task difficult.

I couldn't help but smile at the sight of my family, all gathered to celebrate my birth, missing them now so much that I felt the empty pain of it in my chest. Which was why it was no wonder I could feel tears in my eyes, as I was obviously crying back at the Temple. It was just such a beautiful sight, and one that made me feel so loved it was like a rush of emotions had just hit me. A flash of visions of my very own, and each one making me feel blessed despite all my bitterness at being different.

Because each person there meant so much to me and just looking at the little baby in my mother's arms, I knew just how lucky she was to have so many people who loved her. To have so many who were willing to lay down their lives in protecting her.

In fact, it made me feel ashamed that I had run from them

all, knowing how worried they would be. I shouldn't have done that. I should have handled it better. I should have stayed like Lucius had said. I should have shouted, I should have screamed and fought for my answers and reasons...*I should have stayed and listened.*

And right in that moment, I wanted to see my mother so badly that it hurt. Because one look in those stunning eyes of hers as she looked down at me and I knew that I must have been mistaken somehow. No-one could do that to someone they loved as much as my mother loved me.

But now was not the time for that vision.

No, first it was time to witness something else entirely.

Because there in the corner, watching all this, was the one man I had given my heart to, despite all the hurt he had caused. Hurt that just kept coming and in this moment, it was the root of it all. It was time for the truth he had been terrified of telling me. And who could blame him, when he had been the cause of my humanity, stealing away my birthright of an eternal life with those I loved.

A royal bloodline I had been entitled to receive.

But just the sight of him and I found myself gasping. He looked more formidable than I was used to seeing him. This then prompted the natural question to ask myself... *Had I been the one to change him?*

Because this way he seemed more edgy, as if at the ready for action, not some baby celebration. He wore dark jeans, a burgundy t-shirt and a leather biker jacket, as if he didn't intend to stay long, just enough time to give his mandatory congratulations. It was clear he was uncomfortable being there and the tense fist of his gloved hand was making it obvious only to those like me who were taking the time to look closely. Me, *and my mother*, who looked up and sought him out in the crowded room. Then, when it was safe to do so, without making it obvious, she met his eyes as Lucius was now staring back at her and she smiled as he bowed his head in return.

In fact, he reminded me very much as he had that night. The one when I had foolishly entered his club believing it might have been the start of something new and exciting, seeing as even then I had been convinced we were meant to be together. That we were destined by the Fates and I was his Chosen One. I had believed this was something he would have recognised instantly, but how wrong I had been. Of course, since then I knew the truth. I knew that he had discovered me being his fated one long before I had. And now, I was about to discover why he'd fought against it for as long as he had.

I then watched as my mother reached up, kissed my father's cheek and left him to continue his conversation with my Uncle Frank, telling him that she was going to put the baby down. Then she walked over to where Lucius was stood, a bottle of beer casually held in one hand, his gloved one tapping behind him on the dark panelled wall at his back. This was when my vision shifted, taking me closer to them both until I was stood next to what was obviously my crib.

"So, you're a mother now," Lucius said in an easy tone that looked forced to me. My mum laughed once as she placed my sleeping form down in the crib that was near where he stood.

"Yeah, although I think the usual response here is to offer congratulations."

"Mazel Tov," Lucius replied just as he touched the bottle of his beer to his lips and then took a swig.

"That would be great if I was Jewish and all, but hey, I guess I will take what I can get." He winked at her in reply making her roll her eyes, telling me where I got that sassy response from.

"Shoot, I forgot her nappy bag, hey can you just watch her a sec," my mum said making him frown instantly before snapping,

"Do I look like a fuc…"

"Hey, watch the language, buddy! Now all you have to do is coo at her if she wakes, it's not saving the world, Luc!" my mum snapped after first smacking him on the arm to stop him from swearing, then she said,

"I have faith in you…oh, that's her name by the way, in case you wondered… Amelia Faith Draven." Lucius scoffed a laugh making my mum put her hands to her hips and said,

"What?"

"Nothing, now go get your shit bag," he said making my mum huff before going to do just that. Then I watched as Lucius eyed me suspiciously. Even as he took another swig of his beer, his eyes watched me with a frown. Then I started to wake, and I couldn't help but smirk at the same time Lucius did when the baby me burped.

"Cute," he admitted on a laugh, making me smile as he actually decided to take more notice of me. He finished his bottle before putting it down on a side table and decided to come closer to me as I started fussing more.

"Who would name their kid 'work' in Latin? Although, with a father like Dom, then that's exactly what it will be for you, kid, and having Faith won't hurt either. Well, at least being cute will go a long way with this lot," he said scoffing another laugh and I had to say I was shocked that this had been our first conversation.

"Shame you're human, 'cause not gonna lie, kid, that shit is gonna get harder when you're older. If I were you, I would think about becoming a nun." Lucius laughed at his own joke, meanwhile I nearly choked on the irony of it all! But then, it also meant that like everyone else, at this point he thought I was human, which made me have to question why, if I wasn't?

But then I started squirming more and he shot me an irritated look before rolling his eyes and telling me,

"Aww, come on, kid, I wasn't exactly made for this shit, you know. Can't you just wait until your mother comes back or something?" I obviously wasn't ready to do that and started crying more, making him turn to me and mutter,

"I'm a fucking Vampire King for Devil's sake, not a fucking nanny!" But then I started trying to reach out for him and again the irony wasn't lost on me.

"Alright, fine, you've got my attention, but I am not picking you up or any shit like that," he said putting his gloved hand in my crib and I swear my mouth dropped open in utter shock as he started tickling my belly, making me giggle and smile as I looked up at him.

"Well, it's got to be said, you sure do have pretty eyes... even prettier than your mother's but ssshh, don't tell her I said that," he said softly making my heart melt at just how sweet he was being to me as a baby. Even though admittedly, it was all a bit strange. But before I could dwell on this thought too long, something started to happen that made him frown down at me before muttering,

"What's this?" I looked down to see what he was seeing and my eyes widened just the same. Because I had started glowing, with my skin looking as if it had just been dusted in the sunrays breaking through the clouds. Like a golden hue that illuminated my body and Lucius looked up, obviously about to tell someone. But then this was when my tiny baby hand suddenly reached up and grabbed his glove before tugging at it. His eyes went back to inside the crib and quickly they widened in shock as he discovered what else was different about me.

"No...no, no... it can't...*can't be possible?*" he questioned as he pulled his gloved fingers free of my tiny grasp and used one of them to open my mouth. My gummed little mouth started sucking on his leather clad finger as if he was trying to find something there. What had he been looking for…surely not…*fangs?*

Either way, he released a relieved sigh when he saw nothing, but then he looked up obviously wanting to tell my mother about my glowing skin, when suddenly he hissed in shock…and he wasn't the only one, as I looked down to see that I had bitten him!

But not just that, I now had little fangs and had bitten him so hard with them that it had gone straight through his glove and into the hand he always kept hidden.

"Gods, no!" he hissed in fear, but it was too late!

The deed had been done as my glowing skin started to travel up my body and straight into his hand, one I now held to my mouth and was feeding from, as I was actually sucking at the infected blood on his hand. It only took seconds for two things to happen, one of which was him ripping his hand free of my hold and the second, was that for him to realise that it had been too late. Because the glow on my skin was soon gone, along with the fangs.

The baby me then burst into tears, screaming now in what sounded like baby agony, making Lucius stumble back a step before looking down at the black blood seeping from his hand and the tear in the leather.

"Lucius, what happened?" my mum said coming to pick me up, looking no different to how she had put me down, only now I was in tears.

"She started crying, he said in a tense tone after first fisting his hand and hiding the evidence of what had just happened by his side.

"Is that all? Well, yeah, she is probably just hungry," my mum replied, as she cooed at me to calm down and walked back to where my dad was with me in her arms. My dad looked over with a brief moment of concern on his face.

However, Lucius turned his back on them both and after looking down at his hand once more in utter shock, he muttered a horrified,

"Yes, I think she was hungry."

CHAPTER SEVEN

ORDER OF FORGIVENESS

I swear if I'd had my body with me, I would have fallen to the floor in utter shock. I just couldn't believe it! I was so stunned, my mind was stuck on the jumble of questions and none of them felt as if they made any sense. Because it hadn't been Lucius' fault after all. No, he had merely wanted to protect me from the truth.

A truth that had meant only one thing…

This had all been my fault.

Alright, so I had been a baby at the time, but I had been the one to bite him! I had been the one to lose that part of my soul to him and he hadn't been able to do a damn thing to stop it…*or fix it*. I knew this when the next part of my vision began to come into focus and pretty soon it started to knit together twenty seven years of reasons why.

It started with Lucius in his office and he wasn't alone. Adam was in there with him and in that particular moment in time, it quickly became obvious that he was trying to calm Lucius down.

"How the fuck did this fucking happen!?" he roared and grabbed the nearest thing to him, which happened to be a bottle of whisky, and threw it until it smashed into the wall opposite his desk.

"Luc, you need to calm down."

"Calm down! Are you fucking shitting me? How the fuck can I calm down, I stole part of the girl's soul for fuck sake!" Lucius roared again making Adam release a sigh before replying with an obvious statement,

"It was not as if you planned it."

"Oh, so that makes it okay does it, when I go to Keira and tell her that the reason her child is fucking human and no doubt facing a lifetime of danger, a life, that I might add, will be considerably shorter now, that it's okay because I didn't fucking plan it!?" he snapped making Adam shrug his shoulders and say,

"No, I just wouldn't say anything." I sucked in a surprised breath. I couldn't believe what I was hearing. That it was my Uncle Adam who was the one to advise this and I wasn't the only one who looked shocked.

"What the fuck are you suggesting, Adam, that I don't tell them at all!?" Lucius' tone said it all. In return, Adam released a heavy sigh and rubbed a hand at the back of his neck in frustration before telling him,

"What good would telling them do, Luc?" Lucius growled low in reply but Adam ignored it and added,

"Think about it, it's not like anything can be done right now and you would gain nothing by telling them, not when it would more than likely start another war between you and an ally, one that I will remind you, has only just been healed." Luc scoffed at this and said,

"War or not, I accept what I did and if it causes a…"

"What *she did*, Luc... not you." Adam interrupted but Lucius slashed an angry hand through the air before telling him,

"She is a fucking baby, she can hardly be held accountable here!"

"That may be so, but neither can you, for it is not as though you expected that to happen." Adam pointed out and I had to agree with most of what he was saying. Okay, so keeping that type of thing from my parents was hard to accept as being the right thing to do, or condone, but his reasons for suggesting it were also hard to argue against. What I most definitely did agree with was that Lucius wasn't at fault here, yet the way he blamed himself was heartbreaking to see.

"I doubt Dom would fucking see it like that when he is trying to kill me with his bare hands," Lucius said dryly.

"Something we know he can't do seeing as now it would not only kill his Chosen One but also his daughter." Lucius hissed through his teeth as this thought only just came to him thanks to Adam thinking clearly.

"She is now linked to your life as much as Keira is, no doubt even more so and that is something no-one will be able to overlook, including Dom, should he ever find out."

"Then you are right, there really would be no good to come from telling him...*fuck!*" Lucius admitted hissing the curse at the end more to himself.

"Not when it has taken this long for all the Kings to finally come together and work as one. For you and Dom both know the lengths it has taken in the past to even try and get it to this point. You can't jeopardize that now...you know you can't," Adam said and it was easy to see why he was Lucius' voice of reason and right hand man. The respect Lucius had for his honesty could be seen from across the room, despite his lingering anger.

One that erupted again.

"Gods in fucking Hell! How the fuck did this happen!?" Lucius asked now dragging a hand down his face before grabbing a glass of whisky that had survived and knocking it back in one.

"I am not exactly sure, seeing as everyone assumed she was merely born human." I frowned at this and I wasn't the only one as Lucius snapped,

"She was fucking human, Adam… even I saw that!"

"Then what happened?"

"I don't fucking know! Just one second she was human, and then I touched her, and something started to happen. It was as if another side of her was suddenly being called to the surface."

"Your presence clearly triggered something." Lucius growled at this assumption before snapping,

"Yes, but why!? I have nothing to do with the girl!" I flinched at the disdain in his voice, forcing myself to remember that at this point I would have been nothing but a new hindrance for him to deal with.

"Well, I wouldn't say that," Adam muttered, but Lucius naturally heard it and his tone said it all…he hadn't liked it.

"And just what do you fucking mean by that?!" Adam released a sigh, one that no doubt silently asked for patience and told him,

"You're the first Vampire of your kind, an entire race of beings all connected with you as their King, they each have your blood, Luc."

"What's your fucking point here, Adam?" he barked,

"She was not connected to you through blood, she wasn't made. She was born that way and I don't need to point out to you that not a single being can claim the same. Not a single one of us has been born into our vessel as a Vampire, Demon or Angel," Adam said and Lucius was left digesting the words with a harsh, stern look upon his face. Then, once again, he was left with no other option than to listen further.

"Keira gave birth to three souls, two of which are being kept safe until their Chosen vessels come of age. But this child, Amelia, is different, she is the only one. Now we have to ask ourselves why...why was she born this way?" Lucius finally stopped pacing and deflated into a chair and the frustration of all these questions mounting up was easy to see was taking its toll on him.

Meanwhile, I was in utter shock at all that I was hearing.

I was the only one?

"I don't know why, but I know that she was not only born a Vampire," Lucius admitted, making Adam's eyes widen before he raised a brow in question.

"What do you mean?" Lucius released a heavy sigh and again dragged a hand down his face before telling him,

"She was born an Angel also." At this Adam now sucked in a quick breath in shock.

"Gods," he muttered, making Lucius scoff,

"Yeah, my fucking thoughts exactly! Now how the fuck did that happen?!"

"Well, there must be a reason." Lucius rolled his eyes before sarcasm took centre stage in his reply,

"A reason why she was born that way, sure...but a reason why it only showed itself to me and doing so just before I fucking took it away...sorry, my friend, but I am coming up fucking empty on that one!" Lucius snapped making Adam frown.

"The only accountability to it all would be..." Lucius growled low before whipping a hand up and warning,

"Don't fucking say it! Don't you even fucking think it!"

"If not the Fates, then why? Why would she be connected to

you?" Adam braved to ask, making Lucius close his eyes against the idea that the Fates were involved.

"I don't know," he muttered.

"Why wouldn't her own parents know what she truly was?" He continued to ask and I could see that Lucius was losing what shred of patience he had when he forced out through gritted teeth this time,

"I don't know!"

"Why would she be tied to your soul if she wasn't destined to be your..."

"I don't fucking know, alright!" Lucius shouted this time, bolting up out of his seat and making Adam shake his head to himself.

"I am sorry, Luc, I know this isn't easy for you," he said, watching as Lucius looked down at his gloved hand with nothing but disgust and Adam's comment only made him fist it in anger before he ordered,

"I want you and Pip there for her."

"But of course," was Adam's instant reply, but this wasn't enough for Lucius as he turned a little to grant him a stern look over his shoulder, so he could demand more from him,

"I want you to become the girl's guardian, watch over her, keep her safe, do you understand?"

"I will guard the girl with my life, but then this isn't exactly a shock, Luc, not seeing as my wife would have my balls if I did anything but die for her." Lucius huffed and said,

"She has no doubt become quite attached."

"You were at that party, Luc, who do you think was up with her inflating four hundred fucking pink balloons until five in the morning whilst I watched my wife drawing condoms and smiley faces on them all." Luc scoffed again, no doubt unable to find the same humour in the thought as his friend did.

"Good, then that will be another guardian for her," he said and it broke my heart with how responsible he obviously felt.

"Trust me, even beyond the walls of Afterlife she will have many," Adam commented and I smirked, knowing he hadn't been wrong there.

"I also want all the research that can be done about this… done with discretion of course."

"No one will find out, Luc," Adam stated like this was obvious, well that was before Lucius pointed out the most indiscreet person on the planet.

"That also means your wife, my friend," Lucius added making Adam now look uncomfortable before admitting in a tense tone,

"Yes, *I know.*" After this Lucius walked up to where he sat and squeezed his shoulder, telling him silently that he knew he was asking a lot, especially considering how much Adam adored his wife and was as faithful as they came. But then, he was also faithful to his friend and his King.

"And what about you?" Adam asked after Lucius took his seat behind his desk, making him pause slightly as if he was affected by the question.

"What about me?" he asked in return after lowering himself into his seat and speaking in a tone that said he felt agitated by the question.

"What will you do regarding the girl?" At this it didn't take him long to answer.

"I will tell you what I am going to do and that is keep as far as I fucking can away from her, that is what!" he snapped and suddenly with that one statement alone, the last twenty seven years of his treatment of me started to make sense. As it was clear that now had been the starting point in time.

"You think that is wise?" Adam asked, clearly taken back.

"You think it's not?!" Lucius threw back as if he couldn't

believe what he was hearing in that question and holding up his gloved hand to make a point.

"And what if you are destined to…"

"Don't fucking finish that sentence, Adam, for I would like you to leave this office still a friend." Adam released a sigh and said,

"Think about it."

"I refuse to, for she is a fucking child, for Lucifer's sake!" he bellowed, banging a fist on the desk and making me wonder how it had even survived all these years of Lucius' rage.

"Yes, but she won't always be, and you know that," Adam pointed out and Lucius grimaced.

"Yes, and she will grow into a human woman because of me, so you really think I want to be around the reminder of that!" he ground out through clenched teeth and I had to say it hurt, despite the circumstances that surrounded it.

"So, what, you want her protected her entire life but have nothing more to do with it?" Adam pressed, proving exactly what he could get away with around his friend and the answer was a lot.

"Yes, that is exactly what I am saying! After all, it is the least I can do, for if she is now forced to live as a human then this way she will do so for as long as humanly possible… *without being hurt,*" he said emphasizing this last part and trying to make his point.

"And if there is more than that destined for her?"

"Then she will live out that destiny without me fucking in it, that is what!" he snapped making Adam sigh in exasperation.

"Luc, come on, think about it…"

"NO!" Lucius roared and this time when his fist hit the desk he was back to standing and staring down at where it had cracked. Then after needing to take a minute to calm, he told him firmly,

"I won't risk the life of Keira's child...*not again*...keeping her safe is all I will ever offer the girl and that I can promise you." The pain of his words cut deep but what did manage to ease the hurt was that I knew that this was one promise he would have no choice but to break.

However, it did at least answer so many questions as to why he had held me at arm's length for so long. He feared that if he was ever to give into the temptation of being near me, then it could have happened again, that much was obvious.

Which just made me wonder exactly how long had he continued to blame himself for what had happened? The entire time most likely, as he clearly felt ashamed enough to keep it from me. And I had to admit, that this hurt the most. That Lucius hadn't trusted me enough with the truth for only one reason…

He thought that I would blame him, *just as he blamed himself.*

But little did he know that in my eyes there was nothing to forgive, as it was like Adam had said,

This had all been fated.

But I knew it would first take years of my life to be lived through before he would feel this way and go back on his promise. Especially as this image started to fade around the edges, doing so to the sight of Lucius, who was now scowling down at his fisted leather hand. It was as if pure hatred for it was all he was capable of feeling.

And the sight, well…

It broke my heart.

CHAPTER EIGHT

DEPTHS OF AN OBSESSION

After this time in his office ended, it once more became a merging of time, all now featuring Lucius and me. Most of which was unbeknown to me at the time. This started with him watching me from afar. Something that only happened after he saved me the night I had sneaked into the Devil's Ring. And looking at it now and seeing his reaction, well it was obviously when he was hit with the knowledge that I was his Chosen One after all…that Adam had been right all along. And after this point, well it became clear that there were times he found it too difficult to do as he promised he would, which was to stay away from me. Because the next lot of visions of his past only showed one thing… an obsession as it grew in its intensity. As there was something I quickly discovered…

Lucius had always been there watching.

He would watch me as I played the piano, telling me now why there had been one in my apartment that he had purposely decorated for me next to his own in Transfusion. I believe I even questioned this when first seeing it and asking myself why he would even care enough to bother.

And then there were the times when he had been forced to be at events and celebrations that I never knew he had even been there. But there he was and as usual, spent his time watching me from afar. Watching me from the shadows and seemingly questioning why it was that I looked forlorn or even lonely. This as I sat on the sidelines secretly waiting for my prince to come and sweep me off my feet by asking me to dance. There were even times that I saw him taking a step forward before stopping himself as if he had been about to request the next dance. And every single time he saw me, it seemed to end in the same way, as he clenched his gloved hand and scowled before walking away from me, without looking back. It happened so often that it became almost like a habit.

In fact, the amount of times he was part of my life really started to impact me after I turned up at his club the first time and ran from it heartbroken. The true depth of his obsession became even more blindingly obvious when I saw a barrage of visions that started the moment I left the safety of Afterlife.

This even included him buying my building in Twickenham and then arranging to have all the money spent on it to ensure it had top of the range security. I even witnessed his meeting with Queeney, the lady who had helped me that day in the Underground, telling me of a flat for sale. It had all been his doing, not that of my father's!

Gods, but even Ben across the hall had been one of his people! I knew this the second an image of Lucius now sat at his desk emerged, telling me exactly who he was speaking to on his phone. Also telling me exactly who he was getting an update on my movements from and all the while during the call he was tapping on the surveillance pictures of me taken from afar.

I was utterly astounded at all I was discovering, especially the levels that Lucius had gone to throughout most of my life! Which always seemed to have only one theme in common...*my safety*. But despite this and his good intentions of keeping me safe, it was no different to what I had mistakenly blamed my father for doing. It was a huge intrusion of privacy in my life and one he had not only kept from me but continued to allow my father to take the blame for. Something I most definitely did have a right to be angry at him for.

But then there were the other intrusions of my privacy, the more intimate kind. Like when he was in my room, watching me sleep. I remember one time when I had called in sick, suffering with the flu and Lucius looked frustrated when I would cough in my sleep. I had to say, as good as the times for him to be in my room with me went, then this was one of the most embarrassing he could have picked. But then knowing Lucius, it was most likely the reason he had picked to show up, because his daily update of me had mentioned my being absent from work due to sickness. And what sight met him, but balls of used tissues dotted about the bed like little snot bombs and me with one fisted in my hand. This so I could rub my red and sore nose in my sleep, one cracked from blowing it so much.

However, the only move he ever made towards me was a slight stroke of my cheek before he left. He visited me every night after that until I was over it and back to being healthy again. The sight seriously made my heart ache for how much he cared.

But that intense care he only showed me in secret was something he continued to hide and the night he pretended to walk back into my life, when in fact he had never left it, was no exception. As now the not so distant memories started to play back to me, showing me a very different view of the past, one I was finally allowed to feel a part of.

This started with Lucius watching me as I entered the gala, doing so like all those times before, hidden in the shadows. But unlike those nights when he held himself back, this time when he took a step towards me, he kept going. But the second before he made this decision, I saw the way he looked down at his gloved hand and made a fist with it, and I knew why. Even years later, he still blamed himself and again, it made my heart ache for him. To now know the truth about why all this time he never felt comfortable letting me touch it.

Of course, he remembered what happened the last time I did.

And it all made sense now, every single time. Even including the last time not so long ago, where I had kissed his palm in bed. It had ended up being the longest time he had let me touch him there without pulling away, making me ask myself...had he started to trust me more?

But of course, that was now, and this uncertainty *was then*. The reason he fought himself so hard on what he wanted and what he believed was right. What he believed would keep me safe from something he classed as my biggest threat...*himself.*

However, despite this, it became obvious that he still couldn't let me go completely. And after first unclenching his fist, it was like I said, he had made his first move towards me, instead of this time walking away. I swear I almost laughed at the sight of myself as I tensed the moment I heard his voice behind me, remembering my utter disbelief that it was really him. Thus, marking the start of his charade in making me believe he didn't care and that I was just a job to him... or more like a favour he carried out because my father had asked him to.

But the vision didn't skip that far ahead, not like I thought it would have. Which made me wonder if this night was considered an important turning point in Lucius' life and was considered a favoured memory of his? It was most certainly a hopeful thought as I found myself back in the gallery where I had held my tour.

It was strange reliving it and witnessing again how those steel blue eyes of his barely ever left me. I even got to relive the moment when one of the women had come on to him. I remember questioning what it had been he had said to her to make her storm off like that, as she had clearly been slighted in some way.

Well, now I was about to find out as the memory played back. And I could barely believe my ears when I heard what he had said to her. Telling her firmly that she had no chance in Hell or beyond it, for there was only one female he intended for his bed, then he finished this crass statement with a nod towards me and telling the once hopeful woman exactly who he had in his sights.

Clearly insulted, the woman had left, and I remembered it now, wishing at the time I knew why. But there were other times, ones more playful, like when I had been at Wendy's flat texting him. Unbeknown to me at the time, he had been in a car travelling to the airport. And as his driver did all the work in getting him there, he had spent the journey grinning down at his screen, looking…well… *happy.*

But then a very a different grin was what greeted me next as the memory shifted to one of a very different kind. And I knew exactly what it was when I found him watching the security footage with that knowing grin playing at the corner of his lips. It was of me trying to sneak into Transfusion when I had been intent on stealing from him.

I felt a blush rise at just the thought of him watching it all and even more so when I became a spectator to my own first erotic experience. Of course, this had been a life changing memory for me and just knowing that despite all his past sexual encounters, it was a meaningful one for him too and one that made the cut. In fact, it made me question why none of his past sexual encounters with other woman had ever made it through to the montage of memories. Did that mean none of them had been important enough to him?

However, my questioning of this died the moment the time came for my kidnapping. First came the look of pure rage before utter agony took its place. This was when he was forced to endure seeing the distance between us grow as I was taken away from him in a helicopter.

I watched as he stumbled into a wall in the lobby outside his apartment. It was as if in that moment he felt the exact second that I had fallen into the water and couldn't breathe.

"My Šemšā'... my Šemšā... Še...mšā," he whispered over and over again, and my heart broke for him. But then he roared out in undiluted fury before he hit out at the wall behind him. Then he was suddenly running to his apartment with speed, as if he had just had an idea on how to save me and time was crucial. Once he passed through the door my view changed just as he grabbed the vault door with his hands, morphing them to that of his demon. There was such strength and power in them that I felt breathless just watching it, as he brought forth what seemed like flames directly from his link to Hell. Doing so enough that soon the metal could withstand it no more. Gods, but he looked ready to take on all of Heaven and Hell if it meant getting me back, as it was as though he knew something I didn't.

Had I been closer to dying than I had first believed?

It looked like I was soon to find out as the door gave way granting him entrance far quicker than opening it the usual way would have done. Then he walked straight over to the sword and knelt down as he whispered its name. It was done in a way as if calling forth the one who bestowed it upon him the honour of owning it.

"Caliburnus."

He placed his hand upon the blade, bowed his head and then purposely sliced his hand down its length before making a vow,

"My Šemšā .... 'Save my Šemšā, my Electus born. Save her and my blood is yours... *that's all I fucking ask*!" He shouted this last part then roared out his demand,

"SAVE HER!" This was at the same time as hammering a fist down on the floor and cracking it around the sword. After this the weapon began to glow with blinding white power, like an eruption of the Gods gifting him his wish and taking away the sight of anything else in the room. All until a slight figure could still be seen, holding onto the blade and utterly determined not to let go, as if he were hanging on not just for his own dear life but mainly for mine.

The sight had me in tears, for the love this man had for me seemed to have no bounds and it took my breath away, tearing it from my body with the force of my emotions. That was when I knew that I would have drowned in that river had it not been for Lucius.

He had saved me...*saved me again.*

After this I had been ready to break the connection, no longer needing to see anymore, when it seemed as if the Keepers of Three weren't yet done with me.

For there was one last vision left for me.

That of a...

Mistaken Lovers' Kiss

CHAPTER NINE

HELLISH HARSH REALITY

I was quickly transported to that fateful day I had left Afterlife or should I say…

The day I left Lucius.

I almost begged not to see it, as I didn't know if I was strong enough to witness it a second time around. Although, I was surprised that the memory hadn't just taken me straight to the library, but instead I ended up back on the rooftop. It had been where I had left Lucius after our argument but this time, he wasn't alone. And it looked as if I had just entered into the middle of an argument. Because I saw my mother's frustrated sigh before asking the retreating form of Lucius,

"Luc, where are you going?" He shot her a look of anger before snapping,

"To find her and tell her the truth…to tell everyone the fucking truth, like I should have done years ago!"

"You really think that is wise?" my mum asked making me frown, because surely this response was only going to back up the theory of an affair. But the way Lucius was acting towards her didn't make sense either.

"You really think continuing to lie to her is?!" he threw back, before walking through the same door that he had locked in an attempt to keep me from leaving during our own argument.

"Lucius, wait!" my mum shouted desperately, which was something he ignored as my vision followed his angry escape.

"Lucius, please just think about this!" My mum now pleaded after she had caught up with him, once back inside the walls of Afterlife. I also found myself wondering where I was while this was going on. Was I still back inside the Temple of Janus, opening the box or had that time passed and I was back inside the library? Had I been on my way to try and find Lucius, ready and excited to tell him what I had discovered?

These questions faded from my mind the moment he answered my mother.

"I have thought of nothing else!" he snapped angrily as he continued down yet another of the many grand hallways in Afterlife. Yet this was one I recognised as leading towards the library. Which meant that this was it then, the moment that had haunted my dreams and my every thought since this day. The greatest heartbreak I had been forced to endure, despite what happened seven years ago. Now all I could hope for was that after witnessing this, I would still love him the way I couldn't stop myself from doing before it.

Finally, they reached the library door and I knew this was it. It was time for me to witness the truth, one Lucius had been trying to get me to believe was not what I thought it was.

And it all started with a question.

"You love her?" my mum asked, and I sucked in a sharp breath, waiting for his reply. One that came quick and with certainty, as he shouted back,

"Of course I do, she's my Chosen One!"

I swear, but just hearing those words and I knew that I didn't need to see a single moment more, even though it continued. For Lucius had just told my mother of his love for me, not even said as a confession but more as a resounding statement. One that she looked to have already known.

And it was one that I knew in that moment, that the entire world should have known. It suddenly became so clear. What Lucius had been trying to do all this time. All he had wanted was to tell the world the truth, declaring me as his. But mainly to have been given the chance to declare his love for me to my father. That was what they had argued about. That was what every single word referred to. *I knew that now.* Every single word that had sounded like a secret love affair was all quickly turned on its head. I listened to it all playback to me and now that I knew the true context of it, it all became so clear.

His love for me was the only love he spoke of.

Not a secret love for my mother.

Gods, but I had been such a fool! *The biggest of fools.*

They had long ago entered the library and my mind raced as it made sense of every word spoken and it all led back to his love for me, not for her. And when it eventually came time for that fateful moment. The one that had devastated me, I now had the chance to see it from the angle I should have. Because now the ghost of my image stepped into my mother's place and I watched as her hand raised to his cheek, offering comfort as an old friend, *just like he had said it had been*.

He then lowered into it, accepting it at the same time he told her,

"Amelia needs to know, and I can't keep pretending anymore, especially here, *it's fucking killing me, Keira.*" He was talking about pretending in front of my father, about not being able to tell the truth and tell him about me being his Chosen One.

I looked towards the staircase and I just saw a glimpse of myself as I kept my head turned away, hiding from the sight like a coward. I had foolishly let my past insecurities rule over my heart. Whereas, in fact, what I should have done instead of running from the fear of what might have happened, is stayed and discovered the real truth of what *did happen*. Because there must have been a better way than running scared.

I knew that now.

That was why Lucius had been so angry that day. Because I had put him through an equal amount of heartache and all because I didn't trust him. No…because I hadn't trusted myself to be worthy enough for him. When the truth of it all was, he too had held himself back all those years because he felt the same way. He believed that he had been the cause of what I had become, the parts of my soul that I had lost. That he had somehow done this to me and if I ever found out, then I wouldn't just run from him, but I would run and never return. That my love for him would be lost in the shadows of my bitterness for the eternity he hoped to have with me.

Which was when I realised, I might not have trusted him enough to stay that day, but he hadn't trusted me either. He hadn't trusted me enough to love him despite the past. I now knew that our relationship would never have worked, *not like this*. Not when the foundations of our love were built upon a crumbling ground of lies and mistrust.

But that was all before.

All before this day, that I now knew the truth. The real depth of his love for me, something I knew it was now my chance to show in return. The guilt I felt was no doubt as immeasurable as his own. Only the difference was that mine would only last until

I could tell him the words to make it all right again. Lucius' guilt had lasted all my life.

All until this day, for anything beyond it I vowed was no more.

"Enough!" I suddenly shouted after closing my eyes on the past, fully intent on only looking towards the future.

I felt myself gasp as I staggered backwards after the Keepers of Three had finally released me once I had commanded them to do so.

"So now you see."

"The same as us Keepers Three," they said, only this time instead of the one who couldn't speak even trying to, he merely nodded towards my destiny behind me, as if silently telling me the time had now come to make my move. But before then, I had to be sure of one last thing.

"And the Tree of Souls, you're sure it is only me who can fix it?" I asked quietly, so Lucius wouldn't hear. Because I knew why they had shown me how Lucius had damaged his hand. That had been the start of the infection. The Venom of God had spread, and it had taken nearly thirty years to reach the first of the souls he had turned in the Vampires.

"One sacrifice made to start an infection."

"One sacrifice is born to end it."

"Mit mmy tmay."

The Keepers told me, as if seeing for themselves this all playing out in my mind. I nodded before taking a deep breath, telling them that I understood.

There was no other way.

I finally took a deep breath and turned around to face the man I loved and the sight that met my eyes nearly broke me. Lucius was now down on his knees, looking exhausted as the tunnel around him was nearly in ruins from his rage. He knelt in a mass of crumbled rock and I had to wonder how the thing hadn't caved in around him. He kept his head hung down, as if he couldn't even bear to raise it up to witness my reaction to all I had been shown. Because he knew all that I had seen, I could see the devastation written across his pained face.

The one secret that he had hoped to keep from me, for what could have been for my entire life.

And in all honesty, I couldn't find it in myself to blame him…

Not. At. All.

But he didn't know that. Not yet anyway.

He heard me approach and without even looking at me, he started making his next vow.

"I will find a way," he said, with his voice strained and hoarse.

"Lucius." I uttered his name on a whisper, but it was one he ignored.

"I promise you, I will find a way to get you back, if it takes me a fucking eternity, I will do it! If you run, I will find you. If you leave, I will find some way to make you stay. If you say that you no longer love me, I will stop at nothing to make you give me your heart again. This I vow, Amelia…This I fucking vow with not only my own life, but also on every single one on that fucking Tree of Souls I own! *I swear it to you on my blood.*" At this I sucked in a shuddered breath as tears started to roll down my cheeks, and with emotions almost too thick to speak I knew I had to push through.

"Lucius, lo…look at me," I asked, barely getting it out. He didn't, but instead he tore his face to the side, as if he were too afraid to and I found my hands near shaking.

"I…I have something to say," I told him, and he started shaking his head, as if he wasn't yet prepared for it. I knew then that he would never be prepared for what he thought I was about to say…that I wanted to leave him. That I no longer loved him. Words that all seemed like his own personal nightmare and one he didn't want to face.

But he couldn't have been more wrong.

"Lucius, please…please, look at me," I pleaded this time and he physically tensed before finally he granted me my wish. And I swear the sight caused me to hold my breath, as I hadn't expected to see the unshed tears in his eyes, tears that he looked too ashamed to show me. It was then that I could stand it no longer and the sight brought me to my fucking knees. There I was, just a foot away from him, with a barrier shimmering between us and all I wanted was to throw myself into his arms. All I wanted was to put my hand on his cheek and caress away the single tear I knew was threatening to fall. I wanted to place my forehead against his as I framed his face with my hands and told him everything I felt with my lips against his skin.

But in the end, all I had to rely on was the strength of my words.

"Gods, Lucius…I am so sorry!" I cried making him suddenly jerk back as if he was questioning every word I'd said. He frowned through it in that questioning way of his, before he whispered in disbelief,

"What…what did you say?" The sound of his utter uncertainty again broke something in me as I sobbed harder and my hands shook,

"Lucius…*oh, Honey*… I am so fucking sorry!" I shouted this time and I wished I had been free to slip through the portal just so I could have said it to him whilst finding comfort in his arms. But I knew that I wouldn't have made it through. Not when the fate of his life rested upon me to save it.

"Amelia?" He said my name still in question as I covered my face and cried.

"Oh, my Khuba, my sweet girl, why do you cry? Because

you think this is goodbye?" his gentle voice asked me, and my head bolted upright.

"No!" I shouted suddenly and then I let my anger at the idea fuel my emotions further and snapped,

"You will never fucking leave me! Do you hear me, Lucius! You will never leave me, and I will never be so foolish as to ever leave you again!"

"What?" Lucius asked in disbelief as though he could barely believe what he was hearing.

"I was a fool, so fucking foolish to believe...well, to believe what I thought I saw...I was so wrong! I was wrong about it all. You were only trying to tell everyone the truth about us and I took it the wrong way, I let my stupid insecurities get the better of me and push me into thinking I could never be good enough for you, not like my mother... so I ran. I ran because I was scared, no I was fucking terrified! So, I ran...I ran from you... ran from the only man *I've ever loved.*" After I finished telling him this, he closed his eyes and that single tear he had been holding prisoner slipped free. Falling at the same time as he took in a deep shuddered breath. Then he looked up at the ceiling and whispered,

"Thank the Gods, she saw the truth of that day."

"I did! I saw it all." Lucius frowned before opening his eyes and looking back at me, a pained expression taking hold of his features before he said,

"You didn't see it all, Amelia, for if you had, then you would not be saying all of these things...*you would be running again,"* he said sounding pained and I knew what he was now talking about. Especially when he added,

"You didn't see what I did to you." I closed my eyes, took a deep breath and shook my head before telling him,

"Lucius, I did see...*I saw it all."*

"No," he answered firmly, as if completely unwilling to

believe that if I had seen, then I wouldn't be acting this way now.

"Lucius, listen to me, the day you first saw me, when I was only a baby..." he sucked in a harsh breath realising that what I had been saying was true.

"...I saw what happened and..." I tried to say but he interrupted me,

"No! No, it can't be...how can you be here saying all this to me now, after what I did to you...after what I took from you?!" he demanded in a severe way as if it were impossible.

"Lucius, it wasn't your fault, it was mine." At this he growled before tearing his eyes from mine, turning his face away as if he couldn't entertain it.

"I saw it all, I bit you, Lucius," I told him trying again to get him to listen to me. But he sliced a hand through the air and snapped,

"No! It was my fault, I should have been more careful, I never should have touched you!"

"Lucius, come on, you didn't ask for what happened to happen, it just did. I bit you and something was taken from me, but it wasn't your fault...it was just all fated and..." Again, he cut me off as if it pained him to hear me blaming myself.

"Amelia, you need to stop."

"No, Lucius! It's you that needs to start fucking listening to me and right now! This wasn't your fault and I don't blame you, so why do you blame yourself? It does not and will never change how I feel about you, *how much I fucking love you!*" At this he finally looked at me and I could see now that desperate spark of hope in his eyes before I told him,

"You have to trust that I will always love you, no matter what...Hell, even when I thought you'd kissed my mother, I still couldn't stop myself from loving you! Nothing will ever change that, and you need to trust me when I say that," I said again, getting more and more worked up as I did and I knew that if I had been able to touch him, then I would have probably started shaking him by now!

He took a deep breath, making the heavyweight of his shoulders rise and fall before telling me,

"Then step through the barrier, Amelia and say it whilst my arms are around you, for this feels more like a dream than the reality you are trying to get me to believe it is." I released a deep sigh as I knew this was where things were about to get complicated.

This was where I couldn't use actions to strengthen the claim of my words. And my reasons he would soon find to be…

A Hellish, harsh reality.

CHAPTER TEN

ON THE OTHER SIDE OF HEARTBREAK

I took one look at his outstretched hand, waiting for my own to fill it and hated that I couldn't give him what he wished for. Hell, but it was what I wished for too, as I wanted nothing more right in that moment than to step through this damn thing and cry in his arms. To prove my commitment to him and back up my words with actions. But I knew that if I did that, then he would never let me go. He would never let me do what I knew was needed to save not only his race but also his life. And well, after everything I'd just learned, then it wasn't only my mother's life that was linked to his but mine as well.

All I could hope for was that I could get Lucius to understand this and that started with telling him the thing he hated the most…

No.

"I'm sorry, but I can't do that, Lucius." He fisted his hand and let it drop before snapping,

"Why the fuck not!?" I released a sigh knowing just how difficult this conversation was going to be.

"Lucius, please, I can't do that right now, you know I can't."

"Yes, you fucking can! Look, just reach for my hand and take it, I will have enough power to pull you through, I am certain," Lucius said raising his hand to me once more and I found my own fisting at my side so I wouldn't be tempted to just reach out and try it.

So instead I looked behind me and asked,

"Is he right, could he pull me through?" The Keepers of Three all nodded and then said,

"As the Souls' Keeper he has that power."

"But not the power to save us all." At this, Lucius roared in anger before the mumbler had a chance to try and speak. Then he ordered,

"Silence! She is coming with me!"

"What if what they say is true, what if I am the only one who can…?" I started to say but again Lucius wasn't having any of it.

"NO! No, Amelia, no fucking way am I going to let that happen! Now you listen to me, we will figure this out, but we will do it together once you have first given me your hand," he snapped, getting angry and I looked back at the glowing portal that obviously led into Hell.

"Hey, hey…come now, look at me, don't look over there, just look at me," he said bringing my attention back to him and I was met with a serious gaze.

"We will figure it out together," he stated firmly once more.

"But how?" I asked, curious to see what he would say and to see if I was right in how I thought Lucius would act.

"I will go in there and I will fix it, but you have to stay safe."

"You won't take me with you?!" I asked, clearly annoyed

and upset that I had been right. He released a deep sigh before telling me,

"It is too dangerous for you…" I opened my mouth to protest making him snap at me,

"Gods, Amelia, this is Hell we are talking about, not a fucking hot vacation!" This pissed me off, so I snapped back,

"Yeah, I got that, thanks!"

"Yes, well then, you should also know that you could fucking die there and if that happens, then it will be the permanent kind! So no, you will not be fucking going there, as mark my words, Amelia, it is not something I will ever allow to happen!" he growled, whilst holding himself tense as if he was holding back on his demon from making an appearance and adding more rage to this order.

"And what if I am the only one who can set this right, what then?" I asked after folding my arms.

"Then we find another way," he stated without hesitation.

"And if there isn't one…what then?" I asked making his features harden into an anger he was trying to control before he gritted his teeth and said,

"We. Will. Find. A. Way." So, I thought to make my point and turned to face the Keepers.

"Is there another way?" I asked making Lucius growl angrily, losing his cool now.

"Don't say another fucking word!" he snapped, ordering them to be silent. So instead they each shook their heads telling me no.

"Can they lie?" I asked and Lucius calmed enough to tell me,

"They don't know everything."

"That is not what I asked, and you know it," I said now looking back at him, knowing all too well from past experiences how he had been the master at wording things. This without breaking promises made but getting what he wanted, nonetheless. Which was why Lucius snarled the truth,

"No, they can't fucking lie!"

"Then they speak the truth, I am the only way," I stated making Lucius argue back,

"Yes, and like I said, they don't know fucking everything!" I stared at Lucius as he stared back whilst we were both caught in a moment of silence. He, no doubt trying to think of a way to stop me from doing something he deemed too dangerous and me thinking of a way I could convince him to let me.

Needless to say, we were at a standstill, both staring at a crossroads. He wanted to take my hand and lead me down the safe path, one where the end of the journey was uncertain, and I wanted to run headfirst into the one I believed would save us all. Which was why I broke the silence first and said,

"I am sorry, Lucius, but it is not as if we can take that chance." His reaction was instantaneous as he started shouting at me,

"No! Amelia no, I will not let you do this!" But I simply made a point of looking all around the shimmering barrier between us and said,

"It is also not as if you can stop me." He growled low and menacingly at this. He then pulled back a clenched fist looking ready to try and punch his way through it, when I stopped him,

"If you do that then it might knock you unconscious again." Lucius listened to me and instead turned at the last second and embedded his fist into the already crumbling wall.

"RAHH!" he roared making me wince, knowing I was the cause of his anger.

"I don't understand," he said after a few moments of trying to rein in the fury by panting through his rage. Then he pulled it calmly from the wall as I asked,

"What don't you understand?"

"How you could tell me how foolish you were for running from me and yet here you are telling me that you're about to do it again, only this time you are running to a place you have no idea how to survive in!" he shouted, holding his arms out to the sides as if that world he spoke of was all around us.

"This time it's different," I told him, hating that on some level he was right...but really, what choice did I have?

"Yeah, how is that, Amelia?!" he snapped,

"Because this time I am not running from you!" I shouted back, trying to make him understand.

"No, you are just running to certain death!" he threw back, and I winced before feigning the hurt in my response.

"Thanks for the vote of confidence," I said dryly making him roar at me,

"This is not a fucking joke, Amelia! What you're talking about is fucking suicide!"

"Then if that were true, why does this whole thing seem fated...why would I be the only one able to stop this if me getting there wasn't even possible!" I pointed out and this was when he made what I knew he would consider his mistake.

"Gods, you're as stubborn as your fucking mother, for she too believed she could take on Hell to save your father!"

"What?" I hissed and the second I did, Lucius flinched as he knew he had just let something major slip.

"No, no, no do not even think of going there, my girl, for it is not the same fucking thing!" he snapped.

"Why, was she a Vampire when she did this?" I asked in return, honestly wanting to know and when he looked as though he didn't want to answer me, I said his name again,

"Lucius?" He released a frustrated sound and a second later I was questioning what his reply would have been had he been given the chance to answer. Would he have lied to save me yet again or would he have trusted me with the truth? Like I

said, I never got to find out as the answer came from behind me,

"No, just the blood of a King, but nothing more."

"For she was human when she walked through Hell's door."

"Mmanbknne."

Lucius released a threatening growl at the Keepers of Three when they told me what he should have.

"Then how did she survive?" I asked Lucius, with my arms folded.

"Dumb fucking luck!" he snapped, but I had heard enough. My mother had done what was needed to save my father and she had done this whilst still being human, with only my father's essence inside her. How would that make what I was about to do any different?

I mean, did I want to go into Hell to save an entire Vampire race from dying out, no, not particularly…in fact, fuck the pun here, but that was more like a Hell no, I really didn't!

But, what choice did we have? Because I knew that if I let Lucius convince me not to do this and instead, I gave him my hand so he could pull me back through the barrier, then he would never allow me to do this. He would never have allowed me to go into Hell, not even if it was to help save his life and that of my mother's.

No, he would most likely send me on my way to be safe with my family as had been his original plan when taking me there the first time and well, we all knew how that had ended!

Which meant that I couldn't chance it. I couldn't chance giving Lucius the power to stop me, doing so because he valued my life over his own and that of his people. Because all Lucius ever wanted was to ensure my safety and had gone as far as to keep away from me all these years believing this course of action would achieve it. But we had come too far for that now and Lucius had crossed the point of no return even for himself, as it was clear he couldn't walk away from me now and I felt blessed knowing this. Despite what I knew my next actions could potentially do to our relationship, one that might not last as long as I wanted it to, should I fail in stopping this curse.

But I felt sure that he wouldn't leave me. Because, if there was anything other than the truth I had got from his lifetime of memories, then it was that he was too deep in his obsession to walk away now, *just as I was.* Which meant that, unfortunately, this only left me with one choice and as for Lucius, well he was not going to like it...

Not. At. All.

And he knew it. He could see it all playing out in the emotions on my face. He knew what I was planning. It was why, instead of shouting at me again, he tried a different tactic.

"Just give me your hand and at least let us discuss this together without this fucking barrier between us!" Lucius asked in a tense tone that told me exactly what would happen the moment I did that. And if I were honest, then by the Gods how I wanted to! How I wanted nothing more than to just give him my hand and let him pull me into his arms. How I wanted my apology for running from him to be sealed with a kiss. How I just wanted him to hold me and allow myself the time to process all I had seen of his long life and for us to focus on moving forward now that I knew everything. Because it was not knowing that was sometimes worse. It was the things you convinced yourself that could be. The nightmare hiding in the shadows playing with you like a toy box filled with insecurities. When all that was needed to burn it to ashes was for the light to cast its truth back into your reality.

And it had turned to ash...it truly had.

But now I faced a new nightmare and this time no amount of light was capable of casting it aside into a forgotten realm. Because this was no longer a matter of the heart.

No, for this was a matter of the soul.

Because that was what faced me when I walked through that doorway...that portal into Hell. And Lucius knew. He knew with just one look back towards the tree what I planned to do, and it now fed his desperation.

"Think about your parents, Amelia. Gods, girl, just think about what this would do to them!" Lucius said making me tense as I lowered my gaze from the tree and down to the floor. Then I thought about my parents, who would be heartbroken if they knew. Lucius was right, I had so many people who cared about me and if I didn't walk away from this alive, then the hurt and pain I would cause would be...*immeasurable.*

Gods, just thinking about my poor mother who I had foolishly believed capable of kissing Lucius. Who I had wrongly accused of not only being the cause of my broken heart but also of cheating on my father! A man she adored and loved more than any other in all the world. It made me ashamed to think of all I had put my parents through and now this. Something I was still putting them through. The guilt I felt caused tears to cloud my vision before they fell from my eyes and to the ground. But then the moment I saw the effect they had on the roots once more, it brought my mind back to what I felt I had no choice to do. I had to try and save my mother!

Oh yes, his desperation would make him try everything, but he was soon to discover that it had backfired.

"I love my mum and dad," I said, mainly to myself as I needed to hear it spoken aloud.

"I know you do, my Khuba," Lucius replied in a tender tone, but then I wiped my tears away and looked at him, taking a few silent moments before I spoke. Because I wanted to just look at him with the anger and tried not to focus too much on the hope I saw in his stunning, steel blue eyes. A hope I killed the moment I told him,

"I am thinking about them, as it's not just your soul I intend on saving, Lucius." Then I turned away from him before I went back on my decision and I was forced to witness the catastrophic mistake that might curse our future.

"NO! Fuck, no Amelia, just look at me!" he shouted making me tense, balling my hands into fists as I sniffed back my tears.

"I lost you once, don't make me lose you again, Amelia, please don't fucking do that to me." His plea made me suck back a sob, holding myself rigid as I closed my eyes against the pain that I knew I had no choice but to continue to cause him. But right now, I couldn't look back at him and I knew that it made me a coward. Because after all I had unknowingly put him through, he deserved to have his decision granted. He deserved to have my hand in his.

But what he deserved and what I had to do quickly became two vastly different things. Because I knew that my father would never have let my mother go to Hell and back for him, but she had done it. Just like I knew that Lucius would never allow me to take the same risks.

So, without looking at him I told him,

"I love you so much, Lucius, by the Gods, I do."

"Amelia, sweetheart, then prove it, prove it by just giving me your hand, that is all I ask." I shook my head and started walking towards the tree, knowing that if I looked back at him, I wouldn't be able to go through with it. That my steps would falter to the point of stopping completely. The tears that continued to fall told me that.

"NO! COME BACK HERE!" Lucius roared but I ignored him and continued telling him,

"I love you so much, that I would go to Hell and back for you." But he wasn't listening, despite how each word I said managed to somehow give me the strength I needed to keep going. But Lucius didn't hear me, for he was losing himself to his rage.

"I DEMAND YOU FUCKING LET ME INSIDE NOW!" Lucius bellowed at the Keepers of Three for them to grant him access so he could stop me. But one look at them all shaking their heads and I wasn't sure whether or not they would survive when he finally did make it through. And even though I knew my words wouldn't help the matter, or even ease his pain, I couldn't help but tell him,

"I am so sorry, Lucius, I hope one day you will forgive me."

"NO! No... no I will not! Do you hear me, Amelia! If you do this, I will never fucking forgive you!" he shouted and I felt that reply freeze my whole body with the pain of his words, a declaration I was hoping was only fuelled by his rage and nothing more. That it was something that didn't have the power to stick, and when he calmed down, he would then find it in him to forgive me.

"I'm sorry," I said again just after I braved a look up at the tree and seeing more than just a whole world of souls. I saw his council, people I had come to know and love. I saw Pip and Adam, who had unknowingly been my guardians my whole life. I saw my beautiful sweet mother who I had treated wrongly. Then I saw my own soul. That of a crimson rose I so wanted to see entwined with the roots of Lucius' soul for all eternity. Something that was unlikely to happen should the Tree be left to die.

So, as a single leaf fell it became symbolic. It became just one more sign from the Fates of why I should do this. So, when it turned to black as it fluttered to the ground, floating away to ash before it could make the journey, I knew I was making the right decision.

"AMELIA, WAIT!" he thundered, just as I was about to take my first step inside, making me pause and finally look over my shoulder at him. As I knew that if all of this went wrong and death was all that met me on the other side, that I couldn't just leave without looking at him one last time. It pained me to think that I was the one who brought such anguish to his features as he looked like a man desperate not to lose his soul.

"You said you wouldn't run again," he said in a tone that spoke only of his desolation at the events. So, I took a deep breath and told him,

"This isn't me running, Lucius."

"But don't you see, it is! It fucking is, Amelia, and you know it!" he tried gripping to the sides of the tunnel and I could see the stone he held cracking under the force of his pain.

So, I told him,

"No, this me choosing to save our world."

He shook his head and I could see from here the angry tears he held back, with his gloved fist ready to cause no end of destruction.

"Amelia, I fucking swear to every Gods be damned being out there, that if you do this…"

"But I don't plan on doing this alone," I interrupted quickly and then before he could issue another threat or finish the first, I told him,

"Don't worry, if this all goes to plan, then the second I step through this portal, the barrier will drop and it won't be goodbye for long, Handsome…" He growled low and I added just before slipping through the portal,

"As I will see you on the other side."

Then I simply stepped…

Straight into Hell.

CHAPTER ELEVEN

DOWN THE SPIDER HELL HOLE

The second I stepped through the portal the very last thing I heard was the sound of Lucius' bellow of demonic fury, along with that of my own screams echoing around me. Because it hadn't just been like stepping through some glowing doorway, but in fact stepping through some kind of Hellish womb, one that gave birth to you on the other side!

It felt as if I'd had every piece of me analyzed and tested and sections of me pulled apart as the pain sliced through me. As if my blood had needed to be tested before I had been granted access. But then, even when I had, I fell into another world as though being spat out of some small opening barely big enough for me to fit through.

I fell to the ground barely saving myself from greater injury as my hands shot out before my head could follow. I continued to take deep breaths, dragging them into my lungs and struggling at first as the air felt thick and heated. As if I had just stepped off the plane after arriving in some ridiculously hot country. And for a moment I couldn't move. I don't know why, but it was as if my body just needed the time to adjust. It was like two sides of myself were fighting against each other and the battle inside of me needed to settle enough to call a ceasefire.

So there I remained, curled in a fetal position for how long, I wasn't really sure. My arms were up over my head protecting myself and trying to calm my ass down as I listened to the pounding of my own heart in my ears. It was a strange feeling and I found myself questioning if my mother had experienced anything like this when she too had crossed over?

I also had to ask if this was because the stolen part of my soul was Angel and I knew that they were forbidden to enter this realm. But then my father was half Angel, as was my brother, Theo, and neither had a problem crossing over. But then I could also class Lucius as the same, which had me questioning were those three the only exceptions? Did I come under the same category too? Was this like some kind of calling to that missing part of my soul or was it the Vampire part of me that was crying out in this place?

I didn't know and had no answers for myself. But I was smart enough to know it was the reason my body struggled as it did. Because I was alive and I was human, and down here, the two didn't exactly mix. For there was nothing down here but demons, the Devil's creatures and the dead that powered the whole realm. Layers upon layers of Hell that made up a whole world. There were villages, towns and even cities and each made up individual Kingdoms of Hell. Each had their own ruler and with it, their own laws to enforce upon their land. But with this being said, this world could still claim only one overlord the other Kings obeyed and that was Lucifer, better known as the Devil.

I finally felt my body twitching as life seemed to flow back into me and I sat up to take in my surroundings. Because I had to wonder where that portal had led to. I knew as well as being home to many cities of demonic life, there were also vast planes of space in between. Lands filled with deserts, mountains, oceans and even forests, just like the one it seemed I was in now. I pushed myself up on shaky feet and stumbled at first as if the world had tilted on its axis.

I rubbed the dry dust from my eyes that had covered my body and face after my fall into this world. And when I did, I finally managed to blink my eyes clear, despite it sticking to my contact lenses, doing so enough that I could see the strangest forest staring back at me.

I was thankful that I didn't exactly frighten easily, but even I had to admit that I would be thankful when Lucius finally got here, despite how mad he was going to be. Gods, forget about just being mad, he was going to be furious. Although, I was hoping that when he realised my idea of having him follow me through the gateway, like I had always intended him to, would help with the forgiving process.

However, like all best laid plans, this was one of those times it utterly went to shit! I turned around and couldn't even see where I had come from. Dread then suddenly started to creep its way in, as I spun around over and over again in panic, trying in vain to find that damn portal!

"Where is it!" I snapped and I looked from one direction to the other and all that met me was a forest of eerie dead trees that twisted and knotted like gnarled, old fingers. But the air was strange, not exactly dark but as if the whole world had some strange filter on it. As if it was some old vintage photograph I had just stepped into, where everything had that strange burnt touch to it, that looked like the calm before the storm. As if the air was statically charged, ready to join forces with the sparks of lightening that felt as if just at the ready to blaze across the strange sky.

I had to say that when I thought of Hell, (not that it was a regular occurrence, because…well, morbid much) but when it did happen to be in my thoughts, I never really imagined it to have a sky. The land, the trees, the demons and the famous rivers of fire I had all associated with it, but the sky was something that I had not been ready for. A burnt orange hue with no blue in sight, seemed to tell me that it was still day and night hadn't yet fallen, making me wonder that when it did, what colour it would be.

Would it be black the same as when the sun disappeared and set for the day? Because the strangest thing of all was that I had no idea where the light came from, as there was no sun above us. Of course, these would have all been things I could have asked Lucius after he had stepped inside the portal for himself right behind me. But unfortunately, he was still yet to appear and I had to admit, that the longer it took, the more time it gave me to allow fear to take over rational thought. Because I knew that I couldn't do this alone, and I never had intended to when walking through that damn tree!

Of course, now I was regretting my decision not to speak up about my plans, instead of letting him know at the very last moment before stepping inside. My reason for this had been the Keepers of Three. I couldn't chance them trying to stop him in some way, as they were obviously the ones who controlled the barrier, and they might have refused to bring it down had they known he intended to follow me through and potentially try and take me back before I had completed my mission. Of course, I knew this was also mostly on the cards for my future as this would be Lucius' main focus. But my hopes had been that once here, then I would have a greater chance at convincing him for us to stay and work together to try and beat this curse.

Of course, that looked to be all in vain now and had me questioning, was this why he seemed so panicked? Because he knew for some reason he wouldn't be able to follow me through into Hell? The Keepers of Three had said that one person at a time could enter, so surely that meant the barrier between us would have been lifted the moment I made it through here. Which still remained the biggest question of all… *why wasn't he here now?*

Had I got it all wrong?

"Oh, Gods…what have I done?" I whispered, now turning around and no longer looking for an opening. No, now I was looking at the Hell I had just foolishly stepped into, with every plan I'd made being labelled useless. A plan that was solely based around Lucius being by my side and guiding me through this.

And now I was alone.

This was the moment I slumped to the floor, pulled my legs up to my chest and sat there, now praying that he would step through a slice in the very fabric of time that made up the edges of this realm. That he would come for me. That it just might take him some time, but he would come…

"He will come for me," I muttered to myself quietly, as I eyed my surroundings with caution and unease. Because I couldn't stop thinking that here I was, a human with no powers whatsoever and the pointless skill of being able to kick human ass. And what had I done…?

I had stepped into Hell…*alone.*

"Gods, you fucking idiot, Fae!" I cursed myself and smacked the side of my head, wishing I had known the biggest danger in coming to Hell was ending up here all by myself! Because Lucius had been right… *this was a fucking suicide mission!*

"No! Don't think like that…don't you fucking dare, Fae,

you're a Draven, now it's time to fucking think like one!" I chastised myself whilst shaking my head and telling myself I couldn't just sit here any longer, waiting for something that was obviously not going to happen.

Because Lucius wasn't coming and sitting here waiting for him to suddenly appear out of the thick Hellish air and save the fucking day wasn't going to happen! Besides, I didn't exactly think that being out in this dead forest was going to be wise when it did turn to night, whatever the Hell that looked like...*pun, most definitely intended!*

So, I forced myself to get up off the ground and hated the uncertainty I felt as I looked for even a single clue on where to go. There were no roads or even a path, just a vast and endless looking mass of twisted trees that looked as if they had been frozen in time. For they were long ago dead and pointless even being here. For what they offered this place, I didn't know. No creatures lived here, a small grace to be thankful for I guess, seeing as I didn't exactly hold out much hope for animals in Hell being the cute and cuddly kind!

Which meant that I picked a direction and started walking, because I couldn't wait around any longer. Not when it felt like I would just become a meal ticket waving my flag of humanity at anyone hungry enough to come sniffing.

So, I walked and I walked and I walked some more. And I did this without coming across a single soul, something I no doubt had to be thankful for. Because the moment the forest began to change, I was wishing for the seemingly endless dead trees and nothing more. This was because now the land became harder to walk across, as the floor became a series of roots, all snarled up in a mass of angry twists and knots. Naturally in a place like this, there wasn't an inch of green to be seen, for they were in tones of oranges and burnt reds. A mass that spanned across the forest floor like millions of snakes that had been baked by the nonexistent sun as they slithered towards the trees. Then, like veins providing a live source to the trunk, they flowed up covering the entirety of its girth in different thicknesses.

"Oh, Gods!" I muttered in a cry of horror before my hands flew to my mouth. Because it was only when following the sight up that I noticed the mummified bodies that were suspended about ten feet up from the ground. They each had their backs to the trees and at one time had been lifted up there when naked. And they still would have been, had it not been for the roots that covered most of their bodies as all that was left on show was their chests.

Their arms were held slightly out to the sides and entwined with the same roots that looked more like restraints, with their knees bent and the pads of their feet held flush to the rooted bark. But it was their heads that made the sight even more haunting. With their chins raised up as if looking to the Heavens and silently asking why their prayers hadn't yet been answered. Their mouths were open as if they had died screaming before the roots had swarmed in between their teeth from all sides.

The next tree had a woman's figure, as her naked breasts had roots circling them and the flare of her hips had been left exposed. She too was in the same position as the one before her and it was only when I let my eyes travel the length of the tree line, did I see the true horror…*there were thousands of them!*

A whole forest where human life and tree had merged like living tombstones displaying the bodies instead of letting their hosts rot underground. No, instead the trees looked to have fed from their now withered flesh, and it became harder to see where human life had ended and where the life of Hell's trees began. It was so startling that all of a sudden, I found myself running, as if my feet had made the decision for me and my mind was left playing catch up.

But then, as I finally broke through the edge of the forest, I soon discovered that by getting away from one horror, it had only ended up giving way to another. Because this time it wasn't trees of the dead I had to contend with, it was trees that held the living that I needed to be fearful of.

This part of the forest had tall branchless trees that looked more like black pillars lining the way to some Hellish Roman temple. This time a line of columns framed a path of ash toned dirt. Dirt that could have been made from the bones of man ground up into powder for all I knew, as I was starting to understand that anything found in Hell wouldn't surprise me.

"Well, at least it seems to lead somewhere," I told myself, needing to hear at least one sound or voice, even if it was my own. However, the life these trees held was one I discovered to be even more sinister the further down I ventured. The pathway was probably wide enough to drive three cars down side by side, which at least helped me avoid them. However, what had looked like a canopy of thickly dense grey leaves above, I could now see was something else. It looked more like rain clouds, thick enough you could have scooped them up. But the more time you spent looking at them trying to discover what they were became yet another mistake made out of many. Because what they represented was one of the things I was actually scared of. It was masses and masses of webbing.

"Oh shit…oh no, no, no, please…anything but spiders!" I pleaded to no one, but as I backed away from one tree, I only ended up having to do it again from the one behind me. This was why I thought it best to travel directly down the centre, which I had to admit, felt more like a trap when doing so. The long cleared road looked as if there was a darkness at the end, that I was hoping marked the finish line to this new nightmare.

I hated spiders!

Which meant that I also hated everything that came with

them. Like the massive treetops filled with one giant web, that instead of holding the classic shape, was nothing more than a mass of sticky webbing the size of cars that all seemed to connect together. Then the further I travelled, the scene changed once more, adding what looked like huge egg sacks that hung down from thinner webs. These were in giant white teardrop shapes. Ones that looked to be defying physics as the weight inside of them looked too great for the thin lengths of web they were attached to. They hung down from the tops of the trees as if the forest was weeping the poor souls that looked to have fallen victim to whatever beast had made them.

I could just barely recognise the shapes of boned limbs inside the layers and layers of sticky thread. It also looked silver in some places, whenever the light from the sky above managed to break through the canopy. But then I felt the ground start to tremble and couldn't help but comment,

"Not a good sign, Fae…definitely, not a good sign." Of course, this was then backed up by the jolting movement coming from the pods, as they seemed to suddenly vibrate as if whatever I had foolishly thought dead inside them had started to waken. The sacks then all began to swing at the same time as the webbing that encased them started to stretch. This allowed me to see the limbs that were moving beneath the layers, obviously trying to break their way free. Which, naturally, I took as a very bad sign!

Especially when there were hundreds of them all hanging there, now jerking as though a silent timer had gone off, telling their maker her creatures were fully baked and ready to go. However, it wasn't long before I discovered that this had nothing to do with the rumbling on the ground, as I had expected. No, because that sound was emanating from behind me, the one I had named the rooted forest of the dead and where I had just come from.

What by the Gods was happening here now?!

I had to say when asking myself this in my head, I had wished the answer never came to me. That it had simply passed me by to remain forever unknown. However, this unfortunately didn't happen. Instead what did happen, was that all the sacks started to split and tear open. It made the webbing look more like the stretching of old grey chewing gum as you pulled your shoe from where it had got stuck on the sidewalk. The long holes that appeared started where most movement was made. This being the stretching of the head, as it folded back on itself, thus creating great tears at the neck as it started to appear. Then came a ladder effect all the way down the spine as it stretched before snapping completely.

After this what appeared was truly monstrous, as it looked as if a new creature had been born from what must have once been the husk of a human vessel. Now making me wonder where did they even get these bodies from?! Did they suck them from the very ground we thought to have safely buried our dead in?!

A white, almost bleached flesh appeared that was like dead skin without the decay. Almost translucent in places with more bone beneath than that of any muscle. An overly long neck and long stretched limbs came down from the torso that no longer looked to have any shoulders. Its bottom half was even more sickening, as if it had been twisted completely, so that now the pelvis faced opposite to where it should be. This meant that the legs bent at a pair of pronounced knee joints of gnarled bone behind the creature not in front as on a normal human. This strange angle therefore meant that when the creatures started climbing down, escaping from their sticky pods, they did so with an odd bend to their bodies. As their stomachs dipped lower at the hip bones, making them move like a two-legged spider.

I screamed when I saw that instead of just climbing down the bare straight column tree, some were using the webbing they had been born from to jump and leap from the sacks to the ground. I could now see their faces had been stripped of any distinguishable features other than white eyes permanently held open due to the removal of the eyelids and a space where their nose once was. They all spotted me and snarled in some kind of demonic call that stretched the remaining webbing coating their bald heads. This was due to them throwing their heads back and opening their overly large, spade shaped mouths that were lined with tiny pointed teeth, reminding me of a pike fish.

This was naturally when I started running the other way, as they all started dropping from above or scurrying down the trees all around me. But then that thundering sound started to get louder and seeing as I was now running towards it, I could soon see why.

The root covered forest I had just come from had released its captors just as this part of the spider forest had done the same. But this only became obvious once the rumbling sound grew louder, doing so now as I could see mounds of earth rising and travelling towards me at speed. It was as if giant worms were slithering beneath the surface ready to burst free any moment and I really didn't want to be where I was when they did. However, I was trapped, as I couldn't run to the sides without getting caught, as the spider creatures started to close in around me.

But wait, there looked to be one place left to escape if I could just get there quickly enough! It was a break in between the two sides of the forest where the creatures looked as if they would soon come head to head. I started running towards it but then found myself suddenly screaming as the earth started to quake harder. It then split open and the bodies that had been captured by the trees now emerged in an explosion of erupting earth. They rose up like giants, made bigger by the extended roots that heightened their limbs, making them look like giant tree people. Wow, Groot would be right at home here, I thought as I skidded to a halt, wishing now I knew exactly who the good guys were and who were the bad.

Although, I was in Hell, so chances were high that there weren't any good guys and I was just the human bug about to get squashed. However, the question of who was who, seemed to be the least of my concerns right now as I saw three powerful looking figures emerge from what had potentially been my only escape. It was the only side of the forest that hadn't yet been overrun by creatures and one that was now a hope that seemed dead in the ground, just like I was soon to be.

The three beings were each riding massive creatures that looked more like mighty battle beasts, as they were covered in spiked armour, each one snarling and equally terrifying.

I looked behind me to see the line of spider creatures mirroring those of the tree people, now lining up in front and I soon realised the true horror of my situation.

For there was no place to run. Not when I was surrounded and in the middle of what my mind quickly realised was nothing short of...

A Demonic War.

CHAPTER TWELVE

FOREST WAR OF THREE

Frozen…that's what I was.

It was that moment your body braced itself for the impact. The coming pain and damage you weren't sure you would survive. But then I didn't know what they were waiting for. It was as if some sort of signal needed to be given before the battle could commence. And looking at both sides, well it meant that the word suicidal was looking less like an exaggeration and more like a certainty. As let's just say I hadn't foreseen this day ending with me now smack bang in the middle of what looked like a war of nightmares. And the battle line was more than just a symbolic statement, as the two forests that met at this point couldn't have been more different from each other. And at the place where burnt orange roots covered the ground like fire snakes, it was mirrored on the other side by deathly grey powdered earth and dead trees.

And at the centre of where two nightmares met was where I was stood, with each opposing army either side of me, that had come to claim their rights to the other.

This became apparent as I looked left then right over the wave of creatures. One side that had moments ago been born from thousands of spider webbed eggs, and the other that looked to have been waiting for this very moment to be allowed to finally break free from the prison of their trees and fight, as thousands emerged up from the ground of roots.

But then, I wasn't the only one that looked to be stood in their way of domination. The three mighty figures that had arrived still remained waiting on the sidelines, as if their only reasons for being there was to jump in at the ready in case they were needed. They had approached from the only side that wasn't overtaken by creatures, cutting off both my escape and any others caught in the fray that didn't want to fight.

They each sat upon large beastly creatures that looked battle ready, telling me that in all likelihood they never intended to just watch to see how this war turned out. But more like they were at the ready to pick a side. Each of them were different in size, and so was their choice of ride, but from so far away it was hard to make out the details. All I could detect was that the one on the end was considerably larger than the other two and he carried what looked like a massive hammer of war.

He was sat upon a great snarling beast that didn't exactly look built for speed with its huge hanging belly barely held above the ground on its thick scaled legs, reminding me of a demonic crocodile. However, its tail curled up like that of a scorpion with a deadly bulbous stinger that was tipped into a point. Its head was covered in some kind of plating and the huge curled horns that came from its head acted as a way for the big rider to hold onto his beast.

The other two were similar in size to each other, with the one positioned in the centre sat upon a creature that had the body of a scaled horse. It had dark red horns running down its back framing where the rider sat. The head was a snarling lizard shape, that was also covered in armour, one that looked bolted with chains attached to it so the rider could use them as reins.

The last of these men was at the other end and sat upon a figure of a bird, covered in hard feathers that looked like rust coloured metal plating. This continued over its head and its snarling mouth was biting around a gleaming silver bar that had chains attached to the ends so this too became a way for its rider to control the beast. And like all three of these Hellish creatures, the masterly figures that sat upon them were all covered in armour, ready for battle. Each wore a horned helmet of black pointed plating, with each section interlocked in such a way that all three looked like dragon heads. They stood at the ready, looking demonically regal and proud against the backdrop of the changing sky behind them.

In fact, it made for a startling sight and I think it was the reason Hell was always depicted as a reddish place, because the sky beyond the dark clouds looked as if it was on fire. It was reds, and dark oranges without the yellows and pinks of a pretty sunset. However right now, the clouds were parting above them and instead of the blood night sky, an eerie greenish dark glow was breaking through.

Then a mighty roar could be heard coming from behind me, and this quickly answered my question, as this had been the signal they had all been waiting for.

This was when all Hell broke loose…*literally!*

The two sides started running towards each other as the ground shook and I was left with nowhere to go. I was only wishing that I had some kind of weapon in my hand, just so I knew I wasn't going to go down without a fight, no matter how pointless it seemed against such hellish odds. But then, something drew my eyes away from the oncoming danger, as the middle rider pulled a flaming blue sword from his side and raised it up in the air. The action made sparks of power light the space around all three of them before he then pointed it towards the battle. This was a signal for the other two to join him and charge as one. But this wasn't all he did with his sword and soon I was thankful, as he wasn't done yet. Because instead of keeping it raised and pointing to the enemy, he lowered it to the ground and leaned to one side on his beast's back. This was so he could scrape the tip of the blue sword along the ground as they travelled into the fray.

It sparked blue before the forked flames suddenly turned into icy shards that now shot forward and travelled straight ahead of them. In fact, it didn't just travel ahead but it came right at me before I was quick enough to escape the impact, I turned making it only a single step before I was completely surrounded. Massive shards of ice shot up from the ground like the teeth of some icy dragon as it rose up from beneath me trying to swallow me whole.

"AAAHHH!" I screamed and dropped to my knees and covered my head trying to protect myself from whatever was trying to consume me, closing my eyes tight and waiting for the end. However, it was one that thankfully never came. So, after a few seconds longer of cowering, I braved opening my eyes and found myself encased in an icy cage. It indeed looked like teeth that had interlocked above me, with wider gaps in the thicker parts of the surrounding arch of fangs and ones I would only barely be able to fit my arms through.

It looked like some kind of domed cage made of ice and the second the two battle sides collided I was more than thankful for it! Because this was when I realised, it wasn't breakable like ice, but it was more like clear granite that looked wet to touch and something I didn't think wise to check, fearing the ice would travel up my skin.

However, the moment the first spider creature decided to investigate, I realised that this wasn't the case, as touching the ice wasn't a problem. What was a problem was the long clawed limbs that reached through and tried to grab me. Naturally, I moved back into the centre and was left with nothing but a prayer that the cage would hold up against them.

But I wasn't without my uses, as I did manage to kick out at some of the tree people when they used their roots to reach me at the centre. However, without a weapon, I was pretty much spending my time trying to prevent them from getting to me and causing damage. And the moment there was a break in their attack on the cage, it gave me the chance to look further beyond the ice that surrounded me.

I found the rider in the centre, the one with the sword, watching me, despite swinging his weapon and taking out any creatures within its radius. His focus was on me not the battle he had become a part of. My own focus, however, was on all the madness that was going on around me. This included the way the creatures started tearing into each other as the war truly began.

The tree creatures would lash out with their great rooted limbs, swiping across the spiders who either managed to scuttle away as they jumped back to the dark trees they were born from or were merely flattened and died. On the opposing side of the battle, the spider creatures took a different approach, where they worked together in groups, using the swarm of bodies as a collective to consume the whole of the tree people. This worked effectively in overpowering them as they would spit out streams of webbing and cocoon them in seconds. And this was how the battle was fought.

But as much as I was thankful for my protective cage, it didn't stop my mind from questioning the motives of the three that were battling in a war of two sides, for they seemed to fight for neither side but for themselves. So, what they had in store for me, I didn't yet know. All I did know was that it was obvious they hadn't come here to pick a side.

Although, I had to say, from the looks of things, the three fighting were an army in their own right! The larger one steered his beast into the most crowded part and started swinging his hammer and taking out wave after wave of any creatures that foolishly tried to surround him. His weapon looked like the foot of some demonic oversized elephant that had been dipped in black steel and decorated with a gilded band.

It ploughed into them, knocking the tree people on their backs and squashing the spider creatures in a burst of broken bones and sticky webs, that clung to his hammer making a mess. This effectively proved that out of the two creatures, they were the hardest to kill. The difference was that once the tree people were down, then they struggled to get back up and had no choice but to let the ground absorb their bodies, taking them back into the forest from which they came.

The last of the three, who was sat upon the battle bird was also getting ready to fight but he did so from further away as his creature took its position on the sidelines. He then pulled a gleaming gold and black bow from his back and I watched in utter awe as he pulled the string taut, before creating the arrow to fill the void. He did this by blowing a line from where his fingers created the tension, all the way to where his other hand held the bow.

I was amazed to see that what followed the air blown from between his lips was the creation of a flaming arrow appearing from nowhere but his deadly breath. Then, once whole, he let it fly after first aiming high. It soared through the sky in a graceful arc before coming down to inflict the terror it was intended to. It hit the ground and burst like a small explosion of flames, igniting the creatures as easily as if they were made from sun baked kindling. He continued this move over and over, which became an effective way to break up the masses.

As for the one with the blue flaming sword, he travelled directly towards me with speed. At the same time swiping out with the glowing blade and turning all it touched to ice before the beast kicked out its hind legs behind him, shattering them on impact. After this he skidded his beast to a halt right in front of me. He then dismounted and used the reins to smack the creature's rump, creating a loud thwack sound. This made it go charging off through the battle, killing all in its path as it did, mainly with the front of its armoured head, as it butted out like a bull. After this the rider came close enough to the cage, one he had created to ask,

"Are ye alri…" I cut him off quickly just as one of the spider creatures started to attack the cage from the other side, making me shout,

"Quick, give me a weapon!"

I couldn't see his features under his black helmet, other than the dark auburn hair trailing from underneath it. Which meant it gave nothing away regarding what he thought of my demand. But well, seeing as he hadn't yet handed me anything, I kicked out at the long boney arms that tried to reach inside again and grab me.

"NOW!" I shouted as another one grabbed my ankle and yanked me towards it, this was after my kick hadn't been as successful as before. The rider saw this and without thinking pulled another blade from behind his cloak and slipped it through the gaps, barely just making it fit.

"Here!" a stern voice replied, and I reached out as far as I could to grab the handle, doing so just in time before I was about to become a meal. I turned quickly and stabbed straight through the spider creature's skull. He twitched around before releasing my foot. I then pushed myself back, kicking against the strengthened ice at the same time removing the blade from its head. After this I swung it around and took off any limbs that were inside my space, making them howl and screech in a high pitched scream of pain.

Then I reversed my steps so my back was up against the cloaked rider, now with only the icy wall between us. He took up this stance as if trying to protect me from anything that would have reached my back. Then with a skilful roll of his blade twisting in his hand it signalled to all that approached that he was ready to do battle. He sliced through the first wave of creatures in front of him, turning both halves into ice as they separated and slid off the blade.

Meanwhile, I continued to hack at any limbs or roots that tried to get to me, feeling uneasy when the thicker roots managed to make the cage crack.

"Look, I don't know who you guys are and I have no idea what the fuck is going on here, but I am not sure this cool little cage of yours is gonna last much longer!" I shouted before lashing out again, this time stabbing a spider creature in the chest and finding myself fighting against the sticky webbing when trying to get it out again. Note to self, stick to chopping limbs and stabbing heads.

The rider grunted before whistling and raising a fist in the air to signal to the others. He then extended two gloved fingers out and jerked them first left and then right. This must have been a silent, 'clear the path boys' as this was exactly what they started to do. The bulkier of the three, started to swing his rounded hammer from left to right so it created a seesaw effect. This became a very effective way of clearing a space, as the impact managed to take out at least five or six spider creatures at a time. As for the tree people, he took a different approach and hammered his weapon down into the ground, creating a wave of earth to travel at speed towards them. As soon as the flowing hump hit their legs, it caused them to go down as it took them off balance.

As for the other rider, he let more flaming arrows land, doing so as if lighting a landing pathway framing both sides of where the big guy stood in the centre, then he called out,

"THREE, TWO, ONE…"

"And the flaming deed is done," the rider in front of me muttered as the big guy suddenly twisted the handle of his hammer, igniting the whole thing in a lightning of green sparks. Then he dropped to one knee and pounded his now glowing weapon to the ground, twisting his body into the movement. The effect of this managed to create a green gust of power to blow back the arrows at just the right moment as they all exploded at the same time. The force from the hammer's power on the ground made sure the destruction caused blew away from him in the right direction.

This epic move managed to destroy hundreds from each side all at once and just as the wave of annihilation was now travelling this way, the rider in front of me turned. Then he raised his blue flaming sword up and touched it to the top of the ice cage, making it blind me with light, as if he had just created a forcefield to envelop the cage.

This lasted only a few seconds and I found I was still blinking away the spots as my vision cleared enough to see the two other men now walking towards their comrade. Their beasts were following behind them as the space had been cleared enough for them to do so without needing to fight, thanks to the perfect and effective explosion.

"Well, look whit we git 'ere boys, nobody said this jab cam wi' a bonus prize!" The one with the bow in his hand said as he approached, doing so in a heavy Scottish accent; a handsome lilt to his voice that was easy and playfully teasing. And the closer he came I could see that he was definitely more stealthy looking than the other two.

The only way to describe how he was dressed was more of an assassin than that of a warrior like the other two. A thick leather coat was fitted tight to his body due to the black chest plate that was strapped to his torso. It came down to his knees and a strip of what I assumed was his clan's Tartan was seen underneath. Padded brown suede was another layer that acted as a protective lining and matched the heavy boots that reached to his knees. Armoured shoulder pieces matched the scaled dragon helmet and was strapped across the chest plate at multiple points.

What completed the look were the dangerous elements; daggers and spiked throwing discs were also strapped and hung from different points on the three rows of belts that tapered in at his narrow waist. His gleaming black and gold bow could be seen from behind where a leather holder for it was buckled over his shoulder and at his waist.

Gods, but I could just imagine how long it took these guys to undress at the end of the day! Not that I was thinking about them getting naked or anything. And well, as for the biggest one, who was most definitely all brute strength and reminded me of Ragnar in size, he was dressed more like a God of war.

But, unlike the other men, he didn't seem concerned about having as much armour on as his comrades did, as he was near naked from the waist up. A crisscross of thicker leather and metal straps kept a massive shoulder piece in place. It was one that had been decorated with hammered steel and stitched leather that held rows of demonic teeth and horns, a theme that continued down one arm with the rest of the armour to match that covered his skin. His other huge muscular arm was left bare, with nothing more than a series of symbols tattooed on every inch of skin, with only strips of his natural tanned flesh colour peeking through the ink.

Around his waist he wore the same clan tartan in a sash that was fixed at his waist by the thicker belts which were also decorated in fangs and horns. He wore trousers that looked as though they were made from a scaly brown animal, with boots similar to the archer and as he rolled his shoulders, his large muscles bunched, showing an impressive display of abs at his belly.

The guy was terrifying and looked like a killing machine!

"Aye, well fur now I suggest we continue tae focus oan th' job." This was said by the one in front of me in answer to the archer's comment, doing so at the same time he lowered his sword, telling me that he was also Scottish, although his accent wasn't as strong.

I wished I could have seen their faces, but with their helmets on, then it was only in size where they differed. All three of them were tall, with the muscle clad one being half a foot above the rest. But the one with the sword had wide square shoulders telling me he wasn't short of an abundance of muscle himself. The joker of the group with the bow was the slimmest of the three, but his height put him in between the other two.

As for my personal saviour in front of me, he wore a thick, dark grey cloak, that was strapped to his body over what armour I had managed to see. The bare hint of a kilt in the same clan tartan colours could be seen worn over black trousers and the heavy holder for his sword created a point in the cloak at his back.

The big one with the hammer grunted in his reply, whilst the archer muttered,

"Ye'v always bin a spoilsport."

"Aye, 'n' ye won't be saying that if we git oot of this wit'oot managing tae wake up th' queen." The guy with the sword said but then, as if on cue, a huge battle cry sounded and the trees from the darker, spider forest started to bend as if a bomb had exploded and a tornado had suddenly gripped them. They quaked as if some invisible force was trying to tear them from the roots and all the remaining pieces left of the spider pods shook wildly.

But after this the roar ended and the trees sprang back to their upright positions and that darkness at the end I had once foolishly believed might have been a way out, started to move. This was when I realised exactly what it was.

The entrance to the lair of something truly monstrous.

And the archer said it all when he muttered,

"Tae late lads, th' bitch is awake!" and he was right, it most certainly was...

Too late.

CHAPTER THIRTEEN

CURSED QUEEN

"Damn she looks mair pissed aff than lest time!" The arrow guy said before the biggest one rolled the handle of his hammer in his large meaty hand, making the end spin in anticipation before he grunted in a deep gruff Scottish voice,

"Aye, let her come, fur mah hammer wull feed fae her rotted soul!" The archer patted him on the back once and said,

"Yeah, ye dae git tis nae a pet, dinnae ye, Gryph…Aye?" Okay, well as far as Scottish accents were concerned you couldn't get much heavier than that one, so I was officially clueless on everything the two of them just said! But whatever had just been said it made the big guy, who I now assumed was called Gryph, scoff a deep guttural sound, that in all honesty, could have been a laugh.

"Kin we git back tae focusing on th' one who started this war now?" the swordsman said, who most definitely seemed to be the one in charge…that or he just wanted to get the job done and was the more focused one of the lot. Of course, now considering myself as one of the gang, I thought it best to speak up now before I lost the opportunity to figure out what exactly was going on here.

"Erm...I hate to be the annoying addition to the party of three here, but I feel like I need to ask at this point...who is this Queen and what makes her so dangerous?" The second after I asked this the ground rumbled just in the same way it had done when the tree people had risen from their side of the forest. Only this time it had enough force to make it difficult to stay on my feet and more of the ice cage started to crack.

This was because I could now see what was emerging from the cave and even from this far away, it looked like a gigantic demonic spider!

"Ah okay, never mind," I said referring to the sight of true horror appearing in front of me, one that had me wishing this to be nothing more than a nightmare I could wake up from.

"Aye, noo she gets it," the archer said sarcastically.

And I did...*oh, I sooo did.*

"Probably not the best time to mention I am scared of spiders," I said making the big one grunt and I think it was another laugh before saying,

"She's a funny wee lassie."

"Yeah, weel buy her flowers after ye impress her by killing this bitch first aye or Trice is gonnae shit roses 'n' nae th' type ye wanna give tae a lass," the archer said in that easy joking tone of his telling me yet another name...*Trice.*

That was the name of the swordsman who had still remained closer to me and in his reply, he gave me the name of the archer,

"Vern, cut th' shit 'n' fire an arrow towards th' bitch already, ye ken how she hates fire," the swordsman said who I now knew as Trice.

"Wi' pleasure...time tae light this bitch's fire!" Vern said pulling back on his bow and blowing along the length from hand to hand, only this time, he did so in a spiral motion. This was so that more than one arrow appeared as now there were six all bunched together. He aimed the tips up at the sky, getting the right angle before letting them all go. They flew up higher than before and then all six started to rain down the centre clearing, the one I had been walking down before all Hell erupted from the ground and the trees above. I followed the glowing lengths of each until they landed down by the darkness at the end where the Queen had emerged from.

The fire erupted in an arc around the monster no doubt in an effort to try and push her back inside the cave. Although, it also ended up illuminating the true nature of the creature and it was the personal stuff of my nightmares, as this was going to take my fear of spiders to a whole new level!

This was because the view I now had of the Queen was utterly terrifying! It was as if two entities had been merged together, starting with the figure of a human woman and that of a gigantic demonic spider. A spider I should add, that looked as though it had captured it's human host and forced her to become one with the beast.

The woman was wearing a flowing black gown that trailed well past her feet as she was suspended at least twenty feet in the air. The material of her dress looked as if it was floating, as though she was a ghost slowly moving under water. Her waist length black hair was the same and captured at the top of her head where a crown sat as a collection of silver, spider's legs. One that rose up higher in the centre of her forehead like twigs. Most of her breasts were exposed by the deep slit in the front of her dress, but her pale white skin was painted both black and red, like you would find on a poisonous black widow spider.

And speaking of the spider element, she looked held prisoner to the colossal spider's legs positioned behind her.

They rose up and around her small frame with spiked knee joints before the legs bent back down to the ground, providing her with the motion of walking where her human legs were no longer needed.

Two shorter spider's legs didn't touch the ground but instead framed her shoulders with huge stingers. They each looked to have the means of shooting webbing from beneath the razor tips, telling me this was how she created all her webbed egg sacks that had once hung from the trees. Two giant pedipalps rose up above her head and looked more like clawed horns that opened and snapped shut making a clicking sound.

It clearly didn't like the flames, but despite its fear of fire the woman at its centre merely screamed at it, screeching in that high pitched wail, before the clacking sound of her legs moving echoed down the centre of the trees.

She moved in jerky disjointed movements where the pointed ends of her black legs jabbed at the ground when they raised up and down at the multiple knuckle joints. Frighteningly quick movements that swiftly had her avoiding the fire and doing so by making use of the trees on either side. This, however, meant that the figure of the woman was left suspended over the fire, making her cry out in fear and pain as the forks of flames licked at her feet.

It was strange, as if the two were one but also not, as they didn't seem to work together. Almost as if she was a host that had been punished by being given to the creature to merge with. Either way, they both made it past the fire and were now coming right at us.

Meanwhile, the creatures that had been held back by the explosion had also made it over the bodies of the dead. The ones caused by the three men and as effective as it had been, they were now also coming at us from both sides. However, the Queen cared little about her army as she trampled over her children, spearing some with her deadly steps and adding to her legs as they got stuck there, like adding meat to a demonic kebab.

"Gryph," Trice said nodding to the biggest one and Vern blew out another arrow and twisted his body just enough so he could fire it behind him this time. It hit its mark, this being one of the tree people who was closest to him and the arrow set him alight instantly. He had done this in seconds and with barely a glance to mark his aim.

"Fine, let's see it then," Vern said sarcastically after his arrows obviously hadn't had the desired effect on the Queen. Gryph then rolled his shoulders and said in that gruff voice of his,

"Whit urr ye waiting fur, unleash yer hell!"

Trice then stepped away from the cage, leaving me for the first time since appearing to save me and when he did, the one named Vern ducked his head to catch a better view of me. This was so he could grant me a comical little wave. It was one I felt equally rude not to do in return, just as I felt silly doing it. However, politeness won over shame and besides, so far these guys seemed like they were on my side, despite me still being in a cage.

Trice rolled his sword around in his hand, doing so with as much ease as if he had been born with it in his grasp. Then he stabbed it into the ground making the surrounding area glow with an icy spark of power. Then he twisted his sword and the brightness grew, telling me that it was time to cover my eyes. So, I threw my arm over my eyes and looked down. It was only when I saw the hint of it starting to die down through the small gap, did I then brave lowering my arm.

I could see the effect it had caused as there was an icy path from his sword to Gryph, where it had exploded next to him into a frozen eruption the size of a boulder.

"We tried fire, noo tis time fur this bitch tae cool aff," Vern said making Trice look back at him over his shoulder. Then he shook his head making the archer shrug his shoulders and say,

"What, action heroes always hae th' best yin liners."

"Aye, emphasis on the word best," Trice said dryly making Vern give him the middle finger. This was as Gryph was stepping up to the icy boulder the size of Lucius' Mercedes SUV. Then, just as the Queen was getting closer, he twisted the handle of his weapon once more, igniting its power. Then he swung the hammer and smashed it into the centre of the boulder with such force, that it shattered into hundreds of deadly shards that all flew towards the oncoming horde of spider creatures and their Queen. The second they hit their intended victims the spider creatures froze on impact, making me shout out in victory. And as I was yelling out one for the team in excitement, it made Vern shake a thumb over his shoulder at me and say,

"Git a load o' this yin, talk aboot bloodthirsty."

"Aye, juist th' wey I lik' em," Gryph said before erupting into laughter but stopped when the freezing shards hit the Queen, only managing to freeze the bottom parts of her legs for a short time. After this she screamed in anger and started running at them.

"Och bugger, ah think we made her mad again!" Vern shouted before firing arrow after arrow at her, but it was having no effect.

"Ye know what this means!" Trice shouted back after being forced to deal with the battling forces of the army as they continued to swarm around us.

"Ah fck! Aye it means needing tae kip fur a fucking munth is whit it means!" Vern snapped and the big guy just growled in annoyance. Meanwhile they may have understood what it meant, but I had no clue as to what they were talking about. No, instead I just focused on stabbing and chopping where I could as both creatures were still trying to get to me.

"Weel look at ye go…hey, who gave doll face a weapon?" Vern said after kicking one tree man hard enough the roots snapped his leg off.

"I did. Now we need tae try and drive her back tae th' cave, lead her away from th' girl. Vern release th' call tae release oor beasts so thay don't git hurt in th' crossfire. Gryph, open up th' ground, that should slow em down 'til we figure a wey tae kill this bitch!" Trice said who was definitely the one leading this show and I noticed his accent came out stronger when angry.

Vern nodded before he blew out a flaming white arrow and shot it, directing it up in the air above our heads making it explode like a firework, whilst releasing a high pitched whistle. I could just see the beasts they had rode in on when joining the battle, charging their way towards the clearing and in the direction they had come from. I wondered about the one Vern had travelled here on, when suddenly I saw the huge winged creature take to the sky and start flying away like a giant eagle. Meanwhile, Trice nodded to me and said,

"Hang tight… I'll be back." I frowned and was about to ask how long that 'hang tight' comment was meant for when Vern said,

"Ye know that yin is taken, right?" This was referring to what I assumed was the 'Action hero one-liners'.

"C'moan, jackass, time tae do what ye do best," Trice said after walking away and hitting Vern on his back as he went, making him stumble forward a step before asking,

"Aye 'n' what's that, ye bastard?"

"Piss off women," Trice replied making the big guy, known as Gryph, bellow in laughter before he hit out at the ground and this time instead of creating a booming shockwave effect, he split it wide open, making me cry out in shock. He seemed to be able to control the damage as he centred it around where I stood, so it now created a little island around the cage, splitting it away from the rest. This was so it made it more difficult for the creatures to get to me. Of course, it also made it impossible for anyone to free me, which was something I would have pointed out had they not already started running towards the angry Queen.

They moved with such speed it was nothing short of incredible and made me wonder what supernatural beings they were. They all split up, so the Queen didn't know who to grab, but then something they weren't counting on happened, which looked like it was game over for the three riders. It started when two pedipalps reached down over the Queen's human head, covering her face. Then they continued even further as they pushed their way inside her mouth before stretching it so wide, I thought it was going to rip her face in half!

She screamed in haunting agony as the two shorter legs that produced the webbing reached over and entered the stretched mouth, gagging her on them both as they tore their way forcefully inside her body. This was just before her stomach started to expand, as if something was being deposited in her belly before it grew so big, it made her look nine months pregnant in seconds.

I felt like gagging too at just the sight but managed to keep down the vomit that threatened...*unlike the Queen*. The spider legs were quickly turning her and just as the three riders were making it to the cave, the legs pulled from her mouth and the two pedipalps held her jaw open as she spewed a seemingly endless amount of sticky wet webbing at them. This had been what was forced to grow in her belly, making it land over the three men like a hot blanket, capturing them in her thick webbed net.

"NO!" I screamed as she quickly spun extra webbing

around the captured three, until they were completely covered in a cocooned sack. Then she gathered up her new kill and made off towards the cave, her treasure nestled up against the body of the woman. One whose head now hung in what looked like utter exhaustion.

"Oh shit, no! Fuck…FUCK!" I shouted in anger as I felt utterly helpless to do anything, especially now being stuck on a fucking island surrounded by a horde of battling creatures all around me! I also felt sad, because I was starting to like those guys and now it felt as if they had died trying to protect me. The pain of which made my chest ache for them and their gallant efforts now seemed in vain, for their deaths happened so swiftly.

I felt tears emerge as hopelessness settled bitterly in my gut. I tried to tell myself that maybe they weren't dead. That maybe it wasn't too late to save them and as soon as I discovered a way free, then perhaps I could sneak inside the cave and cut them free once this war had ended. Because surely it had to end right? I mean just how long would it take for them to all kill each other?

Obviously not soon enough I thought as suddenly the creatures from both sides were trying to discover ways of getting to me. Something that ended up being successful when the spiders backed up enough to jump across the massive rupture in the land. The tree people also managed it, as the roots unravelled from their bodies so they could launch across the gap. They latched onto the cage to anchor themselves in making it across when the rest of their bodies soon followed.

"Ah, just fuck off already, will you!?" I shouted as I swung my weapon around which was a smaller sword, reminding me of a Roman Gladius. I managed to keep some at bay, but with the lack of my protector to help me out, it was soon becoming obvious that the three riders weren't the only ones about to lose their lives in this battle. As the ice cage around me was starting to crack under the pressure of so many of them.

"AH!" I shouted in pain as one of the hands from the spider creatures managed to reach for me. The second I tugged my arm out of its grasp, its claws scratched deep gouges into my skin, tearing into my shirt and leaving me bleeding at the top of my arm. I ignored the pain but it distracted me long enough that I didn't spot the roots gaining access through the gaps of ice. But just before I could dodge one, the other had wrapped around my ankle and was yanking me hard to the floor. I dropped the blade as I fell and cursed myself for the deadly mistake.

"NO!" I screamed as I kicked out and thrashed, trying to get free and twisting my body so I could reach the handle of the sword, thinking I could cut myself free. However, another root reached for it and just as my fingertips grazed the handle, it was cruelly yanked out of my grasp before being lost completely with no hope of ever getting it back.

"Fuck!" I snapped knowing this was it, there was no recovering from this. Not when even more roots wrapped themselves around my body, letting me know that this was what it wanted. To drag me back to one of the trees to imprison me there, so it could add me to the demonic collection, like making me part of the Borg and its collective.

I knew this when the main part of the tree man's body was using his rooted hands to try and pry open the icy cage, making it crack even further. Meanwhile the roots had wrapped themselves tightly around my torso, making me shudder in revulsion when they circled my breasts, before moving up towards my neck. Soon my movements became too limited, with nothing left to do but strain my neck away from the vine as it worked its way up from tightening around my chest.

But this was when something unexpected happened. A

Gods' almighty roar erupted from where the spider Queen had disappeared and it was so powerful, it created a wave of air to come bellowing through the forest. It was a warning to all the creatures, as if they knew what it was and they feared it. I knew this as after the demonic sound was made, the roots loosened their hold on me a little. I managed to twist slightly, and it was enough to see what had caused the terrifying sound as suddenly a huge winged beast erupted from the cave, one that had three snarling heads.

It also emerged with the spider Queen grasped in the six feet that were on the underbelly of the dragon-like creature. Each clawed foot had a spider leg in its grasp and just as the woman started screaming, the creature roared again before ripping the Queen apart. This made the woman fall to the ground, with the rest of the demonic body in a bloody mess of broken spider limbs.

Her spider spawn all cried out in a high pitched sound that made me wince against the pain it caused to my ears. Of course, this didn't last as one of the heads of the dragon started breathing fire in great streams of spitting lava, setting the main part of the horde alight. I could barely make out the details of the huge beast as it just moved too fast. This was as it started to swoop down killing all in sight, putting not just an end to the war but also burning down the entire demonic forest.

Then, as it flew back on itself doing another round, it came closer to me. I didn't realise what its plans were until it was too late. As it wasn't just trying to get to the creatures around the cage but it had other ideas, ones with me in mind. Because it continued to get closer and closer until I had to close my eyes against the dust that flew up around me. This was thanks to the multiple sets of wings that battered the air, making it whip at my skin. Then the next thing I knew I was shaking as I heard the sound of ice cracking above me. I opened my eyes just long enough to see the lid of the cage was now in the grasp of one set of clawed feet. This was before it broke it away completely and was tossed aside.

Then I felt another set of feet start to curl themselves around me and I screamed as I was scooped up in their hold, before being lifted out of the shattered ice cage. However, I wasn't the only one, as the tree man that had been wrapping his roots around me also came along for the ride, making me cry out as it tightened around me.

"HOLY SHIT!" I shouted as the winged beast flew higher and higher. But then I screamed again, making the creature respond. One snarling head looked back at me before it swooped down low, now dragging the hanging tree man into the webbed treetops in hopes of getting him caught there. Thankfully, this worked as it snagged him, but the roots got too painful and felt as if they would squeeze me to death. So I cried out hoping that the creature was trying to save me and could understand my panic when I shouted in a pained way,

"TOO TIGHT!" This was when a demonic eagle type head ducked under as if to look and see what was happening for itself. Then the second it saw me caught, it reached back with the spare clawed foot and sliced through the roots, which severed the connection between me and the fallen tree man.

Finally, I could breathe again!

Although for how long I didn't know, as this battle may have ended but I had no clue what Hell had in store for me in the next place I found myself.

And I had to confess, I just hoped it wasn't a giant nest full of hungry winged beast babies all waiting to see what mummy had brought home for dinner.

Oh yeah, Hell was so much fun so far!

CHAPTER FOURTEEN

FROZEN READY MEAL

Well, I had to say, if someone had told me that me my trip to Hell would have included getting stuck in the middle of a battle between spider pod people and men that could have been the new spokespeople for Greenpeace…before being trapped in an ice cage while being saved by three warriors from an angry spider Queen, who was obviously not having a good day… or just hated men in general… to find myself being captured by a gigantic winged beast…then naturally I would have given Lucius my hand, let him pull me through the barrier, then patted him on the back and said, 'good luck honey' before booking myself a flight to Bora Bora until all this demonic genocide stuff blew over!

However, when finding yourself held in the deadly grasp of some winged beast that looked only a forgetful moment away from either dropping you or crushing you to death, then it was of little wonder that I dreamed of being on a beach somewhere. What I didn't want to be doing was flying over the vast barren lands of Hell, held by a creature that I had no idea if it wanted to feed me to its offspring, use me as bait for a bigger meal or just plain old eat me itself. Of course, there was always the other more unlikely scenario of this that might play out.

Like the magpie theory, only instead of collecting shiny objects for its nest, this one collected small helpless animals. Or maybe they believed I would make a good pet to keep them entertained. Or there was even the idea that I could be some kind of offering to a female they intended to mate with? There were also crazier ideas that included a colossal giant, his pet bird-like creature and me, the rodent they brought back for their master like a cat does when leaving 'gifts' outside the front door for you to find.

But this was what happened with your time when you had nothing other to do than just lie like a sausage in between wicked looking claws, staring down at those massive talons like a deadly blanket was wrapped around you…well, then let's just say you start to go a little crazy questioning the possibilities of your fate.

But then I had already spent the first ten minutes analysing the beast that had me in its clutches. It was incredible and naturally unlike anything I had ever seen, or even come across in my research. Because, thanks to the Afterlife library, I knew of most things, even if the tree people and creepy spider Queen and her offspring had been missed off the Demon A to Z's.

However, it soon became obvious that the three headed beast was a combination of creatures, now which of those creatures they were, was only ever going to be at best a guess at this point. Its body, one I could only make out from below due to obvious reasons, wasn't like I would have expected from a dragon type creature. No, instead it looked more like that of a giant lion, but it had yellowish, orange scales at the sides of its body instead of fur. Its underbelly had a mass of feathers that started off as the white downy kind, that were tipped with ice blue and looked incredibly soft.

They then started to change further down the body into larger feathers the colour of rust, that split off into three different tails. One was dark blue and covered in scales that split into two points at the end. The other was black with hints of red at the spikes that ran down its length and ended in an arrowhead. The last tail was unmistakably that of a lion and this time was one that was covered in fur with a bushy end.

As for its legs, there were six of them and each pair was different. There was the one that looked as if they belonged to a large bird, like an oversized eagle that reminded me of my father's pet demonic bird named Ava. She usually only liked my father and my mother and didn't really like children. So naturally she had given me a wide berth whenever she felt the need to land on my father's balcony. But as for this creature, well it was the size of a damn building!

As for the other legs, one pair looked more like large elongated paws covered with rust coloured fur with lion's claws big enough to shred a tree to splinters. As for the last pair, they didn't look like they belonged to a dragon either but were definitely the biggest. They were also the ones I was currently hitching a ride on, as the black talons were curled around my body, making it not exactly the most comfortable ride of my life. Saying this, I was at least thankful that my ass cheeks fit in the curved groove. But then the other edges dug into my skin, behind my knees and at my back, making me wish I was wearing a blanket, not just jeans and a shirt!

Well, at least the pointed ends of those claws were far from my fleshy bits, as I wasn't sure I would have survived much of the ride if they hadn't been. As for the top part of the beast, it was only glimpses I would get and it looked like three different sets of legs and tails weren't the only things on this beast that came in threes. Because I had seen earlier, before being picked up, that it had three sets of wings, the details of which had been too hard to see during flight. And well, I already knew about the three heads.

What I didn't know was how long we had been flying for, but the second we rose higher over a mountain range of black rock, I started to shiver, unable to help shaking in the cage of large claws. It was at this point that one of the heads looked back down at me and it clucked its huge beak. This made me cower back as I thought at first it was trying to bite me. It had dark red eyes, a scaled head unlike a bird, two small slits that I assumed were the nostrils and two tightly coiled horns that framed either side of its head.

However, the second I looked scared of the thing, shaking now from cold and fear, it cocked its head to the side as if in a questioning way. Then it made a loud bird like screech as if communicating with the other two, because soon I was moving.

"WHOA!" I shouted as I found myself being lifted in the claws. Then, as they started to open up, I began to panic!

"NO, DON'T DROP ME!" I screamed but soon found there was no need, as I was being pushed up against the underbelly of the beast into the blue and white downy feathers closer to the neck than the tail. The claws held me in place so I wouldn't fall but could still get close to the belly, but more importantly...*the warmth.*

Oh, by the Gods, it was wonderful, and I couldn't stop myself from rubbing my fingers through the feathers, telling it,

"THANK YOU!" I had no idea if it heard me as when it rumbled a purred response, one I felt vibrating against me, I didn't know if it was from my thanks or my stroking its feathers. Either way, I took the fact it wanted to care for me as a very good sign. Unless of course...

It didn't like frozen ready meals.

But then just as I found myself getting warm and even a little more comfortable, I noticed we had started to descend. I looked around seeing that we had made it over the mountains and were flying over what looked like a field of brown grass with a large hill at its centre.

"Okay, I guess we are coming into land then, rather you than…whoa, okay that's a little…FAST!" This ended on a scream as we suddenly dipped to one side as if the beast was now hurt or something, as now it looked barely able to keep itself in the sky, let alone me as well. Suddenly I found myself tight in its grasp again and being lowered from its belly as it got closer and closer to the ground. Naturally, I screamed as the sight of the field started to come at me quicker and the second the claws released their hold, I fell, hoping it was closer than it looked.

I fell with a thud and tumbled in the grass, thankful that it only knocked the air from my chest and nothing more. I quickly lifted my head in time to see the beast now in all its entirety.

"Holy shit," I muttered in awe as even falling the creature looked majestic and incredible. I had been right about the wings, as they were three different types, that all now tried in vain to work together to make the landing a little easier.

There was a black pair that looked scaly along the finger bones brushed with the hint of red whilst the ends gleamed crimson at the large taloned tips. The other two both had feathers but were different in size and colour. There was a dark navy blue pair that were slimmer and looked sleeker, and I wondered if perhaps this was for greater speed. They also looked as if they had been dipped in ink as they appeared wet and almost shimmery under what was now a red hue soaked sky. The last and biggest pair were at the centre and they looked more like those of an eagle, with burnt red feathers that were long and wide, with white running down the centres.

As for the other two heads, I could barely believe what I was seeing, as one was a dragon! Although it had webbed fins at the sides of its head along with down its neck. It also had I don't know how many rows of teeth, as the details of what I could make out were only what I could see in the seconds of its rapid descent. But it looked like it also had a single horn surrounded by spikes at the centre of its head and glowing red slits for eyes.

The last one had a mane of long floating bright red fur around its neck with the head of an eagle and a set of huge horns that rose up and curled over its head like a helmet.

But as it glided over the field, all six legs started running through the air, ready and waiting for when it landed. However, it didn't help as suddenly the wings just vanished! After this the whole creature crashed over the top of the hill before it tumbled out of sight and down the other side.

"NO!" I shouted as I quickly got to my feet and started running. I don't know what had come over me, but I felt struck with panic that the creature could be hurt or worse…dead. Of course, trying to run up a hill didn't exactly last long, and I found myself having to stop to catch my breath before I did something silly like pass out. But then finally I reached the part of the hill that it had first started to land on. Once there I could now see the deep gouges in the ground that had been taken out where it had tried to use its claws to stop itself.

"Oh please, oh please, oh please be alright," I repeated to myself as I gave it one last push and ran over the top of the hill to see for myself if it had survived.

"What the Hell?" I muttered ignoring my own pun in place of something else.

"Where did it go?" I asked as there was nothing but the three long skid marks that all went off in separate directions.

But what was missing from this picture was the giant winged beast lay amongst the torn up strips of land.

However, what was at the ends of these makeshift landing strips were what looked like three black slumped figures that only when they started moving, did I gasp in realisation…

They were the three riders!

CHAPTER FIFTEEN

SCARRED BEAUTY

The second I saw them begin to move, getting to their feet I panicked! So, just as the first one was up and shaking his head, doing so as if trying to get his senses back, I ran. I didn't go far, but just back over to the other side of the hill and skidded down it a little so as to hide.

"Shit, shit, shit! Okay...just think, Fae," I whispered to myself, trying to think of the best course of action. I mean other than them putting me in a cage, saving my ass and then flying off with me, what did I really know about them? Other than I was pretty sure only moments ago the three of them had been a three headed dragon, eagle, lion mix.

"Gods, just how much more fucking complicated could my life get right now?" I hissed at myself knowing that I didn't exactly wake up that morning thinking my brain would need to be putting together words like dragon, let alone hitching a ride on one and then finding out they were shifters.

"Well, that worked well...*not!*" I could hear being said from not that far away, telling me they were coming this way.

"Let's just concentrate on finding th' lass." I was pretty sure the one called Trice said.

"Well, she sure as shit won't git far if we broke the wee lass' legs," the first one commented, again in the same heavy Scottish accent I had heard before, it was Vern.

I was right, they were shifters.

This put me in two minds as I know that they had saved me before, well twice actually, if I counted the whole dragon thing, but the biggest question was still…why? I didn't exactly think that down here was the type of place where people did things out of the goodness of their hearts. Because let's face it, there was usually a reason people were down here in the first place. But then, these guys were shifter demons which meant that with demons, things weren't always as they seemed. Because with demon souls born from Hell, that didn't always mean that you were evil. My father's world wasn't black and white like that. No, there was an ocean of grey areas just as there was for Angels, who weren't always good.

But then, I also knew the dangers of trusting anyone down here. Because both my father and Lucius had their fair share of enemies, most of which they had no doubt sent back down to Hell at one time or another. Which meant that if I did choose to go with these three, then if they didn't know who I was already, it was probably wise to keep it like that.

"Ah!" I shouted the second a hand landed on my shoulder, making me scramble away quickly before turning around to face what had to be said, looked like one of the jolliest guys I had ever seen.

"Ah fun th' wee one," he said, in a heavy Scottish accent like his friend, and one I barely could understand. I think he might have said that he'd found me.

Now I was looking at Gryph without his helmet on, meaning I could finally put a face to the huge muscled body. He was a similar size to Ragnar and in fact, he even looked as though he could have been a distant Scottish relation, as he too had his hair shaved at the sides in a Viking style cut. Although Gryph had flaming red hair which didn't have even a hint of copper or orange or anything thing else but the brightest of reds. It was also twisted down the centre and held together in sections with black leather pieces all the way down his back to his waist.

But putting his unusual hair aside, along with the massive size of muscles he had, it was his face that set him apart, as he was seriously cute! He had light green eyes that were almost completely lost whenever he smiled as his big cheeks rose up making them narrow. Laughter lines also appeared at the corners of his eyes, along with deep smile lines around his lips.

He had a larger nose and large forehead that suited his face, still making him handsome, only in a more rugged way. The bottom part of his face was covered in a long wiry beard in a shade lighter than his hair. It was also one that was neatly trimmed around his mouth, creating a thick moustache on his top lip. His smile was also one that was infectious and other than the sheer intimidating size of him, he looked far too jolly to be a killing machine. But then I looked down at his enormous hammer and quickly remembered what he could do with it... on the battlefield that was... I had no idea about his skills in the bedroom to comment by making that statement a euphemism!

It also made me question where exactly he had put the thing when he had changed into part of the beast, again, I meant his weapon and nothing more.

"Aye, so he did," the next one said coming up behind him and slapping him on the back saying,

"Pity tis nae finders keepers, eh?" This made the big one, Gryph, grunt out a laugh.

"Aye, she be a wee bonnie lass," Gryph agreed making me blush at being called pretty.

"Uh...thanks," I said making him place a hand on his heart dramatically and say something I could only half understand.

"'N' she haes th' voice o' an angel tae!"

"Aye bit tis a pity she doesn't ken ye, brother!" the slimmer one said who I knew to be the joker of the group and was who they called Vern.

And like Gryph, now that he wasn't wearing his helmet, I could see that he looked like your loveable rogue, with easy going handsome features. He too had red hair, but it was lighter, more a strawberry blonde than Gryph's flaming red. It was also kept trim at the back and sides and longer on the top that fell mainly to one side in a floppy style. It also looked as if he spent a good deal of time running a hand through it whenever it fell into his eyes, like he needed a haircut but just hadn't got round to it. He also had a beard but his was trimmed all around and was not long enough to hide the dimples that looked permanently on show.

His eyes were a beautiful hazel colour with flecks of green and they were framed with arched brows that granted him more prominent expressions, like the cocky sexy look he was giving me right now. He also may have been the slimmer of the two, but his biceps still stood out as being someone used to fighting. This was just most likely more of a stealthy kind, as he looked more like a quick athlete than the heavy weight champion that stepped up next to him.

And by the Gods, the last man was utterly breath-taking!

"Ken ye?" I forced myself to ask, just as he appeared, hoping that my voice didn't sound as strained as it felt. He was definitely who I thought was the most beautiful out of the three, even though they certainly each had their own charm and handsome looks.

"Understand you," said the one named Trice, who had been the creator of my ice cage. He was obviously also the one in charge and his accent was a lot less strong than the other two, with only hints of it.

All three of the men were tall, with Gryph obviously being the biggest at well over six foot seven. But the other two looked about the same height as Lucius, which meant they must have been at least six foot four. However, it was Trice who looked more like some chiseled depiction of a Greek God, one that had also been scarred. This was because he had a serious face with stunning dark brown eyes that were edged with a dark green ring, making them seem to have the power to pierce your soul!

He had those faint lines in the higher cheekbones and a square jaw peppered with a dark stubble that framed kissable lips (for at least one single girl, who wasn't me) as his bottom lip was slightly fuller than the top. And like the other two, his hair was also red, but it was darker, and more auburn. He also wore it in long waves, with half of it tied back off his face in a full and messy manbun, with it reaching down past his shoulders.

Gods, it made him look sexy, even with the blindingly obvious scar on his face that some may have believed tarnished his beauty…I, however, *did not.*

But it looked like a recent injury or one that had only just been made, which I had a feeling wasn't the case. This was because there was no blood on his face or down his neck. Yet it was one that looked red raw and newly inflicted. It ran straight down through his left eye starting an inch from his hairline and ending level with his nostrils. And besides it being strange in the fact that it didn't look to have ever healed properly, the shape of it was odd too. As the top of it forked into two points, making it look like a lizard's tongue and having me instantly question, what had done this to him?

This question died the moment I got a full look at his body, unable to help myself when I scanned the length of him. He was huge, and if he had been an Avenger, then he would have been the Captain America of the group. This was thanks to his large shoulders, and beefy arms that looked like he spent a lot of time hammering punchbags off their chains with his large fists. And this was all seen even with his clothes on, so I didn't even want to think how many muscles there were without!

But then, he wasn't much bigger than Lucius in this department, so it wasn't as if I needed much of an imagination as Lucius was a powerhouse of sheer muscle and strength, one I was missing like crazy.

"Okay, so I am going to take a wild stab in Hell here and say that you three aren't going to kill me any time soon or eat me, seeing as you are no longer a giant three headed Dragon." The second I said this Trice and Gryph both winced before the big guy dragged a hand down his face and said,

"Och na, she's dane it noo." Which I think meant that I had done something I shouldn't have. This became clear when Vern narrowed his eyes and said,

"Och na, she didnae say that!" he said looking at Gryph who shrugged his massive shoulders whilst Trice said,

"Let it go, Vern."

"Na, I will not let it goo," he said slowly mimicking Trice's correct use of words,

"I'm going ta skelp yer wee behind shuid ye ca' me a dragon again, lass!" Vern said making me frown before leaning towards Trice and asked quietly,

"And what's skelp?" Trice's lips twitched as Gryph burst out laughing, after putting his hands on his bare abs and bending slightly.

"To smack your bottom is what it be!" Vern said translating himself and making my mouth drop open in shock.

"You will not!" I said putting my hands on my hips.

"Aye ah bloody wull!"

"Listen here, mister touchy Dragon man, if you even try to smack my behind, I will put you on your ass so fast you will think your head is spinning!" I threatened now stepping up to him and looking up with no fear in my gaze. Meanwhile, his hazel eyes almost glistened as he was obviously finding this threat amusing. Something that was confirmed when he mimicked my stance by putting his hands on his hips and getting closer to my face.

"Is that so now?" he asked, purposely holding back the heavy words of his accent.

"Try it and see where it gets you!" The playful challenge in his eyes was again easy to see and I waited, hoping he wasn't as quick as he looked. But then he looked to Trice who shook his head telling him no, whilst Gryph just shrugged his shoulders. Then, trying to take me off guard, he lunged for me making me side-step and grab his arm, before taking it with me as I ducked behind him. After this I forced his body to roll with it, so he was now on the floor looking up at me with astonishment. This made Gryph boom with laughter and slap his hands to his knees and he bent over even further this time. Trice also chuckled and placed a hand on my shoulder, telling me,

"Alright, lass enough show and tell, consider us impressed."

"Aye, mak' that, bloody impressed!" Gryph said laughing some more. Meanwhile Vern still looked shocked, even as Trice offered him his hand.

"Come on, get your arse up!" Vern slapped a hand to his and said,

"A dinnae ken whither to be pissed off or turned on," as he was pulled to his feet.

"Ah ken which one I a'm," Gryph said winking at me and making me chuckle.

"Alright, so let's make a deal, I won't call you the D word

again if you explain to me what happened back there and who are you guys?" I said folding my arms as I expected answers.

"Well, we are ne no, Drake, Lindwrum, Amphiptere, Wrym or fckin Dragon! I am a Wyvern, hence the name, the big bastard is a Gryphon, gain' hence the name and tis broody bastard ere is a Cock tease!" Vern said nudging Trice whilst laughing at his own joke and making him roll his eyes once in return. This was before Trice swiftly turned and delivered a gut punch to him, making him double over and cough through the hit. Then Trice walked calmly over to me and informed me,

"I am what is known as a Cockatrice, that is also hence the name. We are known as the McBain brothers," he said and considering they all had red hair, then it wasn't really a big surprise.

"Aye, McBain, 'n' we bring th' pain!" Vern added with a wink.

"'N' whit micht yer name be, lassie?" Gryph asked with a great big grin that never seemed to leave his face. But I granted Trice a questioning look making him get closer to my face and whisper softly,

"He wishes tae know ye name, lass."

"Oh, well it's uh Emmie... my name is Emmie," I said deciding this was probably the safest name to give, seeing as it was the one most rarely used unless by my closest friends.

"And exactly how did ye come to be 'ere *uh,* Emmie?" Trice asked mimicking my hesitation whilst circling me and looking me up and down, just as Vern did the same, also looking at me suspiciously. As for Gryph, well he just grinned at me.

"I don't remember, but I think it had something to do with a witch," I said thinking this was most likely the safest thing to say.

"We don't get many humans down here, do we brothers?"

Trice said, stating the obvious and clearly not believing me completely.

"Na, nae unless ye be deid, and ye be tae bonnie fur that, lass." Vern agreed.

"Look, all I need to do is try and find a way back, and seeing as you three seem like the helpful types, how about you help a girl out?" I asked making Trice fold his arms, making the leather of his jacket groan at his biceps. Vern gave me a wry look and for once, Gryph looked slightly less happy.

"We have a duty to our King," Trice stated firmly and Gods, he could be intimidating.

"Okay, so what does that mean exactly?" I asked, not liking the sound of this.

"It means ye be shit oot o' luck, lass," Vern said making me frown, until Trice explained,

"This be his Kingdom we are in 'n' that means everything in it belongs tae him."

"Everything?" I asked with my voice breaking and ending higher.

"Aye, even us, lass," Gryph answered making my eyes widen in surprise.

"We are blood bound to him and therefore we follow his law," Trice informed me and suddenly this wasn't sounding so good.

"And this law means...?" I let that question linger, rolling my hand around,

"That ye belongs to him now," Trice said making Vern cut in and finish,

"'N' we mist deliver."

"Aye, we mist," Gryph added now looking regretful.

But despite this new revelation, what they didn't know was that I was just viewing this as a safe passage and nothing more. As I knew that at least if they planned to deliver me to their king, then they intended to do so with me still breathing and in one piece. Otherwise they would have no doubt just tied me up and gagged me by now.

Besides, I would let them take me as far as I could go and then I would sneak off when they were least expecting it. Getting as far as I could until somehow I could find a way to reach the one man in Hell I knew would help me…

My grandfather, the Prince of Lust.

"So, what now?" I asked, after releasing a frustrated sigh. But Trice turned his back on me and paused just before walking down the hill to tell me,

"Now, lass…

"We walk."

CHAPTER SIXTEEN

KINGDON OF THE DEAD

"Erm, I hate to point out the obvious here but why are we walking?" I asked after rushing to catch up to the three brothers, who were making their way down the hill and past the destruction their crashing shifter form had made.

"Ah think th' wee Lassie likes yer dragon!" Gryph teased his brother Vern, pushing on his arm and making him have to save himself from tumbling off to one side.

"Haud yer wheesht!" Vern replied just as I was catching up to Trice who I thought was the more helpful one in translating.

"What did he say?"

"He told him tae shut up," Trice said granting a brief look down at me.

"Aye, that's whit ah said," Vern said winking at me in that charming cheeky way of his as he passed me.

"So why aren't we…you know…" I asked making a flying motion with one hand, causing Trice to raise a brow at me. This was before Gryph came past and with a chuckle told me,

"Fur this wid happen, lass." Then he motioned with his massive hand a flying motion before crashing it into his other hand with a loud slap. Then as my eyes widened, he burst into a belly shaking laughter before walking past to catch up with Vern. Meanwhile, I wasn't watching where I was going and being clumsy me, I managed to trip in a field of nothing but grass...well, grass and my own feet, which was enough apparently, I thought with an eye roll.

But Trice, who was still walking next to me, caught my arm and steadied me, with nothing but a nod when I thanked him. I seriously had to question how in life I could fight like a badass but be clumsy enough to trip over my own damn body parts! Maybe it was the universe trying to equal things out and create a balance. But then, if that was the case, why didn't I see my sexy boyfriend tripping over his own ass all day long, huh? Yep, totally not fair!

"We kin only combine our shifted forms fur so lang, after that we need time tae recoup our energy before a shift is possible," Trice said deciding to inform me, explaining in greater depth as to what his brother Gryph's explanation was and letting slip more of his accent when doing so. This made me ask,

"How come your accent isn't as strong as theirs?"

"Fur he's a posh bastard, that's how come!" Vern answered over his shoulder making Trice groan in irritation.

"I spent mair of mah time travelling," was his reason, which with the stern look in his eyes, I decided not to press further.

"So, we are walking to wherever this king is then?" I asked making Gryph chuckle when Vern replied nudging his brother,

"Aye, if yi'll waant tae be fifty by th' time ye git thare!" Then he laughed as well.

"Uh...okay, so what's the plan then, are we going to try and get transport or something?"

"Transport! where dae ye think, lassie, th' London underground?" Vern replied after first turning around, raising his arms to his sides and adding,

"Dae ye see a bus or a black cab tae hail?"

"No, but I do see a jackass shifter that I just hitched a ride with that gotta say, wasn't really on my agenda but considering I woke up in Hell today, then I am kinda telling my brain that if a million fucking pixies showed up right now dragging behind them Santa's sledge and nine dead reindeers, then I wouldn't exactly be surprised." At this Trice smirked and both Vern and Gryph laughed.

"Ah knew ah wid lik' ye, lass!" Vern said making Gryph snort an agreement before saying,

"Aye 'n' she be a bonnie lass tae!"

"And bonnie means…" I asked letting that question tail off.

"Beautiful…it means he thinks yer beautiful," Trice said in such a way that it made me blush, especially when Vern said with a wink,

"Aye, we a' dae, isn't that right, brother?" Trice scowled at him making Vern laugh before the broody brother answered with a simple,

"Aye." This signified the end to that strange conversation.

After this I discovered the brothers weren't kidding when they said we would walk, because we did just that…and some! Of course, the brothers didn't get tired but considering they weren't human, then this wasn't surprising.

"Ah kin carry ye if ye lik'?" Gryph said ruffling my hair a bit in an affectionate way.

"Tis not far now," Trice replied for me, doing so in a way that was trying to silently translate something for his brother, making me first frown up at him in question. He ignored this and I smiled up at Gryph instead,

"Thanks for the offer big guy, but I'm okay." He shrugged

his shoulders and chuckled, which seemed to be his answer for most things.

"So not far till what...oh wow!" My questioning ended with my jaw near dropping to the floor as we finally made it over the biggest hill yet. This was because I was now faced with a colossal wall that looked like a giant wave, made not of water but of rock, as if it had once been a cliffside that over millions of years the wind travelling at the same angle had eroded a deep curved gouge along the centre, giving it this beautiful effect.

It also looked as tall as the Eiffel Tower and spanned so far on both sides from where we stood, it went beyond what my sight was capable of. Meaning that the wall was at least hundreds of miles long. It was also made from a rusty orange coloured rock that gave it the appearance as if it was made of sand and all it needed was a giant's finger to come along and run down its length for it to crumble to the ground.

But the real beauty came at the sculptured entrance that honestly left me wondering how such a feat was ever accomplished. Because the size of the opening surpassed that of the height of the wall and looked like an enormous demonic skull with its mouth open.

The skull was carved high above the ledge of the wall, which was topped with a crown of bone underneath the veil of a cloak. One that swooped down the sides to the ground and created the main opening. The skull itself had a sloping forehead from a prominent brow line, that then had two horns curling up out of where the eye sockets should have been. These rose up and framed the crown, with their points ending tipped up at the red sky.

Two slits were recognisable as being the nose, with the top of the jaw hanging down over the side of the ledge. This had a single row of demonic fangs pointing to the ground like carved stalactites that looked ready to crush you into pulp if they were to crack and fall as you passed through.

The whole thing looked like the king of death, with his jaw open ready to consume you whole and devour your soul and I was soon to discover why.

"What is this place?" I asked in an astonished tone.

"This is the Kingdom of Death," Trice answered before he continued on down the other side of the hill. Just looking at the space between us and the sculpture, then I knew that we had at least another hour of walking left before we even reached the massive entrance in front of us.

"But of course, it is," I grumbled making Vern chuckle as he came up behind me,

"Cheer up, lassie, cuid be worse," he then added nudging my shoulder and making me ask,

"Yeah, how do figure that?"

"Ye cuid be traivelin thro' thare alone," he said winking at me and like Gryph had done, he ruffled the top of my hair as though I was some little pet of theirs. But then, I couldn't really argue against this, as he was right,

I could have been alone.

This made me think about Lucius, as I was desperate to know what he was doing right now. Had he managed to get through the barrier into the Temple or had he been forced to look for another way? And if he had been granted access, like the Keepers of Three had said he could, did he then try and go through the portal after me? What if it had closed by then, or worse, what if the Witch had somehow managed to get through and now he was being forced to deal with her and her army alone.

Gods, but there were just too many questions and each one only led to how foolish I felt by coming here. Damn it, but if this place didn't manage to do it first, then by the time Lucius did show up, he was going to kill me!

But then, in my defence, I had believed he would just have been able to follow me. Which made me promise myself that if ever I was faced with making potentially dangerous and stupid decisions, then first I would at least ask about all the variables surrounding it and know all possible outcomes. Because the fault of being reckless was mine and mine alone. I had come here not thinking for one moment that I would have to face completing this journey alone. And well, had it not been for walking into that battle and being saved by these three, then I doubt I would have made it even another hour past that point without ending up dead.

Of course, it also had to be said that since the brothers had flown me here and landed in the field, then we hadn't run into any trouble yet. But all I needed to do was take one look at the gigantic mouth of death we were soon to walk through, to know that whatever was beyond this wall, more likely than not, was going to be my new nightmare.

But Vern was right, at least I wasn't alone and as far as protectors went, then these guys looked more than capable of being able to handle themselves. Of course, I also didn't think it wise to be the stupid cow that questioned why we were going this way. Especially seeing as Vern was right, it would probably take me until I was in my fifties before we walked around it … that was even if there was a way around it.

However, this allowed me to spend the next hour worrying about why the wall was there in the first place? Was it to protect what was beyond it, or to protect the world from it? Naturally, I hoped for the first, but then again, one look behind at the serene looking landscape we had just come from and I knew that this didn't seem likely. Not when we were exchanging the quiet rolling hills of brown grass for barren scenery. One that looked as though it could have been Hell's version of California's Death Valley!

My once red and white sneakers sank into the crusted desert sands and quickly became caked in the orange earth, not exactly making it the easiest terrain to walk on. And jeez, just one look down at myself and I felt like my clothes needed to be set alight, making me cringe at what the rest of me must look like. I felt as though I needed to be soaked in a bath for a week, as I was still finding webbing attached to my jeans. A pair that had started off life as being indigo and were now more of a dirty grey, thanks to the spider forest part of the trip. I had long ago given up on my plaid shirt and taken it off, revealing a slightly cleaner white tank top underneath. Then, so as not to waste my shirt completely, I ripped off a strip of it to use as a makeshift bandage for the scratch on my arm.

Trice had watched me the whole time I had done this and with only a few muttered words, had handed me a flask from his belt. I sniffed at it discovering it was water, which prompted him to say,

"Fur ye tae clean ye wound." I nodded my thanks before doing as he suggested. Then, after I had finished, he silently nodded for me to drink, and well, considering I felt like my mouth had been sucking on a dry loofah sponge this last hour, then let's just say that I didn't need to be offered it twice.

After I was done, I wrapped the material around my arm and when I fumbled with one hand, he silently took over, tying it for me.

"Thanks, again," I mumbled receiving only a nod in return. I didn't know what was with him, was he uncomfortable around me or was he just trying to get this job done and not get attached? Either way, something was odd about him. I continued to try and guess the enigma that was Trice when finally, we had crossed the barren land.

This meant that it had come to the point where there was nowhere else to go but over the cloaked lip of the skull's head, seeing as it was missing the bottom part of its jaw. This obviously wasn't made for shorter legs either as I was just trying to gain friction with my toes when I slipped. But before I felt the painful landing in my knees I was being lifted by a pair of strong hands at my waist, now holding me steady.

I was silently helped up over the curved rock and into the huge dark cave and only when the floor evened out, did I discover which of the brothers it was.

"Try staying on yer feet m'eudail, or Vern will think yer falling for him." This was whispered in my ear before the hands left my waist and Trice walked from behind me.

"Aye, that ah wull," Vern added with a quick turn on his heel so he could poke me in my belly before spinning around again as he walked ahead.

"What does M'eudail mean?" I asked, making Vern wink at me over his shoulder before tapping the side of his nose, whilst Gryph's booming voice came up behind me and answered,

"It means M'eudail." Then he threw his head back and laughed at his own joke seeing as he'd just repeated what Trice had said, only in a stronger accent making it helpful in no way possible.

"Oh great, looks like I found the comedy brothers of Hell," I muttered to myself without malice, making Vern turn around, fold an arm to his waist and bow in a dramatic fashion before tipping an imaginary hat to me. Of course, I couldn't help but giggle.

But then my giggling soon stopped the further in we travelled, as soon what faced me wasn't a Kingdom at all,

It was something else entirely.

CHAPTER SEVENTEEN

NECROMANCER

"Really, this is it?" I asked, my high pitched tone speaking for itself.

"Whit wur ye expecting?" Vern asked as I came to stand in between the three of them all looking up. I, too, gazed up following the twisty path to find the last sight I would have expected after walking through what had looked like the mouth of Hell.

"After that bad ass entrance, a lot more than some shanty town, that's for damn sure!" I commented sarcastically, because that was exactly what it looked like, or at least a demonic version of one.

But then, it was also a bit like stepping back in time. As if five hundred years ago, the earth split open and what fell into it was some broken town from the Tudor period. One that had been crudely fixed over time with whatever the people who were forced to endure this life could get their hands on.

It looked as if the first part of the town had been built inside the huge wall. One that had this section hollowed out to make space for it, as the thickness of the wall alone must have been at least a mile wide.

The town rose up in some sections and then dipped down in others, with a tight knit collection of buildings. These were both narrow and wide and built wherever, despite what should have been the limitations of the rocky foundations they were built upon.

A cobbled street ran up through the centre of it all and looked to be the only safe place to walk as there was barely any space between the swarm of buildings. And each looked slightly different to the next, with some that started off being made of stone and finished off topped with unstable looking wooden structures above. Some dwellings looked solely made out of scrap wood ripped off something else, like a boat or a dock. Some were topped with scraps of material with more holes than swiss cheese and others that could claim more luxury. For these had cone shaped roofs clad in dirty blue tiles or red soot covered triangular pitched rooftops.

But you couldn't tell if these were places people lived in or just a cram packed array of shops, as almost all of them had some sort of faded sign out the front, swinging from curled iron rods.

My complaint ended up making Vern laugh as Trice rolled his eyes and said,

"Let's just git tae th' shop already."

"Wait, that's why we are here, so you guys can do some shopping...hey, wait up!" I asked after they all started walking towards the start of the street, which began with an arch of stone and steps leading up. I started jogging to catch up and walked through the arch, passing under a creaking wooden sign. I muttered the name as I read the demonic script,

"Kingdom of Death" as it was written in what looked like a form of Sumerian, but it was one I understood enough. I

couldn't help but shudder as I entered, as if some sinister force had just passed through my body. But then I heard a whistle and looked up to find Gryph paused waiting for me.

"Come on, ye wee Lass," Gryph said as he patted his thigh as if I was some yappy dog, thus making me decide to ignore the snippy response I would have given and instead asked,

"Seriously, what could you guys want anyway, 'cause unless it's a demon donkey to carry a new arsenal of weapons, I really don't see…?"

"Does she ever stop asking questions?" Vern asked after pointing a thumb over his shoulder at me making me huff.

"Nae, as of yet she doesn't, bit then, that's a bonnie lass fur ye," Trice replied. I huffed at this and snapped,

"Oh, well excuse me for wanting to know a little something of my fate and if it's the type of thing that could get me killed or not."

"Weel yer be in th' right place fur that, Sweetheart," Vern said with a laugh making me scowl back at him.

"Cute, Chuckles," I commented under my breath, making him wink at me.

"What it wull include is food 'n' a bed tae sleep in, if you're interested in that type of fate," Trice commented dryly and right in that moment just the mention of food had my belly rumbling.

"Weel ah would say her tummy wis interested, that's fur sure," Vern said with a chuckle.

"Aye and mine," Gryph said making Vern tug on his long twist of hair down his back before swinging it over his shoulder and saying,

"'ere, chew oan this!"

"Tis mair meat that yer chicken arms, Laddie!" was Gryph's deep reply making Vern give him the finger before saying,

"Ah wis built fur speed, Bucko, nae fur carrying a golden

Mammothant foot oan mah back," Gryph grunted in reply before turning to me and saying,

"He is just sad fur he is puny a' over." Then he wagged his little finger at me, making me giggle as he was obviously talking about the size of Vern's manhood.

"Fck aff, wull ye, th' lasses kin barely handle whit ah hae tae give them!" I laughed despite only understanding half of it, guessing it was about what Vern could give the ladies in the bedroom, when Gryph wagged his little finger at me again, making Vern shout,

"Speak fur yerself!"

"If ye be done comparing cocks, let's git this shit done, th' girl is drawing attention," Trice said looking tense as we made our way up the narrow street making me catch up with him and say,

"The girl has a name you know." At this he just granted me a brief look over his shoulder at me and said,

"I know your name." And it was the way he said it that made me question if he knew something more about me than he was letting on. It was clear something was going on with him. Unless of course it was just as he said, and he was just feeling tense at the fact that we were no longer alone. And clearly, with his hand now resting on the hilt of his sword, he was ready for the possible threat.

I continued along the street, thankful at least that the whole town was lit up because there was no sky to speak of. Most of the light came from the warm glow behind the thousands of windows of panes of red glass in every size and shape. It was also from the tall flaming lanterns that lined the streets and looked like black iron demonic hands holding bowls swinging on three chains.

Some of the buildings were also linked together from above by rickety covered bridges that made for precarious looking walkways. Especially when I could see from below the way splintered dust would rain down every time some cloaked figure crossed one.

We then passed one building that looked little more than a series of scaffolding poles holding up a wooden box the size of a small room. This made it look like some giant insect with lots of skinny legs or maybe something out of War of the Worlds. Then the next one we came across was more rounded at the top from using hammered sheet metal for the curled walls.

But the town itself obviously wasn't the only strange thing about the place, as this was mainly down to the Hellish beings that inhabited it. Because Vern had been right, coming here alone would have been worse…far, far worse. As this part of Hell looked as if it was a mix of lost and wandering souls in tortured human bodies and demons that strangely enough, actually looked like they were trying to make a living.

There were those that scurried along the street like overgrown furless rats with extra limbs, black bodies, spiked spines and heads wrapped in blood soaked cloth. Then there were the more humanoid shaped demons that were tortured skeletons and rotted flesh, reminding me of zombies. Although why zombies had been given a skull full of nails for what appeared to be no reason at all, I didn't know.

There were the full on demons that went from horned beings that walked on two feet and had more muscles than looked possible, to those that were cloaked creatures looking pieced together by some kind of mad scientist with an abundance of demonic body parts.

There were also a few demons that obviously had human hosts, and these were dressed like hunters, or trained muscle for hire. Of course, what gave it away was the mass of weaponry strapped to their bodies whilst walking through the streets elbowing or kicking people out of their way, as if on a mission.

And that became another thing in this town, as you could most definitely tell the strong from the weak that was for sure! Also there didn't seem to be a middle ground with the beings that lived here. In fact, the only thing people seemed to have in common was that everyone looked permanently pissed off. But then this was Hell and not a Florida vacation. Although, I was pretty sure that would have been Lucius' idea of Hell, as let's just say that he didn't exactly strike me as the Mickey Mouse hat wearing type of guy!

Gods, how I missed him!

It was cruel really, seeing as we had only been together for what felt like a mere moment before fate had ripped us apart once more! And once again, it felt as though it was all my fault! But what was I saying, of course it was my fault as Lucius had tried to warn me not to go through the portal. But once again I hadn't listened, and now here I was, in some Hellish slum town looking for a shop, selling I had no clue what.

But then I also knew I had to be thankful for something, mainly that I was still alive thanks to the serious muscle I had on my side. And it continued to show because as it was, walking through the streets with these three surrounding me didn't make me scared in the slightest. Because seeing demons wasn't really going to frighten me, only the situations I continued to get myself into did. Especially when it felt like I was seriously lacking in the weapon department here, that and any fight up against about ninety percent of the demons and I was a straight up goner!

My only problem though was that Trice picked up on my lack of fear, seeing as it was clear he was the silent, observant one of the three, seemingly not missing a trick. Because if my story had been true, that I was human and just woke up in Hell one day, wouldn't I have been a hysterical mess right now?

Shit, I should have thought of that!

Well, it was a little too late to pull the damsel in distress card now because the other two might have bought it, but Trice most certainly wouldn't! So, I decided to ignore the blindingly obvious flaw in my plan at trying to pretend I was 'nobody important' down here. This being my 'I was here by mistake act' and instead continued to be led further into the town. This was until we came across a little shopfront that was different to the rest. This was in the sense that it had a bay window made up of tiny shards of black and grey glass that was pieced together by lead strips.

I squinted my eyes to see that, as a whole, the window made up a picture that looked like black souls trying to rise up, reaching for the sign above it.

One that again was spelt out in lead framed glass letters, this time in blood red.

It read…

The Necromancer.

CHAPTER EIGHTEEN

A TOUCH OF NERO

Vern walked in front of us and pushed open the black door that had a single hand painted sign that said,

'Open to Bitches,
Not Bastards!'

Vern flicked the sign, making it spin round on its hook and commented, "Noo that's cute." Then he walked inside, followed by Gryph, who as usual had a beaming grin and had to duck and turn sideways to fit. Trice then held out his arm and said,

"After ye, Lass." I nodded my thanks and walked in with the rest of them and soon my eyes widened in awe as I looked around at the room that was filled to the brim with so much stuff, it was hard to make one thing out!

I didn't know whether it was a shop or a madman's office who believed in the occult and was trying to prove the existence of the Devil. Of course, being down in Hell and all, well then this could have just been the store that sold cures to a certain type of foot fungus or where Demons got their horns polished and claws manicured.

I started closest to the door and worked my way around, taking in little bits of everything as I went. Like one corner that seemed devoted to crystals, obvious by the collection of polished geode spheres all lined up on one shelf. The next shelf down was filled with hand sized baskets of smaller stones. A huge, quartz geode stood off to one side and it was so high that the arched tip of the sliced rock must have reached my shoulders at least.

Moving along past the bay window that was filled with larger baskets of dried herbs and twisted pale roots, was a ceiling high cabinet. One that had hundreds of cube shaped drawers, each labelled with an alchemist symbol. In front of this was a sort of work bench that was filled with items that looked like everything you would need for potion making, from bowls sat in holders over candles to heat them, to dishes of bloodied meat, jars, and bottles. Stacks of books framed the desk, all piled on their sides. Tools of all kinds were also spread out in that used and haphazard kind of way.

Over the other side of the shop was another cabinet with five glass shelves behind locked doors and it was one that had every inch filled with old fashioned bottles. Each of these had what looked like a different aged label, telling you which were newly made and which had been there for years left unused. The last and biggest shelving unit in the place looked like it took up an entire wall and this was filled with what I would have called 'the body section'.

This was because it was home to the biggest jars and ones that each looked filled with formaldehyde, which was used to preserve the demon body parts inside them. Each looked magnified due to the thick glass and with the heavy booted footsteps of the three men, they started to look alive with the vibrations caused in the liquid.

Among these jars were also smaller ones that looked filled with different coloured powder, that could have been ground up flesh and bone for all I knew. I wouldn't have been surprised considering in the other jars there were teeth and fangs, along with small bones and horns.

Black bottles also filled one shelf, with unusual stoppers in the top, carved like skulls and clawed feet. A huge horned skull of a demon sat in the centre of them, almost like a prized trophy that had provided many of the pieces seen contained behind the glass.

"What is this place?" I asked, as I watched Vern stroll right up to the counter that was right in the centre of the shop. Then he made a show of raising his hand up and then dipping it down onto the buzzer in a comical way. It made a ding sound, but as no one appeared, he got bored and started to stick his finger inside a fancy iron cage that held a simple blackbird inside it.

"What's it look lik', Lass…ah crap, nae this again," Trice said, not answering my question but instead walking over towards his two brothers. And I guess he was right, because if I had to take a not so wild stab in the dark here, then I would have said the shop belonged to a witch and this was her supply store.

"Well, if it isn't the McBain brothers, nice to see you bastards still can't read," the woman said who came from behind a curtain made up of what looked like gold dipped finger bones. This was behind the counter and the shimmery gold doorway was framed by lengths of bunched herbs and dried flower buds.

As for who I assumed was the witch, she was a beautiful girl with the most unusual navy coloured hair. It had a sort of ombre effect where it turned from ink blue to a lighter navy and then to startling white at the tips. It was a mass of waves that were held back in a thong of leather with pieces of it coming loose from the tie, creating shorter waves to lie across her forehead. She had navy blue eyes to match and wore white eye makeup around them, making them look bigger. Peach coloured lips and a thin nose complimented her high cheekbones, and her perfect shaped chin had a tattooed white line down the centre about an inch thick, which had blue symbols down the middle.

She wore a light grey poncho style cape with wide arms and the top part was a tight crop top style that showed off her creamy white toned belly. The neck was wide folds of material from the large hood that hung down the back. With this she wore tight navy trousers, that were tight around the waist and were ruched up by the knee with the gathered material resting on top of oversized leather boots. A thick wide leather belt with pockets and bottles hanging from it completed the look.

"Necro, Ye Bonnie Lass!" Vern said in a cheeky tone, that was definitely considered as flirting.

"It's Nero asswipe, now what do you want!?" she snapped, clearly not impressed by Vern's charm and also I swear that I could detect a little hurtful glint in her eyes at him not getting her name right? I could tell a fake attitude from anywhere, as Wendy was always putting it on when talking to guys, especially the ones she really liked.

"Now, is that any way to treat a customer?" Vern said placing a hand on his heart and pretending to be hurt.

"Depends if you plan on paying for shit this time or just stealing it like usual," Nero said in a dry tone. Vern smirked at her and continued to pop his finger inside at the bird.

"Will you stop that! It took me ages to get them all back inside her the last time you wouldn't leave her alone," she snapped trying to bat his hand away from the cage.

"What can I say, Pet, I am attracted to pretty things," he

replied winking at her, and she just rolled her eyes in return. But then the bird let off a high pitched wailing sound and opened up its wings. This released about twenty white butterflies that looked as though they were made of sparkling vapour. This was all from a ribcage that had no flesh inside, as the bird's body was just all bone.

"Gorgon Balls, Vern, why can't you just leave shit alone, eh?!" she complained as she tried in vain to get them back, after first dumping the contents of a glass jar, which looked filled with used quills, on the floor, so she had something to catch them in.

"Ah, bit o' coorse ye remember mah name," Vern said proudly making her roll her eyes and snap,

"Yeah, whoopie doo, I remember all the names of people I consider a pain in my ass, now what do you want?" I couldn't help but laugh and she looked around Vern to see me.

"And any reason there is a human in my shop…no offence, Chica?" she asked making me shrug and reply,

"None taken, besides, I know when I really don't belong in a place."

"Well no, you're not dead for a start…or at least you're not right now but stick with this one for too long and that's bound to change…walking disaster if you know what I mean, and don't even get me started on the shit he burns!" I laughed making her smile back at me and I had to say, when she dropped the hard ass frown, she was a serious beauty when she smiled!

"Hello, richt 'ere," he said waving and making Trice sigh as it was obvious his patience was waning.

"Oh, we know, right Honey?" I laughed again at her reply, which was when Trice had obviously had enough and got straight to the point.

"We need another Elixir, Nero."

"What, another one?!" she replied sounding shocked and

making me curious to know what it was and what Trice needed it for.

"It wasn't long ago…" she started to say.

"I know, do you have one?" Trice interrupted in irritation.

"Can't you just sleep it off like other shifters, it's not like that shit grows around these parts, and that particular Soul Weed is hard to come by…*for obvious reasons."* After she muttered this last part, I looked to Trice who, after granting me a quick frown, stepped forward and said,

"We have a time constraint here."

"Yeah, and that is my first and last name too," I piped up sarcastically when looking around the large back of Trice's straight at Nero.

"Right," she answered making Vern get back in on the conversation,

"Sae, ye going tae hulp us, beautiful?" She rolled her eyes and said,

"No, I will help your brothers, you however, don't pay for shit and think being charming is payment enough."

"Ah sae ye dae think a'm handsome then?" Vern said bending a little and pointing to her eyes as if he had caught her out.

"Seriously, does he just hear whatever the Hell he wants and it makes sense to no one but him?" Nero asked and both Gryph and Trice both said at the same time,

"Aye."

"Pretty much."

"Och, cheers fur th' back up lads! Jeez, we only share th' same mother an a'll," he complained making Gryph pat him on the back and with a large hand gripping his shoulder, he said,

"Why nae ye pull a flaming arrow oot yer arse 'n' see if that impresses her."

"Aye, she might think yer hot then," Trice added making everyone laugh but Vern.

"Ha, ha laugh it up ye bastards, 'n' just wait till yer wake wi' yer eyebrows singed aff lik' lest time," he replied making Gryph rub his eyebrows with a frown as he remembered his brother doing this.

"'N' as fur ye, Lassie, dinnae ken what your game be bit if ye carry on I'm going ta skelp yer wee behind!" Vern threatened and Nero scrunched up her nose and said,

"I have no idea what you just said you ginger nutcase!" This is when I thought to add my answer,

"I think he said that if you carry on, he is going to spank your ass." At this Nero looked outraged whilst Vern put his hands on his hips and said,

"Aye, what th' bonnie lass said." Although I had to say that he should have taken the threatening glare from a witch more serious as she narrowed her eyes before she slammed her hands on the counter. This made a pot of ink spill before she grabbed the front of his shirt and yanked him to her. Then she warned,

"I've had enough of your cocky Scottish mouth, time to change that!" Then she whispered something I couldn't hear before she pulled him the last few inches and slammed her lips over his, kissing him.

"Och...Tis not good," Trice said as Gryph followed with,

"He's gonnae be pissed," then he scrubbed a big hand down his face. Meanwhile, I was just about to ask why them kissing was a bad idea when the tattoo down her chin started to glow and her eyes turned cloudy white. Although not that Vern seemed to care as he grabbed her in a more secure hold, with one hand fisted in her mass of hair, as he deepened the kiss.

In fact, the two of them looked as if they had forgotten what started it and were now only concerned with how to end it... and that was *in a bed.* It was only when Trice cleared his throat, twice, that Nero finally pulled away. Vern however growled low in his throat, in what was surprisingly a dangerous sound and pulled her back to his lips for another kiss as he was clearly not done with her yet.

"Weel, that's new," Gryph commented on a chuckle, making Trice groan,

"He's a fckin idiot." I frowned wondering what it was that they knew, and I didn't.

"I think I am missing something here," I muttered.

"Aye, just wait fur it, Lass," Trice said before he decided to intervene and he did this by putting a hand on Vern's shoulder, one he tried to shrug off. But Trice had clearly had enough and must have shot an icy blast through his fingertips as Vern jerked back and it broke the kiss.

"What the in the blazes, dear brother…? Hold on a moment, what has become of my voice?" Vern said and I burst out laughing the second I heard it now coming out as a posh old English accent. Something he looked as though he had no control over.

"Why has my manner of speech fled me?" Again, I sniggered trying to hold back a laugh and the other two brothers looked to be trying to do the same.

"You there, you did this to me, and I demand that you return thus the manner of my speech back to me," Vern said and then looked off to one side and mouthed a silent, 'thus' in question at himself. Meanwhile, Nero looked like she was still trying to get over that kiss as her cheeks were flustered and she was fisting her hands to stop them from shaking. Then, as if forcing herself to snap out of it, she said,

"Relax your jockstrap, Sugartits, it will wear off in a day or two."

"A day or two? Good Lord, my Lady, this is not acceptable

behaviour." Nero smirked, crossed her arms over her chest and said,

"I disagree, I think it's a vast improvement…now do you want this shit or what, as I haven't got all night?!" she said nodding to Trice who put an arm to Vern to move him back and said,

"Aye, move aside, Sugartits, we git a job tae dae, c'moan, Gryph."

"Well I never! The utter cheek of the man!" Vern said and his face said it all, asking himself why he continued to say this shit.

"You kin slap me silly later, ye naughty nelly, bit fur now, stay here 'n' watch th' girl…oh 'n' try nae tae git yourself in even more trouble, ye posh git" Trice said before ducking through the curtain of bones and Gryph followed, after first trying to go head on but not fitting. So, he ducked, bent his knees a little and went through side on, telling Vern,

"Aye, catch ye later, Buttercup." Then he winked with a massive grin making Vern scowl at him, obviously not chancing a comeback.

Then Nero pointed a finger at him and said,

"And you, I want all the souls of my ancestors back in that bird by the time I get back, or you will find a posh new hairdo to go with that poncey new voice of yours…you feel me?!"

"I understand you perfectly well, my dear, and as for feeling you, there won't be any of that until we are first courted and then wed." At this Vern slapped both his hands over his own mouth as if horrified by what he'd just said. Nero, on the other hand, blushed scarlet and tried to play it cool by saying a lame,

"Err…whatever…just…erm… don't touch anything!" And then she was gone with a clattering of the gold bones.

"Well, that went well, I think," I commented making him shake his head at me, then he rolled his eyes before making a motion with his hands as if he was going to strangle me, making me laugh. So, I stepped up to him and patted him on the back.

"Don't worry, Vern, just think, it could be worse," I said using his words back at him.

"How so, my Dear?" Vern asked making me roll my lips inwards so I wouldn't laugh and was able to tell him,

"She could actually have given you sugar tits."

CHAPTER NINETEEN

SHATTERED MOMENTS AND BLOOD

After this I spent the next ten minutes watching as a posh Vern tried to catch 'soul flies' into a jar. This mainly consisted of him saying 'darn' and 'dash it all' a lot, which was followed up with him punching stuff in anger. I also had to stop him from taking a pair of scissors at one point as he seemed determined to cut the longer parts of his hair off, as it wasn't becoming of a gentleman for it to be so long. Thankfully, he finally snapped out of that one in some weird wrestling with his own hand type of thing.

It was only when he managed to get the last glistening butterfly back in the cage, did he pick it up and shout,

"Hurrah, tis the most splendid moment, I must go tell Milady, I will be but a moment." Vern winced at his own words and I waved him off and said,

"Don't worry, I don't plan to go anywhere." He nodded and then passed through the curtain of bones with the birdcage in hand. After this I looked around the shop, almost torn on what to do, because if there was ever a time to make a run for it, then it would be now. I also didn't know when another opportunity like this would present itself again. But then, I also knew that my best bet at surviving this was sticking with the three brothers. This meant that all I could hope for was that whoever this King was they were taking me to, didn't order right away for me to be beheaded or something equally as medieval and well...*Hellish.*

Although, surely that was being a tad dramatic?

No, it was time to stop making foolish decisions, as that was what landed me here in the first place. Plus, I was starting to get attached to the big guys, they were funny and sweet. And yes, Trice was a little hot and cold with me, but then I guess seeing as he was the suspicious broody type, then I wasn't surprised that he was going to be this way.

Besides, I was pretty sure that if Lucius were to have a say in my choices, then he would have wanted me to stick with these guys if it meant keeping me safe. Gods, but just thinking about Lucius again and I found tears clouding my vision and I wiped them away angrily the second one fell to the ground. And I don't know why, but the moment it did, I felt strange. I looked around the shop to see if there was anything to cause me to feel this way, but this was when something on one of the cram-packed shelves caught my eye.

So, without following through with trying to find a cause, I walked over to the shelf and focused on the light reflecting off something. It was caught between two jars filled with some kind of herbs in oil, glinting off the candles that lit the shop. Then, without thinking about the dangers involved, I just reached out and pushed the jars aside so I could reach in between and grab whatever it was my mind seemed fixated on.

I curled my fingers around the cool round glass and pulled it free. Then I took a step back and brought it closer to have a better look at it.

"A snow globe?" I questioned aloud as the movements had made it cloud with what looked like tiny silvery grey leaves, ones which looked the same as on the Tree of Souls. I turned it up upside down the second I felt a key at the side, and I turned it, winding it up to see what it did. But then as I put it upright the leaves started to settle and music I knew started to play.

"Phantom of the Opera," I whispered as the tiny leaves soon revealed at its centre a small couple dancing, spinning around slowly in a circle, forever in each other's arms. They were also wearing crimson and featured in a familiar ballroom, with tiny aspects of the room now in miniature, like a grand staircase.

"What the…?" My question died the second I brought it closer and saw the impossible…

It was me and Lucius.

"It can't be!" I shouted when I saw that the couple dancing was a tiny version of us, just as we had been that night of the Masked Ball. But then the music stopped and the moment it did, a hissing sound could be heard, and small streams of red smoke started to seep from between the glass globe and its holder. This made me drop it and as it fell to the floor, the sight seemed far too symbolic for me to ignore as if watching us both falling was a glimpse of the future.

But then, even as the small stream of smoke started to rise up under my nose, I couldn't find it in myself to step away, as the sight of the couple dancing started to turn grey before crumbling away to dust, just like the rogues we had killed did. Then the glass started to crack but not from the fall. The moment it finally shattered was when I came to my senses enough to step back, but it was already too late. I knew that the second I felt the strange smell reach my nostrils… the damage was done. I had already inhaled something that I shouldn't have.

I knew this when my head started to feel heavy and my vision blurred. I shook my head and rubbed my eyes, feeling now how sore they were from having my contacts in for so long. So, I blinked rapidly trying to clear my vision that way, but then the second I opened my eyes, Hell was right there with me in the shop.

"Hello, Princess." The voice of the witch matched that of her scarred face, now staring back at me and the second she lunged for me, I screamed. Then I turned around and fled out of the shop. How had she found me!? How was she here, had the snow globe been a trap? Had she known that I would come here, or did Nero have something to do with it?

I didn't know anything other than I just had to run. I had to get as far away from her as possible! I couldn't let her get to me, not where she was at her strongest and I was alone. Damn it! I should have called for the brothers! But then what if she had hurt them, she was damn powerful after all and they admittedly had been weakened and needed to regenerate their power. Could she have the power to kill them before they had a chance to fight back!?

Gods, I just didn't know and couldn't chance going back there for that reason. I just needed to keep going, to keep running. Although this was easier said than done as the blurriness took over again and every time it did, I closed my eyes and opened them again to find myself faced with a different nightmare.

"Watch where you're going!" One demon said as I must have accidentally bumped into him without seeing him, as all I noticed now was his glowing eyes scowling back at me as I passed him in my haste. Then, as I tried to get away giving him more space, I was suddenly falling, tripping over and landing hard on my knees on the cobbled stones. I rubbed my sore eyes, feeling my contacts sticking and become almost hard around the edges. Gods, I just wanted to take them out! To squeeze my eyeballs just to get the relief of air behind them, so I could blink them away with my tears.

But then my vision cleared and it was long enough to see what new horror I had tripped over this time. A figure of a man covered in soot, caked in the stuff and dragging behind him the charred remains of bodies…bodies who I just knew had been his murder victims. Some still had the remains of their rotting flesh, whilst others were little more than fire damaged skeletons. All were attached to chains, so many chains in fact, that it looked like a cloak behind him. As each thick chain was anchored on to the iron collar around his neck or the shackles around his wrists and manacles around his ankles. The second I accidentally touched one as I tried to get back to my feet, I saw a flash of the past hit me.

A roadside blocked off by yellow tape, a town sheriff's cruiser parked side on with its lights still flashing. Other cop cars parked along the side of the road, with some directing traffic around the obvious crime scene. Suddenly a man in uniform ran from the tree line and barely made it to the roadside before he threw up, letting me know this wasn't a good sign. Moments later I discovered why as men in white coveralls came from the same place, only instead of just one body bag, there were several and not ones that looked big enough to be a whole person.

I screamed and the moment I did, I was back in the street looking into the haunting eyes of a dead girl and her severed head, telling me now that the monster in front had been a serial killer and this had been one of his victims. I quickly scrambled to my feet and saw for myself at least twenty bodies in different states of decay, telling me this was obviously what they had looked like by the time they had been found and laid to rest. Then one look up at the tortured punishment of the man responsible and the evidence left behind of his death, told me he had obviously received the death sentence by lethal injection. As the evidence of it was still attached to his arm with the needle sticking out of soot covered flesh.

Naturally, I quickly ran away from him, utterly haunted by his crimes and the face of a decomposing head that would never leave me. Meanwhile, he paid neither me or anyone else around him any notice, as he continued on his way through the street, dragging his cloak of chains and trail of bodies behind him as if it was just another day in Hell.

But then the blurriness in my eyes started to rise once more and soon my mind was telling me that the things around me were real when I knew deep down they weren't. Like the fog of hands all reaching for me and trying to grab me, making me turn and twist away from creatures that were nowhere near me.

"Fucking human flesh!" One shouted when I felt something hit me in the shoulder and I looked around but could only see the same black arms reaching for me, so I screamed and ran. I didn't know where I ran to but it was in the only direction the arms weren't clouding my vision. Which meant it was too late when I realised I was obviously being led somewhere.

The alleyways between the buildings hadn't looked big enough for a person to fit down, but this one was the exception as it looked like it led to a cellar. However, this had been my last thought when tumbling down the first few steps, saving myself just in time before breaking my neck. Which would no doubt have happened had I made it all the way down the rest of them, and eventually landing at the bottom.

Which meant that I ended up with my back to the steps with my arms behind me gripping on and now looking down into the glowing eyes of a child who strangely enough, was sat under a large red umbrella. I looked up to see there was no rain so I hadn't missed the part where it had soaked my skin, in all my panic. I knew the kid was a demon of some kind and it was not a good idea to get involved in whatever was going on with her. But then, after I was once again steady on my feet, the second I turned and started back up the steps, a small voice said,

"I'm all alone...*Won't you help me?*" I stopped dead and this time my own malicious grin spread before I slowly looked back at her and said,

"That didn't work the first time, bitch, it certainly won't work down in Hell." By the time I turned fully, I saw the whites of her teeth in the dark as she smiled.

"No, I guess not, but then again you never were as gullible as your mother," the witch replied, using what looked like the body of a small horned demon child to communicate with me. Of course, she was referring back to the time in my father's prison, when she fooled my mother into trying to help her.

"Gullible or not, she could still kick your ass."

"She could try but I think not, not now I am getting more powerful by the day, and speaking of days, that poor Vampire King of yours, he is awfully lonely up here without you." Hearing this I tried not to react, knowing that was exactly what she wanted. But then she carried on and I could feel myself losing my shit pretty quickly.

"I would even say he's crazed and very close to losing himself to his demon in his need to have you back. Although don't worry, I have had him locked in chains so he doesn't hurt himself and I have had Layla keeping him company for you until your return. One I suggest happens quickly if you want to see him live long enough for you to say your goodbyes." Okay, so this was where I hit my limit and the second I did, something strange happened as I could feel my blood pounding beneath my skin. It was like when you felt your own pulse point in a random place on your body, only this was all over. It was as if in my utter rage, something that had been lying dormant inside me was waking up and this bitch was the key to provoking it.

It started at my heart and travelled all the way down to the ends of my limbs until my toes and fingertips seemed to vibrate, shaking with the humming of power. I then looked down to see the tips of my fingers glowing and burning almost red hot and the witch's eyes widened with surprise. But that wasn't the only thing to happen as she looked down beneath her, now seeing for herself the pool of liquid that had gathered around her form. She dipped a small child's finger into it and brought it up to her face, now testing it and rubbing it in between her fingertip and thumb.

"How is this possible?" she asked herself but when the liquid started to rise up even further, you could see her panicking. So, I too looked down to see that the liquid rising up through the cracks beneath the cobbles was blood.

A river of blood.

I was summoning it once again and I had no idea how. But the witch wasn't going to take any chances by waiting around to figure out how either. Instead, she decided it was time to use her own defences against me,

"Don't wait too long before coming home, Princess, or your King might find himself on the end of a noose for the second time!" she shouted and just as I let my anger flow further, so did the blood rapidly start to rise. But before it could consume her whole, she looked up at her umbrella, the one that made little sense until her eyes started to roll back inside her head. This seemed to summon something from above, and I watched as shadowy black tentacles came from underneath the stretch of material. Then they became more whole and wrapped around the body of the small demon child she was using. Then with one last warning she said,

"Soon he will burn, just as he deserves!" Then she was

quickly dragged up into the hidden world inside the umbrella. The second after this happened it dropped, now with no one around to hold it. Meaning that it fell with the handle in the air, floating on the now flooded stairwell. Although I didn't yet know how to stop the blood as it rose higher and higher until I had no choice but to back up until I was back on the street. I shook my fingers, trying to get them to stop glowing but as the blood rose higher, it also brought with it the witch's umbrella. The shadows of darkness were still swirling around inside the material and once at the top, they started to grow bigger, until I was finally smart enough to turn around and run.

Unfortunately, I was too late and the second I felt something circle my ankle, I screamed. Then it tugged hard and pulled my leg from underneath me, throwing me off balance so I had nowhere to go but down. I barely just saved my face from slapping into the blood-soaked alleyway, with my hands hitting the ground first. The liquid splashed up around me making me turn my face away, only this became the last of my concerns. This was because the tentacles of darkness that had taken the witch were now trying to take me!

"NO! GET OFF ME!" I screamed twisting and turning, splashing in the pool of blood trying to get it off me. But this was all in vain as more of the creature emerged and soon the entire lower half of my body was encased in the writhing limbs of whatever beast this was that the witch had summoned to get me. It then started dragging me closer and closer to the umbrella, ready to drag me to wherever the witch intended to imprison me.

But I didn't give up.

It wasn't in my nature to. So, instead I fought, trying to push myself out of its hold in order to gain some more movement. An effort I doubled the second I saw the tips of my feet now reach the edge of the stretched material. I thrashed and thrashed, trying to kick out hoping that the splashing of blood it floated on would create enough movement for a small wave that would send it further away. But the tentacles just yanked me hard and the first part of my legs were dragged inside, giving me a weird feeling of being suspended above somewhere in a void.

I couldn't let her take me! Because if she did and if what she'd said was true about her having somehow managed to capture Lucius, then he needed my help to break him out! I would be no good to him if I too was caught and for whatever reason, it was obvious she needed me, and I had a feeling she was using Lucius as bait!

"YOU CAN'T HAVE ME!" I screamed, finally managing to twist onto my belly, my hands dipping through the blood and finding pieces of stone I could dig my fingertips around so I now had something to hold on to. But then, as I looked over my shoulder, I saw the tentacles giving space to something at the centre and I didn't have long to question what. As suddenly a demonic hand burst from the darkness and reached for me.

"AAAAHHHH!" I screamed in utter agony as she caught me and started clawing at my back, making me cry out even more as the witch's long razor talons scratched away at my skin. This made me realise she was trying to dig her hold into my flesh and use that to pull me under.

And pulling me under was exactly what she was doing as I soon realised the fight in me was no longer enough.

As I might have already been in Hell, but where she wanted me to go was far worse.

Back to the…

Death she had planned for me.

CHAPTER TWENTY

DANGEROUS FROZEN KISSES

I screamed in pain and reached out my free hand, seeing the drops of blood I had created dripping down and off my fingers in a sort of slow motion. As if time was on my side and trying to drag out the moment for as long as possible before the witch dragged me into her nightmare. But as I reached out with my hands, all I saw was a crowd of demons coming closer. Snarling beasts on chains and about to be set free by a horned master. One who looked as if he had just found a free meal for his pets and it was time they took a break and chowed down on human meat.

So, this was it.

This was my choice.

To either let this bitch take me or fight for a freedom that meant getting torn apart by wild beasts. I took a deep breath, trying to concentrate past the pain and as my eyes lowered, my cramping fingers were about to accept my fate and let go of the hold I had. But that was when suddenly a bright blue glow caught my eyes and they snapped open just in time to see what it was.

A demonic roar of pain echoed in the night as the blue light turned brighter as it started to tear through the chest of the horned owner, before the tip of a blue blade could be seen as it speared through his body from behind. After it disappeared the demon dropped to his knees and let go of the chains causing the snarling beasts to come running at me.

I could barely see as the cloaked figure from behind him moved so fast, the growling beasts didn't have a chance as he sliced through them one after the other. I could just make out the sight of frozen pieces that had once made a whole beast fall to the floor with a thud.

"AHHH!" I then screamed as the hand dug in deeper and I swear the witch's hand was trying to grip onto either side of my spine! The hooded figure's head snapped up just as my hand lost its grip and I started to get pulled backwards.

"Hold on now!" A male voice shouted and he grabbed my hand, forcing me to grip tight to the one cobbled rock on the floor that was raised up enough for me to do so. Then I looked over my shoulder to see him slice across the witch's hand with his sword, turning the flesh a frosted ice and making her scream before letting me go.

After this I watched as he spun on a heel before hammering down his sword into the middle of the umbrella, making the tentacles freeze and crack before crumbling back down into the darkness like frost being blown off a stone surface.

I felt myself finally free and started trying to get to my feet when a familiar hand helped me,

"Trice?" I looked up into the hard yet handsome face of my saviour and whispered the obvious,

"You saved me." as I stumbled and his hands framed my waist as I fell into him, so now he was holding me upright. My

hands went to his chest and my head fell forward, placing my forehead against him, as it felt too heavy to hold up anymore.

Gods, I felt so weak and the blood I could feel pouring down my back wasn't helping matters. I felt one hand leave my waist and instead raise my face up to his with a gentle grasp on my chin. Then he pulled down the flap of leather that hid the lower part of his face. I couldn't help but look at his lips and realised too late that this seemed to be an invitation to something more, as before I knew what was happening, he was lowering his head to mine. I froze and it had nothing to do with the power contained within his shifter but everything to do with the fact that he was about to kiss me!

Oh Gods, but this was why he had been odd with me…
Trice liked me!

I opened my mouth ready to tell him that I was sorry, that we couldn't do this but then he whispered softly,

"I will always save you."

After this his lips were just about to touch my own at the same time my fingertips pressed into his chest, just about to apply enough pressure to stop him, when suddenly I was ripped from his grasp, falling backwards.

"NOOO!" I screamed again as I was yanked back inside the umbrella, where a single tentacle had sneaked back through and had wrapped itself around my waist. But as another scream tore from me, I was falling backwards and at the very last second, my wrist was caught from above. I looked up to find myself hanging down from a cloud of darkness that had filled the umbrella with a hand I now knew holding on to me and unwilling to let me go.

I looked below to see what had hold of me and sucked in a startled gasp before letting it out again as a terrified scream! The monster below me was like something you would have found trying to drown a ship!

Only the edges of it could be seen, as if it was only half summoned from whichever part of Hell she had been able to drag it from. It had legs like a scorpion and a hard outer shell, whilst its tentacles were too many to count and they flailed around above it. But there at its centre was the witch sat cross legged, surrounded by the shadowed essence of the creature. Her scarred face looked up at me, but her eyes were still rolled to the back of her head, so that the whites of her eyes were all that could be seen. She moved her arms around and I noticed that it was done so she could command its movements.

This was when I noticed that it also looked as if I had been dragged down into someone's void. Then, just as the witch made a coiling motion with her arm, a tentacle snapped out and was now trying to curl itself around me. But this was when a light came from above and the same blue glow emerged as Trice's sword tore through the opening of the void. Then the second it made it all the way through, his hand gripped my wrist tighter and swung me to one side and at the same time he thrust his sword down. This shot a freezing bolt straight down at the witch and the impact made the whole void start to shake with the sound of her pain.

The creature that had become a part of her also reacted, as its tentacles uncurled themselves from around me in order to protect the witch's essence at its centre. I couldn't understand how she had been able to suck me into her void... nobody had that kind of power...*did they?*

I quickly felt myself being lifted up and I glanced down, taking in the private world of the witch's mind around me. I did this in the hope of seeing if anything in her memories could have been useful to us and I wasn't wrong. I sucked in a quick breath when I saw what it held.

Over to one side, was a raised mound of grass with a tree growing at the top. Down from the hill was a woman burning at the stake, screaming about her revenge as the agony she experienced wasn't great enough to stop her vow of vengeance. A whole village of people stood around watching as it happened, and a single cloaked figure was stood in the shadows next to the tree watching it all. The figure was small and most likely only a child, perhaps no more than ten years old and she simply remained stood there, as if frozen and unable to move away from the horrific scene.

The only movement the child made was the jerking of her shoulders, telling me that she was sobbing at the sight of the execution. The tree then started burning after the small hand reached out behind and touched it.

But then, just as I was being pulled back up, I noticed something about the crowd…they weren't villagers at all…no…

They were all Vampires.

I was suddenly yanked hard enough that I disappeared through the darkness above and soon found myself back in the alleyway and falling into the strong arms of my saviour for the second time.

Trice.

Trice who had been about to kiss me.

I fell into him once more and before a re-enactment of events could occur I was swept up into his strong arms and carried from the alleyway, just as his brothers appeared from around the corner.

"You found her!" Gryph asked, his tone clearly suggesting he was relieved but then he narrowed his gaze when he took in the sight of me.

"Oh, thank the Heavens!" Vern said as he too stepped into view and was still clearly afflicted with the 'posh curse'.

"Och! What happened tae her?!" Gryph asked and for once

he sounded hard as nails, without a hint of humour lacing his words.

"Gosh, what befell the poor girl?!" Vern added as he too looked concerned, but Trice growled at him first, before snapping,

"Yer fucked up, that tis what happened tae her! Now both of yer, go deal wi' that fcking Portal Void before something even bigger comes out of it!"

Vern tensed before he was jerked back after Trice's shoulder barged him out the way. Then he continued onto the street, snarling at the first demon that got in his way, making him cower back. And I couldn't say that I blamed them, as like this he was most certainly frightening. So, I raised a shaky hand and touched it to his scarred face to get his attention before telling him,

"Don't be mad, it wasn't his fault…it was…the witch…she lured me out and…"

"I know what fcking happened, Amelia!" he snapped and I winced but then frowned when realisation dawned on me,

"Wait…how do you know my…?" I never got to end this question as I felt myself falling, only this time it wasn't my body, but that of my mind.

And as I did, I at least knew that I was no longer in any danger. Because this time, when I fell, I did so into the arms of someone who…

Cared for me.

CHAPTER TWENTY-ONE

COCK TEASE

The moment I started to hear voices was when I started to come around from my unconscious state. Although, from the sounds of the heated discussion that was going on, I thought it best to keep my eyes closed, so I could listen to what was being said… because it quickly became obvious, *it was about me*.

"Fur fck sake, Vern, tis always th' same shit wi' ye!" Trice shouted making me tense at how angry he sounded.

"How dare you accuse me in such a manner! Are you hearing this slanderous accusation?" Vern said in that new posh voice of his and I would have laughed if it hadn't been for the ear bashing he was getting off his brother. But this last part was obviously said to Gryph, as his voice added to the conversation when he replied dryly,

"Aye a'm listening."

"Well, speak then, man!" Vern snapped outraged.

"'N' what wid ye lik' me tae say?" Gryph replied.

"I would like you to defend my character!" At this even I

knew that Vern was a hopeless case, as that was the last thing it sounded the biggest brother was prepared to do.

"I cannae do that whin yer character is bein' a shite," Gryph said obviously not agreeing with him and from what I could make out from his accent, he was calling his character shit. I was suddenly starting to feel very sorry for Vern.

"Good Gods man, don't hold back on my account, will you!" Vern snapped.

"Ye were give one fcking job, Vern, ye ken how important this one is 'n' by leaving her fur five fcking minutes is all it can tak' tae screw it up fur us all…blood bound Vern, how many more fcking years dae ye want tae be blood bound!" Trice shouted at him, with his accent getting stronger because of it and I winced knowing now that I was only a job to them.

But then, how could I expect anything more than that? Well, at least it explained why they were there at the battlefield and it had little to do with a war between neighbouring forests.

"Well, it isn't like I expected a witch to try and ensnarl the girl…I didn't think for one moment that…" Vern tried again but Trice wasn't having any of it.

"Na, ye dinnae think 'n' that's th' problem, brother! Now piss off before I strangle yer Wyvern arse!" Trice snapped angrily and just as Vern was about to say more, Gryph must have thought it best to intervene, as I opened my eyes a little just in time to see the big guy slapping a hand to Vern's back before saying,

"C'moan, Laddie, let's gaun 'n' git us some devil's rum." I heard and saw, as Vern released a big sigh and turned to face the door, but before leaving completely, he paused and said,

"I apologize, brother." Then Vern left before Trice had chance to say anything more.

"You were a little hard on him, weren't ya?" I recognised Nero's voice but without making it obvious that I was awake by opening my eyes fully and having a good look around the place, I was left only to listen. Trice scoffed at this and I could only just see his large figure stood by the bed I was on, with his back against the corner post.

He looked formidable.

"Nae hard enough, he's lucky he didnae git me fist again!" Trice commented with exasperation.

"Trice, lay off the lad, will you!" Nero snapped back, clearly feeling the way I did, that he was being too hard on him.

"Look, ye maybe sweet on th' lad, bit he needs tae learn some fcking' responsibility!!" Trice replied making Nero gasp in horror,

"I...I am not sweet on him!" she argued, after first needing to clear her throat and if you asked me, this was a telltale sign that she was and Trice was right.

"Aye, alright, whitevur ye say, Lass." I heard Nero's growled response, but she didn't comment more than saying a muttered,

"Asshole."

"So, what are you going to do about the girl?" Nero asked making Trice warn,

"Leave it be, Nero."

"So, you are going to take her to the King then, even though you know what might happen?" I held my breath at this, knowing that it didn't sound good.

"What else can I do, we have bin looking fur a way tae break free of bein' blood bound fur centuries, ye really think we have much of a choice?" Trice said telling me exactly what their payment would be for my delivery...great, bloody great! I had been in Hell all of a day and I already had a bounty on my head! How was shit like that even possible?! Because I really didn't remember posing for some damn wanted poster!

"I know that, but I also know you like the girl," Nero said

and suddenly not reacting to this was difficult. So, I hadn't been dreaming or hallucinating last night, Trice had been about to kiss me?

"Aye, so she be a bonnie lass but me loyalty is tae me brothers," he admitted making Nero scoff,

"Gods' balls, Trice, you need to get laid man!"

"No, whit a'm needin is tae git this lass tae th' fcking King 'n' be on me way with mine 'n' me brothers' souls back where we want em," Trice replied and again, his accent came through heavier where he was obviously frustrated.

"And what if the King…"

"Dae nae say it, Nero." She must have just given him an expectant look in return because he added,

"Th' King's a ruthless 'n' vicious bastard, aye… bit he must want her fur something 'n' I dinnae think it's just to kill her," Trice argued and I had to say, his words didn't exactly incite a world of confidence in me!

"Well, as for the King I can't say, as who knows why the heartless son of a bitch does what he does, but what I can tell you is whoever this girl really is, then there is one really powerful witch out there that wants her!" Nero said and had I been awake, I would have said, 'you can say that again!'.

"Aye, I git that, Lass," Trice said wryly.

"I am not sure that you do, Trice…I mean, do you know how insanely hard the shit she pulled is to do! Hell on a stick, even I have never heard shit like that was possible!" Trice let out a frustrated growl and warned,

"This be the part ye git to explaining, Nero."

"From the way you explained it, this witch tried to pull her through into her own void, one she first summoned Hafgufa in to give her the power to drag the girl in…that's…well, fuck me, Trice, that shit is unheard of!" I started thinking about where I had heard that name before as it was better known as something else. I didn't have long to wait as Trice got there first,

"Ye think 'twas a bloody Kraken inside that umbrella!?" Trice asked in astonishment and once again I had to try and not react to the name. The witch had summoned a fucking Kraken! How was that even possible!?

"Well, I don't think it was a baby octopus in an aquarium, Trice!" Nero threw back making Trice hiss a curse.

"Who th' fuck has that kind of power!?" he shouted and I had to say, after that outburst, then he would be an idiot to think I was still asleep, besides, the pain in my back was starting to come back to me, making me wonder what had been done to it to numb it in the first place.

"Th' salve must be wearing off." Trice said obviously noticing my discomfort as I couldn't help but moan as I shifted in the bed.

"Oh yes, that's what woke her up, couldn't have been your booming Scottish rants at all," Nero replied sarcastically.

"Just go 'n' git me some more, woman," Trice replied with exasperation making her huff and snap,

"Aye M'laird, anything you say M'laird!" Nero snapped mimicking his accent before I heard the slamming of the door.

"God's woman, wake th' dead why don't ye," he muttered and I opened my eyes to see him shaking his head to himself, before turning around to face the bed.

"How do you know my name?" This was the first thing I asked. He dragged a hand along the back of his neck, and I could see now that all his hair had been pulled back and knotted into a messy bun of dark auburn waves. But this wasn't the only thing changed about him as now he wasn't wearing a shirt.

Holy mother of a God, did the guy really need that many muscles!? Although, it was also clear to see now that the scar on his face wasn't the only one. Talk about battle scarred, wow, this guy looked to have survived them all! And with how solid and powerful he looked, well I wasn't exactly surprised!

He released a sigh and came to sit on the edge of the bed, one I knew if I tried to move from, it would only end up causing me pain. Because now I had to say that I didn't quite trust him. Because his reasons, as personal as they were, meant that I was considered collateral damage. And as much as I couldn't blame him for wanting to free himself and his brothers from being blood bound to this King, I also knew that he was fine by taking me to this ruthless bastard, without first knowing my fate.

Not exactly the hero I had made him out to be in my head. But I didn't think it was good time to point out this fact, as well...there was still the whole tying me up and gagging me option to think of.

"Yer were a job," he admitted.

"Was?"

"Are," he corrected making my shoulders slump and I felt the tugging pain of doing so on my back, knowing they were right, whatever had been used on me was now wearing off.

"Right, that's what I thought," I said in a deflated tone, replacing the one of anger that I felt had been rising. So instead, I looked around the room and focused on my surroundings during this silence. One he looked thankful for.

As for the room, it looked as if I had stepped back in time as it most definitely had a medieval vibe to it. This with its plain rustic floorboards and the stone walls of mis-matched blocks that rose up into four connecting arches over the bed. And speaking of the bed, it was big but that was the only bonus, as it was unfortunately lumpy and uncomfortable. However, what it lacked in comfort, it made up for in style, as it was decorated in a colourful array of emerald greens, plum purples and orange reds in the many cushions and different layers of blankets and throws that covered it. There were sequins and tassels, fringes and even some with bells. It also had four posts framing the corners, and each were draped with swathes of matching material, leaving the roof part exposed.

As for the rest of the room, there were different styles of trunks in different sizes and a sideboard that looked filled with everything a girl needed to make herself feel pretty when getting ready in the morning. This included the obvious things, like a hairbrush, a free standing mirror, lotions, creams, pots of makeup and randomly, a bowl of what looked like figs cut into sections.

Over the opposite side of the room was a corner sectioned off by a fold out wooden screen that had an Aztec design of decorated squares and symbols framed in different sizes. Clothes and towels were thrown over the top, along with the same 'girl mess' decorating the few chairs and a green sofa that looked well used. Piles of books, a few threadbare rugs, bottles and other nicknacks adorned the room.

However, there were no windows, so all of the light came from a basic iron chandelier that hung from the ceiling. This and a stone ledge that was two feet down from the ceiling, which ran all the way around the room and was filled with hundreds of candles. These were in every shape, size and colour you could think of and each one was lit, telling me someone either had too much time on their hands or they had been lit by supernatural means.

I was betting my dirty clothes on the second. And speaking of dirty clothes and where they were, along with me,

"Where am I?" I asked.

"This is Nero's place," he answered and I had to say, that even without his shirt on, he still looked at the ready for a fight, as his gleaming sword wasn't far from his grasp. This being on a chest next to the bed, along with all his other weapons, armour and belts. He saw me looking and said,

"Ye lost quite a bit of blood from ye wound, most of which went over me as I carried ye back 'ere," he told me, making me wonder just how much of Lucius' 'protection' I had lost, seeing as having his essence in me was what would have helped me heal. Gods, but even just thinking about Lucius now and not knowing what he could be going through at the hands of the witch! Would she have found a way to torture him?

The pain of these thoughts must have shown on my face as it was something Trice took for another reason.

"Yer in pain," he stated and then he reached to take hold of my shoulders, when I pulled back which made me wince.

"What are you doing?"

"I need tae git yer wound tae heal it, Lass." The second he said this I tensed so hard it hurt my back but despite the pain it didn't stop me from crying out in outrage,

"You can't do that!" He frowned at me, pinching the scar on his face and making me wonder if it hurt him to do so. Just then Nero came back inside with a tray full of stuff all balanced on the small space, making her walk towards the sideboard so she could put it down.

"And why not?" he asked, now raising his brow and this time barely sounding Scottish. Which I had started to notice happened sometimes. I swallowed hard before I shot a look to Nero who had her back to us, and I grabbed onto to his bicep so I could pull myself closer, and hiss,

"You know why!" At this he first looked to where my hand was gripping him, which made me let go and then he looked back to me now with a very obvious smirk playing on his lips.

"Nae, I don't, bit I a'm very interested tae know what ye think it is." I must have blushed to my roots at this and Nero had now turned around and said,

"I see her bloods back at least...better get a shirt on Trice, before the poor girl faints." Then she winked at me and laughed at my scowl in return.

"Fine, you think you will embarrass me by making me say it, but you won't…I am not going to let you give me an orgasm!" At this Nero burst out laughing and said,

"I knew I liked this chick! Right, well I'll leave this one to you, *Cocktease*," she said with a wink at Trice making him groan before grumbling,

"Cockatrice…damn ye, Vern."

CHAPTER TWENTY-TWO

HEXES AND HELL'S RUM

"Not a fan of the nickname, eh?" I commented making him give me a pointed look in return. Then he got up off the bed and one handed, swiped one of the small side tables by the sofa, making the books that had been piled up on it go tumbling. Not that he looked like he cared much, and damn it, I hated that my eyes followed the line of his biceps as they bunched at the movement.

After this he plonked it down by the bed in that heavy handed way, and then walked over to retrieve the tray so he could place it next to the bed. He still wore his trousers (thank the Gods) and now I could see the wrap of the tartan around his narrow waist that was red and green, with slight lines of sky blue. The lines of his hip bones created dips low at his sides, where his waistband had slipped lower due to the lack of the multiple belts. As for his stomach, well it looked like it could have doubled up as somewhere to scrub clothes on, as there were muscles there that I didn't even know the names of!

"Turn aroond," he said making me squint, as if this would help me understand. He rolled his eyes at me.

"Turn a…round," he said, slower this time, making a motion with his finger in a circle.

"But I said…"

"Aye, I know whit ye said, Lass," he replied cutting me off and as he reached out to turn me himself, I batted his hands away and snapped,

"Fine! *I can do it.*" I muttered this last part and did as he asked, only just realising now that I wore an oversized man's tunic in dark grey. But then the tightness around my chest and back suggested that I was wearing something more. I gritted my teeth and turned around but the second he started to pull the material up, tugging it first from under where I sat on the long shirt, I jumped and jerked away.

"Gods, yer as skittish as a whipped mere, just calm will ye, I will nae hurt you," he said and I had to say, hearing how sincere he sounded when saying how he wouldn't hurt me, well it made me trust him enough to do as he asked. So, I took a deep breath and gestured for him to carry on with a nod of my head.

He went back to what he had been doing before my overreaction and gripped the material before starting to lift it up. He did this until he pulled it over my head, leaving my arms in place, so now it just hung down the front.

"I will leave it lik' this," he said making me nod before muttering a quiet,

"Thank you." He made a sound of acknowledgement that was barely a grunted huff before I felt his strong calloused hands come to my back and again, I flinched.

"Easy, Lass," he cooed gently, and when I felt the tugging at my ribs, I looked down to one side and saw that it was bandages that were wrapped around my middle section. He

started trying to unwind them, but I obviously wasn't cooperating as he told me,

"Lift yer arms up fur me."

"Why?" He sighed in frustration and said,

"Because I cannae cut th' damn thing off ye without hurting ye, that's why." I took a deep breath and hated that he was right. But having him here so close like this, about to have his arms around me, well, it just felt way too intimate. To the point, that all I could think about was Lucius and it had me questioning if something like this, *despite how innocent it was*…meant I was being disloyal?

"Alright," I said softly before raising my arms up, but just before I could do it too high, his large hands came from behind and took hold of the tops of my forearms, preventing them from going any further. Then he leaned down and said in my ear,

"If ye go tae fair ye will tear th' skin," he said, his accent even thicker now, along with the timbre in his voice. But because my words had fled me, I found I could only nod, telling him silently that he could carry on. And he did. Oh, boy did he, and I swear that for a warrior for hire, I was shocked at how gentle those large rough hands could be. But they also worked with efficiency and got the job done. However, the problem with this was that the more and more strips of bandages he passed from one hand to the other in front of me, then the less of it was on my body, as my bra was long gone for obvious reasons.

So, the moment he pulled the last strip free from my now naked torso, I sucked in a deep shuddered breath when he grazed my naked breast. It was a reaction he ignored and instead he focused on remaining a gentleman and simply placed his hands at the top of my forearms again. He applied pressure, which told me I was now free to put my arms down, covering my naked breasts with the front of the shirt.

"Now this will hurt," he warned as he started to pull a piece of cloth from the wound the witch had inflicted and he was right, I started crying out, making him stop. Then he let me go and gave me some more space causing me to look over my shoulder to see what he was doing.

"What is that?" I asked watching as he started to pour what looked like some kind of brown spirit into the smallest glass imaginable. Something made possible with the thin red wax spout moulded to the top of the bottle which was covered in a hemp net. Then he handed me the thimble sized glass and said,

"It's something ye wilnae lik' bit it might help, now drink."

"I wilnae lik?" I asked.

"Will not like," he said taking the time to say it slower and making me grimace at the small glass I took from him.

"Oh goodie…hey, it's not like demon piss is it?" At this he laughed, and I had to say the sight of him smiling was a startling raw beauty.

"Na, tis just the Devil's Rum or some call it Hell's Rum, depending on where ye can git it."

"And this is all it will take?" I asked looking down at the tiny amount.

"Fur me, na… bit fur a human, shit aye it will." I frowned not sure that being drunk was a good plan right now but then again, this pain was a bitch, and I had a feeling it would only get worse, so I said,

"Then I guess it's cheers, Laddie!" taking the piss out of his accent, making him roll his eyes, but then he had the last laugh as I shot it back and I swear I thought my insides were melting! I started coughing instantly, and I swear I was close to being able to breathe fire!

Damn but absinthe had nothing on this bitch!

"Holy shit! What the hell is that stuff for, stripping the

scales off a dragon!?" I shouted making him give me a wry look before taking the glass off me and telling me,

"Tis what demons git drunk on."

"Yeah and what humans die on! Gods, that stuff is foul!" At this he chuckled and as he nodded, I interrupted, mocking him with his accent again as I said,

"Turn around...yeah, yeah, I know." He scoffed at my attempt to sound like him. Then I did what he had been about to ask me to do by facing the other way again, already feeling the warmth starting to spread in my belly, making my head swim. But then his hands were on me again and once more I flinched, as a heavy hand took hold of my shoulder.

"Och, ye flinch lik' ye have ne'er been touched by a man," he commented making me tense and tell him quietly,

"Or just by one." At this I felt like crying I missed Lucius that much and wished it was his hands that I had on me right now. Gods, but I would never have flinched and shied away from the touch then. But seeing as I couldn't see his face, I had no idea what his reaction was, other than when his movements stilled for a second before he continued, telling me at least he had heard my comment.

"Now how dae yer feel?" he asked as I could feel him about to go back to removing the strip of cloth that was obviously stuck to my skin with whatever they had used.

"Well, I feel a little fuz...AHHH...Oww!" I said with the scream in the middle being from where he had just ripped it off, getting it over with. Of course, it felt as though he had taken half of my skin with it as well.

"Och, this doesn't look good," was his hissed comment in return.

"No, maybe that's because some big brute just ripped half my skin off!" I snapped making him chuckle,

"Ney, that would all be th' work of a witch wi' her claws in yer bonnie golden skin," he replied and I was sure that had I had the extra blood I would have blushed at the compliment.

"Yeah, I guess that would do it as well," I muttered in annoyance.

"I'm going tae wash it now," he told me and I nodded for him to continue, hissing when he placed a soaked cloth to the wound.

"Aye, she git ye good," he commented with a whistle through his teeth.

"Aye," I agreed in Scottish, no doubt making him roll his eyes behind me.

"So, this witch, a'm going tae tak' a guess 'n' say ye 'n' her..."

"...Oh yeah, we go way back, the bitch and me," I finished for him making him grunt a,

"Aye, she didnae exactly look th' friendly type."

"They never do when they are trying to kill you, but you're right, that would be a Hell no...quite literally as I am coming to discover." He chuckled again and I had to say, talking with him like this helped make me feel more at ease around him. I also had to admit that the Devil's rum had started doing its job, as it didn't hurt as much as it first did when he had started cleaning it.

"So, what is it she wants from ye?" he asked making me scoff,

"Usually it's my blood, and I swear I am close to just bagging the shit for her just to get her to piss off." At this he laughed again,

"So, I tak' it this isn't th' first time?"

"That would be a no," I replied sarcastically.

"Well, I dinnae know about all th' last times she got tae ye, but this looks bad."

"Bad how?" I asked not liking the sound of that.

"What I mean is, I could put more salve on it 'n' it will help, but if I dinnae try 'n' heal this, then it could just git worse 'n' wi' ye bein' human, that means infection." I grimaced at the thought, knowing that he was right and as a human then it wasn't like I could just pop to the nearest chemist and order some antibiotics.

"And Nero, could she…?"

"Aye, she's good, bit nae that good, Lass," he replied making me realise my options here were pretty limited but then something in his voice suggested something more.

"I take it you have something in mind?"

"Aye, that I do," he said before leaning in closer and telling me,

"Tis called healing ye." I sucked in a breath making him chuckle, before he shifted some of my hair off to one side so he could whisper,

"Dinna worry, Sweetheart, when I mak' a Lass cum, tis nae by blowing on her back… 'n' just so ye know... I usually dae so wi' th' intentions of getting something back in return..." I shuddered at the sexual intent in his words, making him grin at my ear before I felt his lips lowering to where my wound was and he said over it,

"But well, I'm a greedy bastard lik' that."

After this was when he started his version of 'healing' me and it started with hands holding me steady, with one at my waist and the other one wrapping around me from behind. This put his large arm firmly across my collar bone and I was just thankful for the tunic that still draped down my front or his muscled forearm would have been pressed against my naked breasts. And well, it felt far too intimate as it was.

"Now tis time tae mak' ye really shudder," he said with sexual intent coating his words and even before he began, I found myself trembling. But then he started and doing so now by blowing along my heated flesh with an icy breath and he was right, as it was one that this time really caused me to shudder.

This soon told me why he had taken this intimate hold on me as my body soon started to shiver uncontrollably, and he cooed softly in between breaths. But the cold was unlike anything I had ever felt before, as it wasn't like someone had just put an ice pack on your back or ice cubes against your skin. No, it was more like someone had injected you with a cooling agent, like having part of your body numbed at the doctors before they stitched you up or something.

At first it felt uncomfortable and almost too much to take but then after whatever he had done started to take effect, it caused the pain to magically fade away, to the point that I released a deep satisfying sigh, letting him know it too.

"Aye, there it be," he said as if satisfied that it was working. He then gave it one last cooling blow and shifted his hold on me, so he was no longer gripping me as tight. Then as I sighed again, marvelling in the pain free movement, he chuckled before asking,

"Was it as good fur ye, as 'twas fur me, Lassie?" This was said in a cheeky tone and I couldn't help but laugh as I smacked the arm that still had hold of the front of me,

"Oi! Behave, you brute!" I scolded, making him chuckle too. But then there came that awkward point of silence after we had both finished laughing. And it came the time for him to let me go, something I wasn't sure that he wanted to do right in that moment. I closed my eyes against the feelings he was invoking, making me feel guilty for the comfort I found being in his arms. It was just the sheer strength of him and being in this place, this level of Hell, that even the witch had been able to find me in, well it was of little wonder I felt this way.

But then I also had to remember that I was just a job to him, as he had made that clear enough to Nero before he thought I was awake.

So, I cleared my throat and said,

"Well, you may be a cheeky bugger, but it has to be said you've got skills, Trice." He scoffed and then let me go, replying with a cocky,

"Aye, bit that's because ye know what I can dae wi' me sword." I granted him a wry look over my shoulder, making him wink at me before he turned back to the table and grabbed a pot of something yellow.

"What's that?" I asked as it became obvious he intended to use it on me.

"Tis a healing salve that Nero mak's," he replied making me frown in question,

"But I thought that your…"

"Ney, that was only tae take away th' pain 'n' help stop th' spread of th' Hex." This was when I utterly froze, and it had not one thing to do with his icy breath but everything to do with what he'd just said.

Because that was when I started to realise the real reason the witch had attacked me. She didn't just want to drag me down into her void at all.

She had been there to deliver a message about Lucius' capture and there to deliver much more still…

To deliver…*A Hex.*

It was at this point that my reactions took over as every memory of a Hex assaulted me.

And naturally…

This was when I started screaming.

CHAPTER TWENTY-THREE

BOYFRIENDS

"**H**EX!" I screamed making Trice jerk back, dropping the jar to the floor as I started to lose it!

"Whoa! Calm yourself 'ere, Lassie!" Trice said as panic gripped me and I was suddenly scrambling off the bed, first getting caught in all the fabric around the frame and hitting out at it in a frenzied way to free myself.

"Hey, come on now," Trice tried, now up off the bed and coming around to my side to help me. But I freed myself just in time, throwing my arms up and walking past him, shaking my head, too afraid to speak. But he snagged my hand and pulled me back, making me fall sideways so he caught me.

"What is this all a'bout?" he asked but I shook my head at him and let my wide panicked eyes do the talking for me. Then I mumbled a jumble of unintelligent words. This is when it must have dawned on him, as he pulled me into his embrace and wrapped his arms around me, soothing me by making me feel safe for the moment.

"Hush now, calm yersel' fur me," he whispered as he

smoothed my hair back from my forehead. I swallowed hard trying to breathe through my panic, knowing that my 'oh shit' situation just turned into an 'oh fuck' situation! But then he told me,

"I dinnae know what Hex ye have come across before, Lass, bit this one dinnae stops ye from talking." I looked up at him, now doing so with wide eyes for a different reason. Then I whispered,

"Are you sure?" He chuckled softly before grasping my chin and giving it a squeeze before saying,

"Aye, I'm sure, pretty eyes." Then, just as I was about to take a step back, he had other ideas. This was when his hold on me tightened before his grip on my chin started to raise my face up a little further, at the same time his head started to dip, making me tense. Then I opened my mouth and his name slipped out,

"Trice, we can..." In the end I never had chance to finish stopping him, as someone else did it for me...two someones actually.

"What happened! Is it the girl, is she alright?!" Vern shouted as he burst through the door. He was quickly followed by Gryph, who stood a full head height above his brother's, looking over him with ease. But it was in this moment they both took in what must have looked like an intimate scene between lovers. Gryph then commented,

"Oh Aye, ah think she is mair than a'lright, Laddie!" Then Gryph burst out laughing making me suddenly tear myself from Trice's arms like I should have done the second he took me into them. Damn my panic and need for comfort!

Meanwhile Trice growled low in the back of his throat and the warning was clear even if his words weren't,

"Git oot noo!" The heavy frustrated accent was obviously understood by his brothers as Gryph said,

"Aye, aye Casanova, keep yer kilt on!" Meanwhile Vern granted him a nod of his head and said,

"I salute you, good sir, but remember to treat her like a lady." I groaned in humiliation whilst Trice roared,

"OOT!" Gryph grabbed his brother by the back of his shirt and yanked him out as he was still saluting with two fingers at his temple. After that Trice stormed to the door and slammed it shut whilst muttering,

"Fcking idiots!" Then he dragged a frustrated hand back over his head and it reminded me so much of Lucius I suddenly blurted out quickly,

"I have a boyfriend!" At this his head snapped up to look at me and it was easy to see the statement was being processed.

"Ye hae a what now?" he asked with a questioning frown.

"A boyfriend…I have a boyfriend," I said, saying it twice and hoping this was enough to make it stick.

"Ye hae a boyfriend?" he asked again, and I nodded, still holding the tunic to the front of my body, glad that it hid everything it should.

"Yes," I said in a sure tone.

"What are ye, a wee bairn?" he asked making me frown before asking,

"Erm…excuse me?" He then walked closer towards me and translated,

"A child, be ye a wee child…a little girl?" he asked again with his emotions making his Scottish come out thicker before he translated for me.

"What?! No, of course I am not a child!" I snapped making him grin and I felt like I was losing something here.

"Aye, I know…You dinnae feel lik' one," he said, again with that wicked grin in place, as he ran his heated gaze down the length of me and I most definitely felt as if I was missing something here…something huge.

"Then why did you ask me if I…"

"Fur real men aren't boyfriends, Lass," he stated firmly and I frowned back at him and said,

"Yes, there are!" But even when I did, I couldn't help but snap back to that conversation between me and Lucius where he had pretty much said the same thing.

"Na, Lassie, they're not." I rolled my eyes at him, and said,

"Then what are they?" But this was when the irritation blew from my sails as he said,

"A man wi' a woman lik' you…" he said nodding at me, making me hold my breath at what the rest of his bold as brass statement would be.

"The keeper 'n' protector of yer heart" he said after crossing his arms over his chest and making every muscle seem to pop out to say hello. And Gods, but if he hadn't just said something incredibly sweet then I would have been able to argue with him even more. But damn him, that was too smooth to ignore. So instead, I focused my irritation on something else.

"Seriously, can't you put on a shirt or something?!" I snapped making him smirk down at me and I swear the cocky bastard tensed his muscles on purpose.

"Why would I dae that, Lass, when ye obviously lik' what ye see?" he said coming even closer so I had no choice but to put my hand out to stop him. This was when he let his arms drop and the last step he made, walked him into my hand, so it was now against his rock hard abs that tensed the second he felt my touch.

"I, uh…I think you should go," I said wishing I had done so with more conviction.

"Dae ye now?" he asked in a knowing tone that was all the confidence of a man who was used to having this effect on a woman.

"Aye, yes, most definitely," I replied making him chuckle

and I felt it under my fingertips. But then, before I could say anything else, he had my wrist in his hold, jerked it to one side and tugged at it so I had no choice but to fall into him, now without my hand against his abs to stop him. Then, before I could stop it, he tilted my head back with his free hand at my jaw so he could grant me a quick kiss on the lips. As I gasped in my shock he pulled back and said,

"'N' just so ye know, beautiful...*I lik' a challenge.*" Then he kissed me quickly one more time and before I could even react, like to slap him, he was gone from my space and walking out of the door without saying another word.

Meanwhile I was left dumbfounded and mortified at the fact I had just been kissed by another man,

A feeling that came out as a muttered,

"What the Hell just happened?"

CHAPTER TWENTY-FOUR

HOPE SHATTERED

Okay, so I had to say the reasons for Lucius wanting to kill me were mounting by the second and I swear it felt like I was a bloody magnet for this shit to keep happening! I thought that I had done everything right with regards to another man making advances to someone in a relationship. I mean, I know I was a novice at this whole dating thing, but I always thought the general rule was not engaging in any sexual act, flirting, reciprocating the advances of others and acting single when you weren't.

So where exactly had I gone wrong?

I questioned all my past actions when it came to Trice and I had to admit, I was coming up empty. I had stopped him from trying to kiss me and told him I was in a relationship, which in my obviously naive mind, had thought that would have been enough...*guess I was wrong.*

"That looks like a heavy mind you got there, Chica." Nero said making me jump. I was currently in her copper bathtub that she had magically filled for me after Trice had sent her up to 'deal with girl shit' helpfully quoted by Nero. But dealing with 'girl shit' actually meant allowing me the means of getting me clean, which I had been more than grateful for. However, as for my eyes, then there was no hope for them.

"Aww shit, honey, there's no reason to be upset," she said putting down what looked like a new tray, one this time that was filled with what smelled like food. My stomach rumbled at just the thought, as I was famished!

"What?" I asked frowning, making her nod to my face, which made me realise she obviously meant my red, sore eyes.

"Oh no, it's just my contact lenses, I haven't been able to take them out as I wouldn't be able to see anything and I don't have my glasses with me…but you're only supposed to keep them in for a day so…"

"Say no more, I got ya covered," she said waving at me and making her navy blue and white hair dance.

"What do you mean?"

"You take em out and I will be right back. But here, I brought you some clothes to wear, because yours were trashed." Oh, holy mother earth, clean skin and new clothes…I swear it felt like my birthday!

"Oh, by the Gods, I think I love you!" I said making her chuckle,

"Yeah, well according to Mr Broody Cocktease, then he thinks I got the hots for his little bro," she said with a roll of her eyes.

"And do you?" I asked making her shrug her shoulders before saying,

"Honestly, Vern's a pain in my ass but…well, it doesn't really matter what, because he wouldn't…you know…he's a bit of a ladies' man," she said in a way that yeah, she totally had the hots for him but wasn't going there because of his past with women. And really, I couldn't blame her, as no one just wanted to become another number or name to add to the list of many… not when you really liked someone.

"Well, I might not know much about his past…*exploits*…"

"Nice," she replied with a wink and a point of her finger at me, for saying anything but women, sexual conquests or any other referral or suggestion of someone in his bed, before carrying on,

"…But I do know that the kiss you shared, wow, now that was hot and looked way more than just an exploit to me." At this she grinned big and said,

"You think?"

"Oh, totally!" I said nodding, and not really having much of a problem with the fact we were sharing this conversation with me naked in a bath. But then, that's what some girls were like and besides, I had grown up around Pip, who let's just say didn't really know the true meaning of modesty…or the skill of hiding it. If anything, her skills came from the other end of that spectrum, where the scale was firmly labelled…NAKED AND ALWAYS.

"You know, I knew I liked you!" she said, yet again making this statement and it was one that made me laugh. Then she added,

"It's true, I gave you the good underwear and everything." Then she winked at me before leaving the room.

So, after this and with the smell of food luring me, I washed quickly, using the fresh bar of soap I found wrapped in brown paper that smelled like it was made from honey and shea butter. It was soft on my skin and smelled amazing, even as I lathered it in my hair, after not finding any other products to use. In fact, I was amazed to find it didn't knot even without having the usual addition of conditioner.

And I most definitely needed it too, as it showed in the water once I got out. Although, after what I had been through in the last twenty-four hours then it was of little wonder the water was now the colour of mud!

I also did as Nero suggested and took out my contacts, making my eyes even more sore in the process. Of course, it hadn't helped with them becoming itchy from the steam of the bath when first getting in.

I grabbed a towel that was hung over the divider and dried myself off. Then I gently wrapped the towel around my back, which thankfully wasn't sore anymore, but I knew the wound was still there. Which meant that Trice had been right, I needed to put some salve back on there and wrap it up. So, I grabbed the underwear, putting the plain black panties on and having no choice but to leave the bra as it would have rubbed on my back in the wrong place. Then I grabbed the trousers that were a soft, stretchy material in a brownish burgundy and dark navy colour with alternating vertical stripes. They were also tight at the top of my thighs but flared out at the bottom and were overly long. I looked down and yanked on the ties so they gathered up slightly, enough so I wasn't tripping over them at least.

Then, as I held the towel to my front, I walked over to the side of the bed Trice had been sitting on and picked up the jar he had dropped on the floor.

"Ye know, I would be happy tae help ye wi' that again." I froze the second I was back to being upright and thankful that my back was to the door, even though once again it was bare.

"Wow, so people really don't like knocking in Hell then," I commented dryly, gripping my towel tight before turning to face him, making him scoff,

"Tis why locks were invented, ye should have a go at them sometime...I know I will be in th' future," he said, adding this part at the end for obvious reasons which included his brothers.

"Okay, I will. In fact, how about you walk back out the door and I will try it right now," I said making him chuckle,

"Och, yer upset a'bout th' kiss," he surmised making me snap back,

"Well, look at that, you do listen after all…funny you didn't when I told you…"

"Aye, aye, that ye have a boyfriend, I hear'd." he said coming in now and closing the door and making me shout,

"Don't you dare lock it this time!" He laughed and raised his hand up in the air before turning around and smirking at me.

"Why… are ye afraid of bein' left alone wi' me, Lass?" I huffed and said,

"Second thoughts, you go ahead and lock it, that way it will give me longer to clean up the evidence of a murder." At this he threw his head back and laughed and I mean really laughed… making me now question whether or not I was happy that even through my blurred vision, he was now wearing a shirt.

"You will have a job, Lass, especially whilst yer still clutching onto th' towel lik' tis protecting ye," he said with a nod at me.

"It is protecting me, from you seeing me near naked!" I shouted in my defence.

"Nay tis not, Lass." I frowned in response, making him say,

"A Cockatrice can see through things." At this I was horrified and screamed whilst turning back around and giving him my back after screeching in annoyance. But then I jumped when I felt him at my back, knowing now of his stealth skills as I hadn't even heard a floorboard creak.

"Relax, me bonnie Lass, I'm teasing ye." Hearing this I let out a relieved breath only to suck it back in again when I felt him taking the jar of salve from my hand, one I had been holding to my chest to help keep my towel there.

"Wh…what are you…"

"What does it look lik', I came up 'ere tae help ye," he informed me after forcing me to give up the jar.

"That's fine, I am sure Nero wouldn't mind helping me," I pointed out, knowing which of the two I would prefer and which one was definitely safer.

"She's busy wi' customers," he informed me, making me grit my teeth.

"Then I will just wait for her to finish." I felt him lean down and after running a fingertip across my shoulder, one I shrugged off he said with humour,

"There be a lot of customers."

"Fine, then I will just do it myself." At this he laughed and said,

"Och, now that I would lik' tae see!" I growled at him, turned and tried to snatch the jar from his hand when he just lifted it up above my head, knowing that I would have no chance of getting it seeing as he was considerably taller than me.

"Well, that's mature," I said stopping myself from folding my arms just in time, because that would have been…bye, bye towel.

"Aye, says th' one wi' th' *boyfriend,*" he said, mocking me with the word and I rolled my eyes at him. Also, if I didn't have my modesty to keep, then I would have fought him for it. His eyes glistened with mirth, telling me that he knew it too.

"You're enjoying this aren't you!?" He grinned big, got closer to my face and answered,

"Aye…Immensely."

"Fine, then I will just forget about the damn salve, you can have it…eat it for all I care…I am getting dressed!" I snapped, no longer playing his games, ones that admittedly if I had been single, I would have no doubt enjoyed playing. As his loveable rogue act was definitely attractive. Damn him!

I gripped my towel tighter in one hand and swiped my top off the bed with the other, walking now towards the bathroom in the corner behind the screens when suddenly a pair of arms enveloped me from behind, making him say,

"Na, dinnae struggle, just listen...I will behave, just let me tak' care of yer wounds lik' I came up 'ere tae dae." I stopped like he asked and tested,

"You will behave?"

"Aye, I will be th' perfect gentleman, ye have my word, Lass," he said making me release a sigh before nodding and he let me go and took a step back. Then he opened up the jar and I watched him over my shoulder as he dipped his fingers inside to get a scoop of the yellow substance. Then he started rubbing it into my back making the scent of it waft up my nose.

"Eww, what is that, it stinks?"

"Ye dinnae want tae know," he replied honestly so I took his advice and left it as an unknown.

"So, I never asked you about this Hex," I said as he continued to rub gentle fingertips over my back.

"Aye, 'n' I never asked ye how ye know of Hexes?" I tensed a second, knowing I was on delicate ground here as I didn't exactly know what he knew, other than my name.

"Witch with a grudge, remember?" I stated. I looked back at him over my shoulder and when he didn't look convinced, I added,

"I did my homework." He nodded as if this was an acceptable reason, before telling me.

"I am na expert bit Nero is, 'n' she said 'twas what looked lik a summoning Hex, a little lik' a calling or way of finding you." I groaned at this and said,

"Marvellous, just what I need, a damn homing beacon on my body!"

"I have prevented it fur now but will need tae dae th' same every few days fur it tae continue tae work...or nae work, should I say."

"Yeah, err…thanks for that," I said, unsure how I felt about him having to blow on my naked back every few days, as one experience of it was quite enough, seeing how intimate it had felt.

"Yer welcome, Lass," he said after he was done, so he put down the jar and picked up a fresh roll of bandages and said,

"Ye wull have tae lift yer arms lik' before." I frowned and looked down the front of myself before asking,

"And what about my towel?" I swear I felt him smile behind me before his head came closer to my shoulder. Then he looked down at me for himself, making me shoot him a wry, sideways glance.

"Lose it," he stated, and I was about to protest when he added,

"Ye have my word, I wullnae look." I thought about it and knew that I had to have the bandages, which would be hard to do by myself without tearing my wound, so I said,

"Fine, give me the end and I will hold it across me until you have wrapped it around a few times."

"Aye, very well," he replied handing me the end so I could do just that. Then once I felt it was at the very least covering my nipples, I tossed the towel to one side and let him get to work. To give him his due, he didn't look, from what I could tell anyway. He also made quick work of getting my torso wrapped up, doing so tight at my request. This was so it also held my boobs up as I didn't have my bra, but naturally, I didn't tell him this.

Once finished, he tied off the end, after first tearing down the length and knotting it at the side of my waist out of the way. It ended up looking like a tube top and I felt safer now being covered up in front of him. So, I muttered my thanks, making him lean closer and say in a husky tone,

"Again…*Yer welcome, Lass.*" After this I stepped away and

grabbed the top Nero had left me. It was two joined together with a blue grey tank top and a darker navy blue strappy top over it, one that fitted under the bust and came down past my hips like a mini skirt.

"So, what's the plan now?" I asked, walking over to where the food was and helping myself to the stew looking concoction and tearing off a piece of bread from the loaf. Then I turned around and faced him to find him watching me curiously. Then he ignored my question and asked one of his own,

"How come ye cannae see properly?" Ah, so he must have noticed the way I felt around for things. Of course, after this I couldn't miss the sight of his blurred figure now coming closer towards me and before I could speak he grasped my chin and raised my face up to his whist I had a mouthful of bread I was then forced to swallow.

"Hey, less of the manhandling," I said pulling my face from his hold but again he ignored my complaint and said,

"'N' yer eyes are now all red 'n' sore...what happened?" I knew he was only concerned, which I found odd considering I was in fact just a job to him and one he still intended to deliver on, despite not knowing my fate.

But then it was clear he also felt something towards me, which for obvious reasons, I was not prepared to encourage. Even if I had to admit that on a survival basis, this wasn't a bad thing and may even mean he might feel conflicted in handing me over to whoever this King was. Now, would it be enough by the time we got there for him to regret his decision or even decide against it?

I didn't know, but the very least I could do, was be nice.

However, it was seconds later that parts of that hope were shattered, as Nero ran into the room and shouted,

"We got a problem, boss man!"

"Aye 'n' what's that?" Trice said after letting go of my chin and folding his arms, once again annoyed at the intrusion, one we were soon to discover, was needed.

"Someone sent an army out to get the girl!" Nero shouted and my mouth dropped.

Because it looked like one thing for sure…

Hell wasn't done with me yet.

CHAPTER TWENTY-FIVE

THE DEVIL'S CUP

After this news from Nero and what was the star of my next 'oh shit' moment, things started to happen pretty quickly. This began of course, when Trice switched from flirty Scotsman to commander mode and was issuing orders in seconds,

"Git ye boots on, Lass, time tae go!"

So, I did as I was told, dragging on a pair of wedge style boots that laced at the sides and put me at least a good three inches higher. I also stuffed my head inside a poncho style jacket that fell around me in waves of navy blue fleece. After this Nero stopped me and as I looked back at her, she opened her hand and blew a light green dust in my face, making me shout in surprise.

"Blink through it, as it should only take a few minutes before the blurriness clears, then you will be able to see," she told me, making me blink rapidly as she advised, as right at this moment in time, my eyesight was even worse!

"You're sure this will clear?" I asked rubbing at them and making her slap my hands away.

"It will but it will take time. I have added enough in this pouch to last you about a week, as you will need to do this each day when your vision returns back to the way it usually is," Nero told me, prompting me to confirm,

"So, it only lasts a day?"

"Yeah, two at most so go sparingly with it, and if I were you, I would time it so you don't waste it, as it's not like you need to see when you're asleep."

"Good point," I said nodding, then I grabbed her to me to hug her in thanks,

"I will repay you for all this one day," I told her, making her hug me back and laugh,

"Yeah, well we will consider it even, if you try and keep asswipe out of trouble," she admitted whilst I was still blinking through the fog in my eyes. At least it didn't make them sore, unlike my contacts had done. But her reply made me comment.

"The kiss was that good, eh?" I asked making her smirk before telling me,

"I'm still trying to convince myself it was just my own kissing skills that made it that good." I laughed once, patted her on the back and said,

"Yeah, good luck with that." It was at this point that Trice came back in the room, now fully dressed as he was before, then he threw Nero a bag of what I assumed was coins and asked,

"Did yer see what flag their wur flying?" Nero shook her head, telling him,

"No, but it's rumoured they were the King's army that were ordered to leave the camp and instead of charging into battle on the Shadowlands at first light, they were told to march here... now, I am no war expert here, but a human girl pops up in Hell and suddenly a piece of land he has been campaigning to claim for three hundred turns of the sky is forgottenand next thing is they are coming to this shit stain of a town…cowinkydink…I think not, my friend," Nero said, sounding a little like Pip with that last comment. Oh, and also, adding to the 'oh shit moment' for me.

"It's nae a coincidence…where be mah brothers?" he asked with his accent showing his frustration.

"Where do you think they are?" she said making him release a groan of frustration and reply with a question,

"The Spiked Monkey or The Devil's Cup?" She grinned before telling him,

"Well, they talked about rum, so I am guessing the Devil's Cup, besides, you know Gryph has a thing for the curvy ladies."

"Aye," Trice replied and when I raised a brow at Nero in question, she mouthed the word, 'pub' at me.

"Well, I hope yer right, as tis closer," Trice said making Nero walk towards the far wall in her room that held what I knew was a bookcase. Then, through blurred eyes, I half watched as she ran her hand in front of it until I heard a click. I stepped closer and could just make out two book spines as they inched forward from the rest. Then she pulled on them like handles and opened the two doors that had been hidden. When she turned back to face us, I could just see the blue line down her chin glowing from the magic.

"Here, go through this, it's a bridge that leads you across to the side the pub is on, first door on the right and down the spiral staircase will lead inside the pub." Trice nodded as he walked to the chest the rest of his things were on and started strapping them to his body, including his massive sword. So, I turned to my new friend and said,

"It was nice meeting you, Nero."

"You too, human," she said letting me see the whites of her

teeth, telling me that she was grinning. After this Trice finished by stabbing a small dagger through the holder at his side and walked towards the open bookcase. I quickly followed, and after knocking my hip into the corner of one of the side tables, Nero added,

"Her vision will clear in a few minutes."

"Right," Trice said before reaching out and grabbing my hand, and I had to say, I was thankful as I wasn't sure how far I was going to get without being able to see through my cloudy sight. Then he pulled me through the small tunnel until he pushed what looked like a fake wall at the end. It was one which seemed to lead out onto one of the bridges I had seen from the street when we first arrived.

"Kin ye run, Lass?" Trice asked making me smile up at his blurred face and say,

"Not saying that I will do well in keeping up with those long legs of yours, but yeah, I can run."

"I kin work wi' that," he said before he broke out into a what must have been a light jog for him, which was a full on run for me. We reached the other side quickly and I yelped when my legs were suddenly pulled from beneath me.

"Whoa!" A shocked sound came out of me in a whoosh of air as he was ducking us both under something I couldn't make out. After this he jumped down to another part of the building and I soon found my feet once more. Then I was being led through a door and down the spiral staircase Nero had spoken about.

The sounds of a busy pub met me and I could smell fresh meat and a sort of hops' scent that wasn't quite beer but came close enough to being recognisable as something similar.

"Och, bloody typical," Trice muttered still with a firm grasp on my hand.

"What?" I asked getting really frustrated at not being able to see now.

"Gryph is chatting up th' barmaid 'n' Vern is gambling... C'moan," he said pulling me through the crowd and growling at anyone that got too close. It was a guttural sound and unlike the type of growl I had heard before, but most definitely effective as the blurred figures soon backed off. And in all fairness, Trice also looked utterly fearless as he shoulder barged his way through the crowd, one that all seemed to be focused in one place.

"Ha, good show chaps, but better luck next time for the gracious lady must be..."

"In trouble," Trice interrupted after leaning down closer to where Vern was obviously sat at the head of the round table playing some kind of game of cards. It was with a pack that were black and flashed with glowing red patterns I couldn't really make out. Vern stood then and started collecting his winnings, telling them,

"My apologies, gentleman, but I must be on my way now, for duty calls in the name of honour." I would have giggled at the sound of his posh accent had the humour of the moment not been robbed by an angry demon. This was one who stood up after first banging what looked like it could have been a giant fist on the table.

"GRAGRAGKO! OGN!" The loud boom of a pissed off demon roared in another language making Vern gasp in horror. Then, just as my vision was starting to clear, it did so as Vern was pulling off one of his gloves. Then I looked up to see as he faced off against the huge demonic beast that looked like he had swallowed other beasts for breakfast. His skin looked as if it still had their remains trying to escape through the dark green flesh, as they looked barely beneath the surface. On his snarling head one broken horn might have, at one time, met the other over his forehead and he was all teeth, claws and spiked bone, standing about seven feet tall.

Then I watched flabbergasted as with the glove in hand Vern slapped the demon across the face with it, making me gasp.

Gryph came up beside us and said

"Why th' fck did ye dae that fur?!" Vern puffed out his chest and said,

"I have not the faintest idea, dear chap, but do excuse me as it looks as if this fellow wants a tussle."

"Oh Aye, he wants a fcking tussel a'richt, he also wants tae knock yer fcking block aff!" Gryph replied making Trice mutter in irritation,

"We dinnae have time fur this shit, Vern, just end it quickly 'n' wi' out th' fcking glove!"

"I dinnae kin, I kinda lik' th' glove bitch slap," Gryph commented making me giggle. Then the demon lunged for Vern and at the same time, Trice grabbed me around the waist and turned with me in his arms, before handing me off to his brother, saying,

"Ere' tak' this."

"Oi!" I shouted as Gryph took hold of me and walked me over to the bar before sitting me down on top of it. This was after first swiping aside all the wooden tankers of what looked like black ale. Then I looked over my shoulder and saw a curvy barmaid with curled horns and reddish skin shrug her shoulders at me before she carried on cleaning, showcasing a large amount of cleavage as she did. Gryph looked smitten.

I looked back to see Vern slip out of the way of the oncoming demon, before he kicked out a chair so it hit him in the face, making Vern put his hands on his hips and throw back his head to laugh like some amused Robin Hood or Peter Pan character. Then, just before he could charge at him, Trice released his blade making it ignite in a blue glow as its steel hit the air. He quickly kicked out at the back of the demon's legs, and forced him to his knees, before grabbing the broken piece of horn. Then after using it to drag the demon's head back, he placed the edge of his glowing steel at his neck and said,

"Dae ye yield?" The demon roared in anger trying to twist from Trice's hold, but this made Trice's eyes glow in a strange dark blue colour that bled into crimson red at the centres. Then the demon's horn started to freeze under Trice's grasp, which prevented the demon from fighting his way free. Then he growled,

"Fine, we dinnae have time fur this shit...Vern, ignite this asshole."

"With pleasure, brother," Vern said rolling his shoulders and taking a deep breath before he shot out a long stream of fire from his mouth. It was one that formed into a flaming sword by the time it was embedded in the demon's chest and to say that I was impressed was an understatement. The demon seemed to die instantly, and Trice dropped him as if he was nothing but dead weight. Then he held out his sword to the rest of the demonic crowd and as angry sparks ignited from it, he said,

"Now, does anyone else wantae piss me off today?" Their answers came in the form of them backing away and clearing a path to the door, making Gryph comment on a chuckle,

"Weel that wis entertaining." After this Trice lowered his sword making the glow simmer down back to steel and then stormed his way over to me. He grabbed me and bent me over his shoulder, making me yelp in shock.

"Right let's go, Vern, lead the way, Gryph, ye behind us."

"Will do, old..." Trice cut him off by pointing the end of his sword at him and warned,

"End that by callin' me Chap 'n' ye shall see whit happens, Lad." At this Vern swallowed hard and ran his finger and thumb across his lips saying,

"Mum's the word."

"Aye, mak' sure tis," Trice said before walking out of the tavern style pub that looked as rough as its name.

"Gryph!" Trice shouted and I looked up after pushing off Trice's back to see Gryph now downing his ale before winking at the barmaid. Then he picked up his hammer, threw it back against his shoulder and walked through the crowd with everyone giving him an even greater distance than they had Trice.

Trice kicked open the old black flaked wooden door and stepped through with me telling him,

"You know I can see now."

"Good fur ye, Lass," he replied in a stern tone making me snap,

"Then why aren't you putting me down?"

"Because pissing in th' wind is faster than ye," he told me making me growl at him. I looked up to see Gryph giving me the thumbs up with a grin, one I didn't return making him chuckle. But then the second we all heard the thundering sound travelling along the cobbled street, Trice stopped dead and the brothers did the same.

"I am going to take an educated guess and surmise this to be the reason for our haste?" Vern asked making Gryph scoff,

"Th' joke there, is yer bein' educated." I watched as Vern fought the posh impulse long enough to give his brother the middle finger in return. However, I kind of wanted to point out at this juncture the impending doom that was now making its way up both sides of the street and closing in on us. Although, at least even through their joking, they still took their positions. One which put them sort of back to back, covering each other as this stance seemed to have been as natural as breathing.

"Oh shit!" I muttered, making Trice respond dryly,

"Aye," he agreed as the black wave of armour came

marching towards us, one that was getting closer and closer and being led on one side by what I gathered was the general of the army. He was huge, being much bigger than the rest, and was wearing similar battle armour as the rest of the army, only just a variation of it. It was all black spiked interlocking plates that covered each of them from head to toe and reminded me of some medieval knights in Hell.

The general's armour rose up higher than the rest in deadly points at his shoulders, along with his helmet being bigger, with the front section rising up like a crown of daggers. He was also riding a winged beast that had the body of a horse but the head of a demonic horned sea creature. It also had eight tails that each looked tipped with deadly barbs and reminded me of black snakes, lashing out behind it.

Both rider and beast were terrifying.

"I think it's time to drink that elixir Nero gave you and let's grow some wings and fly away…yeah, sound like a plan?" I said with the panic in my tone easy to detect.

"Aye, that it would, Lass," Trice replied making me frown at the disappointed way in which he said it and prompting me into discovering our next problem.

"Okay, so what are we waiting for?" I asked making Trice slowly lower me to my feet before looking down at me, the grim expression was soon joined with the reason why, when he told me,

"She didn't have any left." This once again forced a quick flash of deja vu from only moments before as I said,

"Oh shit."

And of course, his reply was what it usually was…

"Aye."

CHAPTER TWENTY-SIX

SOMETHING OUT OF THE BLUE

The moment the general commanded his beast forward Trice released a sigh and muttered to his brothers, "Better leave th' talking tae me, Lads…especially ye, Vern."

"Aye, ye know how he likes tae piss off the' heartless bastard," Gryph agreed, no longer smiling which I naturally took as a bad sign. Then Trice took a step forward and in doing so, tagged the front of my poncho and tugged me in a way that I had no choice but to step behind him. He was protecting me.

"Carn'reau, what brings yer army all the' way tae these shitty parts?" Trice asked the general who I gathered was named Carn'reau. Well, it was this or a Scottish insult I hadn't heard yet. This was when he grabbed the edge of his helmet and tore it from his head, making me suck in a breath at the sight. Holy shit, what was it with the demons with human hosts in Hell! They all looked like damn cover models or sexy superheroes!

Only this one would have most definitely been your

antihero as he looked darker in every sense of the word. He had straight black hair that I couldn't tell the length of as it was hidden, but at a guess then I would have said long and he looked like some kind of royal dark elf, only without the pointed ears.

Maybe he was some kind of Fae being, but I had never seen one before, as they rarely came to Earth. This was said to be because of their well-known disdain for human life, even though they were happy to inhabit one of us as a host. And the utter disgust for my kind could be seen as he looked down his nose at me at the same time he lifted a gauntleted hand my way, pointing a talon tipped finger at me.

"You know why I am here, now give me the girl so I may give her to the King," he demanded in a deep voice, despite the beauty he held, for his high cheekbones and regal features didn't suggest someone that was more comfortable spilling blood on the battlefield. More like sitting his ass on some cushy throne somewhere. But obviously this wasn't the case, as here he was, leading his army.

"Aye that's funny, ye see we wur commanded by th' King tae retrieve th' girl, which as ye kin see, we have done 'n' are now on our way tae deliver th' lass." Trice said making Gryph lift his hammer and slap it to his palm before agreeing,

"Aye."

Carn'reau just raised one of his perfectly shaped black brows in the barest hint of irritation and Gryph had been right, he did look like a heartless bastard. Of course, this was mainly down to those incredible eyes of his that gleamed silver and were ringed black around the iris. Even the skin around them looked darker, giving him a sinister vibe, as if all it would take was a single look before he had the power to crush his enemies.

"Things change in this world, you should know that by now,

shifter," Carn'reau said in a calm and deadly tone making Trice sneer before saying,

"Aye 'n' somethings don't, so despite th' kings plans to get us to find th' girl 'n' you be th' one to hand her over so he still gets to own our souls, is not happening today, my friend." He said this with only the barest hint of an accent, telling me that when he wanted to, he could hold it back to get his point across. And despite the odds against us, I had to say, his tone spoke of deadly intent and determination.

But then Carn'reau looked down briefly as he ran the length of a wicked black talon down the head of his beast, doing so behind the ears and making it purr, as if he enjoyed the contact from its master. This was before saying,

"Tell me Trice McBain, just how do you expect to beat back my entire army, seeing as I know that you've already spent your last shift of the turning sky, on fighting Arachne?" I gathered at this that spider queenie was named Arachne and made a mental note to remember the name so I could do some research...well, that was if I ever made it back to my father's library alive. As I wasn't sure ghosts were known for their reading whilst haunting places.

"I'm sure I wull think of something... I'm resourceful lik' that," Trice replied with a wink making Carn'reau sneer before glancing off to one side and looking bored. Then he motioned one of his men forward and said,

"Bring me the girl and do so unharmed as the King demands." The soldier nodded before taking a step forward and in turn made Trice push me further back behind him. This was before he pulled his sword free, igniting the air around it in a blue glow, and holding it at the ready.

"Think before taking this action Trice, Prince of Three... the girl could get hurt and then the wrath of the King would be on both our heads," Carn'reau said making me skip over the threatening part of this statement and start to focus on the 'Prince of Three' bit. Something Trice didn't like the sound of at all, as he growled low, and the sound was frightening enough to make the soldier falter in his steps. But then it was Vern who stepped forward, making Trice grit his teeth, hissing,

"Not th' time tae piss him off, Laddie."

"Och, Fck." Gryph then said under his breath before swinging his hammer at the ready for all the shit to hit the fan. And I really didn't want these three to fight and potentially lose their lives over me!

Gods, but I just wouldn't be able to bear it and looking both ways up and down the street, then I knew there was only one way to get out of this. Because what type of queen would I ever make Lucius if I didn't do the right thing...*the brave thing*. So, I quickly stepped out from behind Trice before he had time to stop me and took one step telling the General,

"Please, I will come with you, just let these three go and I won't make any trouble!" I said making Trice hiss,

"Amelia, git yer arse back 'ere now!" But Carn'reau held up a hand to stop his men from going further. Then he raised a single brow and looked at me with intrigue as I came to stand next to Vern.

"You wish to sacrifice yourself to an unknown fate just to save these three, when they intend to deliver you to the same fate also?"

"I do," I stated firmly.

"Why?" he asked truly curious.

"Because it may be the same fate, but it's one I chose to make, so as I can save three lives whilst doing it," I said looking up to Vern who was grinning down at me, before giving me a wink. But this ended on me suddenly crying out in surprise as I was grabbed from behind and hauled straight up in the air as

Trice had lifted me off the ground, before setting me in front of Gryph.

"Ere' tak' this," Trice said again, just like back in the tavern making me respond in the same way.

"Oi, you said that before!" I snapped making him tap me under the chin after telling me,

"Aye." Then he turned back to face the enemy, making me hiss at him,

"I am trying to save your asses here!" He paused a step and looked back at me over his shoulder before saying with a grin,

"Aye 'n' we be thanking yer fur it, Lass, but leave this up tae us men tae decide, yeah." I scowled at him and the second I took a step forward Gryph wrapped an arm around me from behind, and I swear the thing was that big it felt like it covered most of the front of my torso. It was like finding myself stuck behind a damn tree trunk!

"Easy, Lass." Gryph cooed.

"Ah, but such a noble act for one so young, humanity at its best no doubt," Carn'reau said, as if truly thoughtful, but then as he nodded for his men to continue Vern wasn't done.

"Now, now, my good man, let's not be too hasty for I believe a solution is to be found, perhaps just beyond the horizon of the King's castle." I frowned wondering what he was talking about, as it seemed as if he was trying to let his brothers know something but with his posh voice curse, this was the only way to do that. I looked to Trice to see him frowning as he too was trying to figure it out when suddenly Vern produced something from behind his back. It was a glowing glass bottle, one I remembered seeing him looking at in Nero's shop before he managed to catch all her 'ancestors'. Had he stolen it when I wasn't looking?

This question died the second Vern looked behind him at his brothers and said,

"Is that not so, brothers?" Then he nodded as if telling them that he had a plan, making Trice shake his head slightly before saying his brother's name in warning,

"Vern." But Vern wasn't listening and instead went on to say,

"After all, it does seem like the most sensible choice...I am just sorry our adventure ends here, chaps. Remember, fly high my brothers," he said and then just as Trice shouted out,

"NO!" was when the last glimpse of Vern I saw was him mouthing the word 'sorry' and then he threw the bottle to the ground behind him so it smashed at our feet. A huge bellowing cloud of blue smoke exploded from it, just before sucking us in and doing so at the same time Trice was trying to reach his brother.

And it was only when the blinding light died, I opened my eyes again to find we weren't where we had once been. No, now we were in some forest, all stood surrounded by trees instead of the army that had once surrounded us. A forest that strangely enough could have been one found in my world and for a few seconds I wondered if that was where Vern had sent us.

But then another thought quickly replaced all others as I scanned the space surrounding us to find Trice. The second I found him my heart started to break at the sight. As the realisation of what just happened started to seep in, and this began when faced with the haunting sight of Trice as he fell to his knees in utter devastation.

He then let his head hang down as he said only one thing...

"Please by the Gods survive the King's wrath..."

"My brother."

CHAPTER TWENTY-SEVEN

SACRIFICES AND SCREAMING

A little time later I found myself curled up on the ground with the hood of my poncho over my head and my hands curled up under by my chin so I could keep blowing on my hands down the neck of the material. I was facing away from the other two just so they couldn't see that I was awake.

And I was devastated.

Vern had sacrificed himself for us all and none of us knew what had become of him. Naturally, the brothers had been upset, displaying it in anger, which first came from Trice who actually sliced his sword through a whole tree trunk when roaring his frustration. Gryph had at least the foresight to grab hold of me and turn us both against the oncoming trunk, as it was near to us both.

Then he ruffled my hair a little and said softly,

"Go take a wee walk, Lass."

I nodded and did as he suggested but it turned out that this hadn't been far enough. I had walked until they were just barely out of sight as I didn't think getting lost right then was going to help matters. So, I had found myself a place to sit. This ended up being a mound of hollowed rocks that were odd in shape, but at the time I didn't think too much of it as for the moment they were just a place to lean against and gather my thoughts. But then the sounds of the forest seemed to be amplified by them, almost as if they were absorbing the sounds. Which meant that the voices I heard were echoed behind me and I ended up hearing the whole conversation between them.

And well, I had to say...

It hurt.

"What dae ye intend tae dae now?" Gryph had asked, being the first to break the silence.

"Exactly what we planned, we git th' fcking job done!" Trice snapped back making Gryph grunt or something. Either way it sounded like he didn't like his brother's response.

"Yer surely dae nae mean that," Gryph stated making Trice scoff,

"And why not, this job's bin nothing bit trouble." I rolled my eyes wishing I could have spoken my own mind about that.

"Aye 'n' this job comes wi' a name, Trice." Gryph made the point of saying and as much as I wanted to slap Trice, I equally wanted to hug his brother. But then I knew I also had to give him a bit of leeway here, as I knew he was upset, worried and angry with what had happened with Vern.

"Aye, one she lied about, dae nae forget who this lass is." I frowned in question, wondering what the hell this meant? Did they know a lot more about me than they had let on? I mean I still didn't know how Trice knew my name, as he had never really answered me on that one.

"Actually, I forgot, who is this lass tae us Trice, fur I can't remember anymore?" Gryph asked sarcastically.

"She's our fcking ticket tae getting our souls back 'n' now added tae that our brother, that's who she is 'n' nothing more!" he snapped angrily, making me physically wince against the pain of hearing that.

"Yer dae nae mean that." Even Gryph said, disbelieving he could be this heartless. However, his response was again another lashing out at me, making me tense when he shouted back,

"Aye, I fcking do!" It was said in such a way that I even felt the vibrations of it against my back.

"Are ye forgetting that th' lass tried tae sacrifice herself fur us, does that nae mean anythin' tae ye?!" Gryph asked in an astonished tone, as even he couldn't believe what he was hearing coming out of his brother's mouth.

"Aye, that she is foolish," he said and I closed my eyes and turned my face away as if I could see them right in front of me and had to cut it off. Gods he was right...*I had been foolish.*

Foolish believing that he cared for me as anything more than just a job to him. A way for them to get their souls back.

"Trice!" Gryph snapped out his brother's name.

"No Gryph, they have our brother, th' one who actually sacrificed himself fur us all 'n' now our only focus is getting him back, 'n' that's it!" Trice said in that commanding way of his, which seemed to have little effect on his brother.

"Aye bit tae whit end, Trice? I want him back as much as ye dae, bit we dinnae know whit th' king even wants wi' th' lass, 'n' whit if tis her life that's on th' line…can we really tak' that risk knowing whit might happen…?"

"Aye, we can," Trice said firmly, making me suck in a deep breath knowing now that I had been played. He had flirted, pretended as if he cared, and it was all just to get me to be compliant. I knew that when their conversation continued.

"Ye dinnae mean that…ye lik' her," Gryph said making his brother snap back, clearly affronted,

"Fck off Gryph, she's a fcking job!"

"Bullshit," he replied calling his bluff.

"Aye yer right, she's th' job of all jobs, th' one that grants our souls back, or did ye forget that?!" Trice said in return but Gryph had his own ideas on what that meant.

"Aye 'n' whit good is that soul if tis rotten by th' choices we make?" Trice growled at this.

"I made a vow tae us all, Gryph, 'n' I am not going back on that noo just fur some bonnie lass."

"Aye, just some lass yer falling in love with," Gryph said making me suck in a startled breath.

"Fck aff ye soppy git, she is a job," Trice said again, making me grit my teeth every time I was referred to as a job.

"Aye, yer keep telling yersel' that, 'n' maybe that shit will stick," Gryph commented in an amused disbelieving tone.

"You're going soft, as yer Gryphon feathers," Trice said

mocking him and he agreed in a sarcastic tone I wasn't used to hearing from the big guy.

"Aye maybe a'm, as Hell clearly turns ye that way or th' other."

"And what th' fck is that supposed tae mean?" Trice snapped and I could just see him now, by the sound of his tone knowing that he was no doubt crossing his big arms over his chest.

"I don't know, ye tell me, you're th' heartless bastard that is willing tae hand over th' lass tae one of Hell's most brutal Kings, 'n' after she wis ready tae sacrifice herself fur us…but hey, ye go right ahead 'n' fool yersel' intae believing that shit is right, just don't fcking drag me intae that lie wi' you, brother," Gryph said and I let out a shuddered breath as the emotions became too heavy to hold back.

"Gryph…" Trice said his name in a remorseful way but Gryph snapped this time,

"No, Trice. I know ye, I know ye better than Vern, than even that our father 'n' our mother did! Ye love this girl 'n' yer running fcking scared. She wanted tae sacrifice herself fur us just lik' our mother did 'n' noo yer fcking scared! Weel, ye may want to believe in yer own shit bit I don't, 'n' when I earn me soul back, I want tae dae it so it comes back just th' same wey that when before we sacrificed it th' first time. We tainted it by doing a deal wi' a fcking Devil, Trice. We became whit we are, 'n' noo when I git it back, I am not doing it just tae taint it again, only this time by coating it in th' blood of some innocent girl," Gryph said and by the time he was finished I had tears flowing down my cheeks, unable to help myself.

"Gryph, come back…GRYPH!"

After this I heard a roar of anger which I knew to be Trice's and I found my legs couldn't hold me up any longer. So, I slumped down against the rocks, trying to process everything I had just heard. Then I lowered my head into my hands and couldn't stop the tears from falling. Everything had turned to shit and now if felt like I was being hunted by most of Hell and the sacrifice was more than just my life, but now the three brothers I cared about.

Despite the betrayal I felt by Trice, I still couldn't stop myself from caring.

Gryph, Vern and yes, even Trice all deserved to have their souls back. Which meant that I had to do something about this, and running was no longer an option. Because I might want to save my own life but surely there was one card I had left to play here. I just needed to get there, and I knew now Trice wouldn't help me. He only had his brother in his mind, and I couldn't find it in myself to blame him, even if it meant him sacrificing my life without a blink. Even if it meant seeing me only as a job.

Meaning, I couldn't trust him to help me.

No, there was only one being in all of Hell that could help me now.

It was time to bargain.

So, a little time later Trice found me and told me that it would be dark soon, as evidently that was what happened in these parts. He told me that he had lit a fire and for me to stay close to it for my protection and to keep warm. It was also obvious that he knew I was upset as I refused to speak to him. But I could tell that at first he thought it was because I was worried for Vern, not because I had heard what he and his brother had said. I knew this when walking past him, intent on storming back to his makeshift camp. He grabbed my arm and held me back, so as to tell me,

"Don't worry, we will git him back." Then, just before I could answer, he heard Gryph's voice calling his name, only with the echo off the unusual rocks, he heard the voice being reflected behind him. This then became obvious what had happened. Because Gryph's voice had been as clear as if he were stood next to him, not as far as way as he was. This was when realization finally hit him, and he had the good graces to look pained by the idea.

"Och, Lass." I cut him off pretty quickly.

"Oh, don't worry, I know you will," I told him in a hard tone before turning on my heel and walking back to where Gryph was, making his hiss a cursed,

"Fck."

I reacted this way because even though I may have understood his reasons, I still wasn't about to pretend to be okay with him ready to throw me to the wolves just to get it. To do it so callously and not even act like it was a hard decision to make.

That was my problem.

So, I walked back to the camp, walked straight up to Gryph and reached up to try and pull him down to me. This obviously surprised him enough to do as I wanted, making him dip his head lower, so I could frame his face with my hands.

"Thank you for caring about what happens to me, Gryph. I will do anything I can to help you get back your soul and I promise you, when you do, it will be untainted and clean," I said, then I kissed him softly making him freeze first under my words and then the affectionate gesture I granted him. Then I tapped him twice on his cheek after pulling back after the quick kiss,

"And remember, ladies like soft feathers." Then I winked at him and turned to find Trice stood there after watching the whole thing. He looked as if he had been punched in the gut but also as though he wanted to do the punching, only most likely to some other poor tree that wouldn't survive it. But I walked past him and as I did, he said my name, my actual name, not 'lass',

"Amelia." I paused long enough to give him my reply,

"What's been said has been said, now let's just get to this fucking castle and finish it, so that what's done is done," I said unable to look at him fully but still I noticed the way his hands fisted in frustration. Then I walked away and sat down by the fire. After this I tried to ignore them both, because it made it easier that way, *on both sides.*

As little did they know that what I said to Gryph had been my goodbye. So, I listened to whenever they talked about things like how far the castle was from here. It was information that I certainly needed for what I intended to do. Which was why I was happy to find out that the forest was only on the outskirts of where the castle was and we were only about an hour away.

A city surrounded it, which was what I really needed, as surely there was someone there that would be willing to get a message to where I needed it to go? But then, even just starting a rumour would do it in this place, as how long had it been before word had gotten out that I was even here?

So, all I had to do now was wait for the two to fall asleep and then I could sneak out. I had thought about telling them, asking them to get word to him, but then I couldn't trust that Trice wouldn't just use that information as a bargaining chip for the wrong thing. Or even just taking me to the King and telling him everything, as they would then know what it would mean. For whom would I have to be for me to have that kind of relation down in Hell?

My Grandfather.

Of course, they would wake and once they found me missing then they would no doubt believe I ran to save myself and that thought hurt. But then no doubt Gryph wouldn't blame me, he wasn't the type, even after my promise. But Trice would.

He would tell his brother 'I told you so'. Well, if he did have even a shred of guilt to feel, then my actions would alleviate him of that burden pretty quickly.

Although, I hadn't counted on him coming over to me as I pretended to be asleep and place the piece of his tartan over me so I had extra warmth... *for who knew that it could be cold in Hell.*

"Get some sleep, Lass, fur we leave at first light," he whispered down at me, making sure to tuck it close to my body and I held myself perfectly still, hating that his kindness was making tears form. Gods, why had his words affected me so much?

Was I making a mistake by leaving?

I asked myself this question even up until I heard Gryph snoring and I braved a look at them to find them both asleep. I purposely made a noise to test if they woke and when they didn't even stir, I braved moving. I sat up as slowly as I could, trying not to make a sound. The crackling of the fire helped and was a long time from going out just yet. I looked to the forest wishing there was a moon or something lighting the way.

But then I looked around and found some of the unused branches Trice had gathered and after tearing a strip off the bottom of the poncho, I wrapped it around the end, making sure it was tight enough not to slip.

Then I got up and held on to the tartan for a while longer. Looking down at Trice's handsome face that for once looked peaceful in his sleep...well, it made my heart ache just knowing this was goodbye. Then I brought the tartan to my face, taking in the scent of the man I admittedly felt something for. Whether it be just as a friend or shamefully a little bit more, I didn't really know yet. I just knew that I had a mission to do and it started with saving an entire race of Vampires. It included saving my mother and the man I loved.

And now, I had no choice but to add three more lives on to that list.

I just wanted to do the right thing.

Sacrifice. That was what my life had become.

And that was okay…*It was okay.*

I just had to be brave. So, with this in mind, I lowered the material and folded it up, laying a kiss on top, in the place of one I couldn't do to Trice, before placing it down next to him. I stepped away and lit my makeshift torch and set off into the forest. One that I thankfully hadn't heard a single sound of life from, beyond us.

I just needed to make it to the city, try and bribe someone to get word of who I was to my grandfather and then enter the castle to try and bargain with whoever this evil tyrant of a King was. Oh yeah, sounds like a piece of cake, Fae, I thought rolling my eyes at myself.

As I had to admit, that the further I travelled, the more I started to see the flaws in my own plan, picking it to pieces. Maybe I should go back and tell Trice and Gryph who I was and that way then they could bargain on my behalf. Surely when Trice listened to reason he would try and save me, even if just by getting word to my grandfather.

"Fuck!" I hissed to myself.

Gods in Hell! I was doing it all over again! Making rash decisions was what had got me in this mess in the first place! But then, could I really trust them to do right by me?

"Fuck, fuck!" I hissed again, stopping now and turning back to face the way I had come. I hadn't gone too far, at least I didn't think so. Oh yeah, that was all I needed, to finally come to my senses only to find myself lost in yet another demonic forest! Well, that would be just my luck wouldn't it?

"Gods Fae, you are so stupid! Why did you even think you could do this alone?" I muttered to myself before deciding to

turn back and tell them everything, taking my chances the safer way. Because the last thing I needed was to end up regretting yet another stupid decision, even if at the time it had seemed like the right one to make. And well, at least this way hopefully one good thing would come out of me being delivered to the King, that three brothers would be reunited back together, along with that of their souls.

I turned around and started walking back towards Gryph and yes, even I had to admit, back to Trice. A man that I was really trying not to delve too deep into how I felt about him, *it was too confusing*. I tried to tell myself as I started walking back that it was just because I was feeling vulnerable being without Lucius. Someone who only recently had come back into my life. I had just learned all about his history and the truth of it that surrounded me.

It was just too much.

All of it.

I felt the emotional overload until the point where I felt I was close to screaming in frustration. But then soon, I was screaming.

Only this time…

It was for a very different reason.

CHAPTER TWENTY-EIGHT

KISSES AND FORGIVENESS

My scream was carried through the trees destroying the stillness of the night. This was because I was suddenly knocked down to the ground and before I could continue screaming a hand was held over my mouth with a furious male on top of me, growling down at my face. The unusual blue and red eyes glared at me, glowing in a powerful way, whilst my makeshift torch had been knocked out of my hand as I fell and was currently setting alight to the dry undergrowth that surrounded it. This managed to light the angry features of none other than,

Trice.

Gods but he looked utterly formidable!

The scar on his face glowed intensely with the stern, hard set of his jaw, one that looked as if he was ready to bite through rocks, he was that tensed up. His blazing gaze burned into mine and there we both were, staring at each other and waiting for the spell to be broken. Of course, the fire spreading would do that, and my panicked eyes looked towards it.

But just as it started to circle around us getting closer, he finally broke away from the sight of me beneath him, so he could look at the cause of my worry. Then he opened his mouth and hissed at it, causing a stream of frost to come from between his lips, which effectively managed to put out the flames. Of course, it also plunged us both into darkness and all I could feel was his body on mine making me feel like I was small and breakable, and not that I was kickass and could usually take care of shit like this. Because now I was questioning why was it that every single move I had learned went flying out of my head. Why was my mind losing focus on anything but those glowing eyes that seemed as if they wanted to consume me.

I needed to stop this. I needed space!

Thankfully, this began by him taking his hand from my mouth but then it ended not the way I wanted, when I started to say,

"I wasn't running." This was when he snapped,

"Shut the Fck up!"

And then he kissed me.

This time it wasn't just the brief and gentle touch of his lips to mine, but an all mind consuming kiss, that he wanted me to remember. That he wanted burned to my soul, branded there, in a way he hoped would stay. And it would...just not for the reasons he wanted.

Trice was kissing me and all I thought was... *oh no, I was cheating on the man I loved!*

I felt the swipe of his tongue enter in between my unprepared lips and his groan was easy to hear. So was the feel of his hands gripping me to him, as he took control, whereas I felt too stunned to do anything other than let him. However, a few seconds later and finally my mind kicked in, but the second I started to squirm under him, he tore his mouth from mine, and suddenly his weight was gone.

Thank the Gods.

But then, before I could question where he went, seeing as I couldn't see anything in the dark, I felt myself being hauled upright. I was lifted off the ground as easily as if I had been a sack of feathers. After which I soon found myself in his arms and being carried back to what I gathered was where I had run from. So, after some time of getting my senses back I muttered,

"I was on my way back."

"Aye, so ye say." I frowned at this in the dark and protested further,

"I was."

"Then why wur ye walking in th' wrong direction?" he stated in that stern tone of his.

"Oh," I muttered shamefully making him grind out a gritted,

"Aye."

After this we were silent and I thought it best, as I doubted in this mood he was going to listen to anything I had to say. Of course, I couldn't see where we were going so I couldn't help but ask,

"How can you see in this darkness?"

"I can see," was his abrupt answer, so I tried to ask for more,

"Because you're a Cockatrice?" I felt him move his gaze to mine and the second I saw his eyes glow a little brighter, I knew he was showing me exactly how he saw in the dark. This was before giving me his usual broody reply of,

"Aye." Something that signified the end of our conversation.

After this I didn't say another word, I just let him walk me back to the camp and once there he plonked me on the floor in not exactly what I would call a gentle manner. I started to walk back to where I had been asleep when he suddenly grabbed me from behind to stop me. Then he growled down at me,

"Stay."

"What am I, a damn dog?!" I snapped making him raise his brow at me and say,

"Nay, they usually do as they are told." I frowned back up at him which didn't seem to affect him in the slightest. So, I ended up just watching him as he unfolded the tartan material I had placed by him, and if he had any thoughts about finding it there, then he didn't say. No instead he just lay it down and once that was done, he ordered,

"Now, lie down." I didn't, but instead folded my arms across my chest and said,

"Why?"

"It may have been a while since I was human, Lass, but I am guessing sleeping is still the same," he replied sarcastically. I heard Gryph chuckling where he lay, obvious not asleep like I had assumed.

"Yeah, well I am not exactly tired, but hey, you go right ahead."

"Tough shit, now lie down before I put ye down," he said making me release a frustrated sigh before saying his name,

"Trice."

"Now!" he snapped making me just give in and lie down. Then I watched as he walked over to the pile of branches and threw some of the bigger ones on the fire before kicking some back into place. Then he came back over to me and I frowned as I saw him get down next to me, making me snap,

"What do you think you are doing?"

"Again, sleeping is the same for a shifter, Lass, we usually prefer to do this lying down," he said wryly, still keeping up with the sarcasm. Again, his brother chuckled making me snap,

"And you're not helping." At this he grunted a laugh and muttered something about this being damn entertaining.

"Now what are you doing!" I asked in a panicked tone the second he wrapped an arm around me and started spooning me from behind.

"I am tired 'n' some Lass just pissed me off by makin' me chase after her in th' damn forest, when all I wanna do is fcking sleep, so consider this me not doing that again." I frowned in the dark before telling him,

"I am not going to run."

"Aye, you're right...*you're not*. Now go tae sleep," he said keeping his meaty arm in place draped over me, squeezing me for a moment as if to emphasize the fact that I wasn't going anywhere. I released a deep sigh and after a few minutes of silence, asked the dark,

"Trice?"

"Um," he muttered behind me.

"Are you asleep?" I stupidly asked.

"No, but tis not fur lack of trying," he replied dryly, something I ignored, even though he could be funny when he wanted to be. I released a sigh and told him,

"I'm sorry." At this I felt him tense next to me before he gave me another squeeze as his answer, but I carried on,

"I was upset, angry and confused. I thought if I went to the castle that maybe I could bargain with..."

"There is no bargaining with th' King, he gets what he wants 'n' that's that," he said cutting me off and me making me sigh again.

"I realised my plan was stupid and really was on my way back...or at least I thought I was," I told him.

"I know, Lass," he admitted surprising me.

"You do?"

"Aye," was his typical Trice reply.

"Okay. So, you're not mad?" I asked making him scoff,

"I am fcking fuming, but I suspect a good sleep will solve that problem," he admitted making me tense and snap,

"Yeah, well you made me pretty mad too."

"Aye, I can see that," he said sounding slightly amused.

"And you upset me," I admitted, this time losing steam in my voice and I felt him tense next to me again, before he pulled me tighter to his frame and whispered in a gentle way,

"Aye, I know that too." After this I didn't know what to say and it was only after it became obvious that I wasn't sleeping that he gave me a squeeze and said,

"Relax, Lass." So, I released a deep sigh and did as he suggested seeing as I knew that I had big day tomorrow, and would no doubt need my strength to get through it. But then, just as I was starting to fall under, giving way to sleep I felt him whisper against my neck,

"Amelia?" I mumbled and mimicked him by saying,

"Aye?" I felt him silently chuckle before he told me softly,

"A'm sorry I hurt ye." And at this I patted his hand that was rested by my belly and said a soft,

"I know."

But what he didn't know was that when I said this, I did so with tears in my eyes. However, what I didn't know was when I finally gave way to sleep and closed my eyes, relaxing back into the wrong arms, it wouldn't be the last time I heard my name being spoken.

As the next time, when it was said in the dark, it didn't come from Trice's lips,

But instead it came from…

Lucius'.

CHAPTER TWENTY-NINE

CASTLES AND THE TYRANTS FOUND THERE

The second I shifted sides, turning to face the other way I felt a pair of arms tighten around me, making me release a contented sigh. I felt safe and treasured, missing the feeling and whispering,

"Handsome." That was when I heard my name being whispered into my ear from behind, where there should have been no one.

"Amelia, where are you, Sweetheart?" It was Lucius' voice and I opened my mouth and cried out silently. Gods, how I had missed that voice! I reached out and gripped onto whatever my hands could find, too afraid that I might slip away from whatever was happening now. Slip away from Lucius' voice as it finally found me.

"I'm here," I whispered, barely hearing it as more than a mumble of sound.

"My Khuba... You. Are. Not." His voice sounded hard, stern as if these words caused him both pain and anger in equal amounts.

"Please...I am...I am waiting for you..." I forced my mind to say, then I felt a looming presence in my mind as if he was now stood over me and I turned my head to look up, finally opening my eyes to find that I was right... *he was there!*

Lucius' masterful figure was standing over me, looking down at where I lay. He had his arms crossed and he looked so angry I could see he was almost shaking from it. But then something snapped in him and he lost his anger the second I reached out a hand towards his own. He released a deep sigh before lowering down to one knee. Then he reached out and stroked my face, making me close my eyes against the emotions it invoked.

Gods, how I had missed him!

I opened my mouth and was just about to whisper his name when suddenly he leaned down closer and said,

"You wait for me in another man's arms?" At this I froze and the horror of what was happening really started to infiltrate my senses. I then looked to what I had been grabbing on to only to find that he was right, I was in Trice's arms facing him in an intimate embrace.

Gods but what had I done?

This was when I started thrashing and I woke with a start the second I heard my name,

"Amelia!"

"NO!" I shouted and started shaking before I felt those arms around me hold me tight and the wrong voice tried to soothe me,

"Hey, Ssshh now. Tis okay, yer safe...I've git ye, Lass... *I've got you."* The last three whispered words came out like a vow, one being said with no accent to be heard behind it. I started to calm enough to stop my body thrashing, but my mind was far from it. Because what he didn't realise was that as sweet as the vow was, it felt like it had come from...

The wrong man.

"Is she alright?" I heard Gryph ask and Trice's hands started to rub up my back as if to help calm me, as he answered his brother,

"Aye, just a nightmare."

And he was right, it had been a nightmare and of the worst kind. As I had a feeling that I hadn't just been dreaming at all. No, the dread in the pit of my stomach now was from knowing that Lucius had been in my Void. He had been looking for me and where he found me, was unbearably,

In another man's arms.

The next day I found myself unable to think of anything else but what had happened last night, feeling ashamed for so many things. But most of all, I hated the idea that Lucius was somewhere in the world believing that I was being unfaithful to him.

It was heartbreaking.

And Trice knew something was wrong, but I was thankful that he didn't push for it, after the one time he asked me and my reply was a simple,

"I'm fine."

After that we had all got up and started the day. I ignored the rumble in my stomach and soon found myself walking through the forest on our way to the castle. Naturally, my mind was everywhere and nowhere, because I knew I should have been questioning what was about to happen to me. But my mind was too busy torturing itself by feeling guilty and now, I was even more worried about Lucius. I needed to save him and the only single thing I had to hold onto was that I knew he was still alive, as my soul was connected with his. I also had a feeling that the witch needed me, and she was going to try and use Lucius as bait. It made sense, as she knew I would do anything to save him.

What she didn't know, of course, was that I was currently on my way to be handed over to a ruthless King, one who for some reason wanted me, and saving Lucius was literally an impossible goal right now. But then, after obsessing about Lucius, I finally started to question why this King could want me. Which led me to believe that he needed me to bargain for something... or worse, could he be in league with the witch? Of course, I hadn't thought of this until now, but seeing as she must have had allies down here, it would make sense.

Gods, if that was the case, I was so screwed!

After an hour of me silently looking worried, Trice put my behaviour down to the uncertainty of my fate and at what was about to happen next. Thankfully, along the way Gryph had scouted ahead and found a brook nearby, so at the very least I could drink away my thirst and throw a couple of handfuls of water on my face. The forest actually looked like one close to where I grew up and its beauty would have been more appreciated had my mind been free to focus on such things.

However, not far from the brook was the end of the forest and a sight that gave way to one even more impressive...

As we were now at the castle.

"Gods," I whispered in utter awe as it was unlike anything I had ever seen before!

It was all made from a grey blue stone that looked carved out of an entire mountain, as its walls looked to be one seamless creation. The whole castle was surrounded by a separate wall, that was a series of wide arches. One so huge, each looked big enough to fit the pyramid of Giza inside of it, and there looked as if there were at least ten of them. All of which were connected by a battlement walkway and enormous turrets and corner towers. The biggest of which framed both sides of the entrance in hexagon shapes, with the highest arch in the centre and it was one that looked as tall as a skyscraper.

It was by far the most intimidating place I had ever seen and suddenly my heart started to beat wildly in my chest.

"I am not sure I can do this," I muttered fearfully.

Both Gryph and Trice heard this and exchanged a knowing look, making Gryph look grim, telling me this didn't mean good things. *The loss of his smile never did.* Nevertheless, Trice nodded for us to continue on and I ended up needing a little nudge from him to get me moving again. My legs felt as though they didn't want to work…actually that wasn't true, they did, they just wanted to put them to better use by running in the opposite direction as fast as they could physically move. And naturally, the closer we got to the building, the more this impulse wanted to kick in.

The castle wasn't anything like I had ever seen before and being who my father was, then let's just say that I had seen my fair share of castles. For starters, what was known as the keep and central building of any castle, didn't look like it should. As for this castle it looked to be made up of many. Almost like a giant network of buildings surrounding a larger one at its core. This central building was surrounded by five other buildings, all the size and shape of skyscrapers.

They were connected by arched bridges and a series of covered parapet walkways hundreds of feet in the air, making them look like veins connecting to the heart of the castle. Although, from way down where we were, they looked far too narrow to be considered safe.

The buildings were of the same style and looked like some powerful sorcerer had just come along and dragged his upturned palms in the air, dragging with them the grey stone beneath his feet. Doing so until colossal shards had risen up, creating the buildings within the surrounding wall. Each were spiked and topped with pointed spires and pinnacles. Spiked iron was also a theme as it framed the battlements and the curtain walls, also topping the turrets and towers. This was with an interwoven lattice effect of iron strips, that almost looked like cages, and each contained a seemingly never extinguished flame. This sinister blue fire rose so high in the sky, I bet that it could have been seen for miles around.

But with this imposing sight of doom in front of me, it was of little wonder why I was a nervous wreck by the time we approached the gate house. Or should I say, guard house as that was precisely what flooded out of it now. Doing so the moment we could be seen approaching. But I also noticed that we hadn't yet passed through a city like I would have thought, making me wonder where it was?

Trice took his domineering and protective stance in front of me, and stated in a firm voice,

"Th' king is expecting us."

They didn't reply but they must have known we were coming as they simply formed a line either side of us and started to escort us through the arched entrance. They were dressed similarly to how Carn'reau's army had been, only instead of black armour, this was more a dark grey, with tints of blue at the spikes. There were about twenty of them that walked us to the main part of the castle and as I looked up when walking through the entrance, I nearly stumbled. I would have fallen too, had it not been for Trice who steadied me.

"Easy, Lass," he said before one of the guards snapped out,

"You're forbidden to touch her!" Trice growled low the second a weapon was pointed his way and his hold on me tightened.

"Come on, Trice, let's nae lose sight of why 'ere now," Gryph said trying to get Trice to let me go and after a few tense seconds, he finally did. Then we continued on walking, doing so now along the footbridge. One that would have made me queasy had I been made to walk near the edge. This was because instead of a moat filled with water surrounding the castle, it looked more like an endless abyss that naturally wouldn't allow you to see the bottom. Although, the constant fog that seem to rise up from it was most likely the reason it gave it this ominous appearance. But like I said, I was thankful to be walking in the middle, as it meant I was as far from the edge as you could get, seeing as it was as wide as a four lane highway.

We were escorted through the main part of the castle, and what you could class as the largest keep, with doors that looked made by giants. Thousands of large iron rivets decorated the two black doors that opened on our arrival and they were so big that colossal redwood trees could have passed through upright. The hinges were also incredible and were a series of black iron points and curls that framed the top and bottom of each door.

Once inside the grandeur continued, only at the very least in a slightly less severe way. Long lengths of crimson cloth as wide as banners hung down the walls and held symbols and what looked like a demonic crest at the centre. One admittedly, I barely took notice of, as I was more focused on the doors at the end that mirrored the ones we'd just walked through. Doors, that I knew would lead us into the throne room. I knew this because as they started to open, that was the very first thing my eyes met.

Because there now, in front of me,

Was the King.

My steps almost stopped completely as I saw the dark figure sat upon the throne. The doors opened fully to a pale arched space that reminded me of a marble cathedral and instead of an altar at the end, raised steps led you to only one place...

A demonic throne fit for a ruthless King.

Although, I hadn't expected the King to be covered in a cloaked jacket, looking more casual than I expected. Although, saying this, he still wore armour, just solely on his arms. This was made up of silver polished plates of smooth steel, which rolled down from large shoulders like waves crashing towards his elbows, ending with curled edges. A bare muscular chest was on show as the sides of his cloaked style jacket were left open and the pointed hems reached the ground either side of his legs which were covered in simple trousers made from some sort of animal hide.

However, his brutal features said he was anything but casual and as he raised a gloved hand to motion me forward, I sucked in a deep breath. Because this silent order told all the guards to suddenly point their spears at us, telling us what to do next.

"Keep going, Lass, I am 'ere wi' ye." Trice's voice behind me gave me strength and I took another deep breath and continued to walk down the great hall, one framed with even more of his army. It was also one where the decoration was sparse, telling me the King obviously didn't have time for frivolous furnishings.

There was also no one other than his guards, as I had to admit, that I expected at least the sight of some of his repressed kingdom, all down on their knees being forced to adore such a rumoured ruthless King. But there were only his guards, ones that were stationed closer to his throne and dressed slightly different, to signify his personal guard no doubt. Crimson red armour gleamed as if they had each been coated in blood and I tried not to let their towering appearance intimidate me. Especially knowing that those massive swords could no doubt cut through me like butter. Ones they held pointed at the ground and I knew they could quite easily be turned on me at any moment.

"Ah, so finally this is what all of the fuss is about…bring her closer now, for I am curious," the King said making me frown and question if he knew who I was or not, as why would he be curious?

When I didn't move, the King nodded to Trice to be the one to step up and take charge. I knew this when he gripped the top of my arm and whispered down at me,

"Just do as he says, Lass, and this might be over quickly." Then he walked me up the steps and the closer I got, the more of his face I saw. Like the warm bronze skin tone, dark hair, full lips and almond shaped eyes that were incredible. Eyes that were now staring back at me in a questioning way. They were light olive green with a strange amber starburst at the centre that circled the darkness of his pupil. He was also annoyingly handsome but then, was I really surprised.

Everyone else seemed to be in this damn place!

The throne he sat on was all darkness compared to the light in the room and was made from what looked like thousands of demonic horns in different sizes. All were curved in the direction they naturally grew, being placed and positioned so it suited the purpose of a King sitting there. They were all black and highly polished with razor tips of gold plating, as if they had each been dipped before being set into place.

"M'laird," Trice said as he approached making the King smirk,

"Ah Trice McBain, I have to hand it to you, you're certainly resourceful and a man of your word, for when you say you can deliver, well, you weren't' wrong."

"And me brother?" Trice said getting straight to the point.

"Alive," the King replied, making Trice visibly take a breath, obviously relieved, as I also did the same.

"Although naturally not everyone was pleased to see him, but I am sure you understand why, given the circumstances," the King said making Trice grit his teeth, no doubt now worried about what state he would find his brother in.

"Now come here, girl," the King demanded and after receiving a little nudge from Trice, I did as I was ordered to do. But then, as I made it to the top step, I stumbled and stupidly fell into the King's lap, meaning he had no choice but to catch me. I sucked in a startled breath and slowly looked up to find him grinning down at me. Only then his cunning eyes left mine and narrowed the second his gaze travelled down my shoulder, as if something offensive had caught his eyes. Then they didn't just frown, they hardened dangerously.

This was when he grabbed me and before Trice could move, the King had spun me around and suddenly flipped up the back of my poncho before tearing down the back of my top. I cried out in shock but then when he touched a fingertip to my wound, I knew he had managed to tear straight through my clothes and the bandages with them. After this he gripped me tighter and hissed only word,

"Witch!" Then he suddenly shoved me forward so I went falling down the steps and was thankfully caught by Trice before I could break my neck. He held me in his arms and looked down at me with true pain in his eyes. Eyes that then closed the moment the King barked out an order and what was to become of my fate.

"Take this witch to the dungeon! For we will let the wrath of her executioner also be that of her judge when he returns, for he can decide which manner to end her life!" The King shouted making me gasp. Because that was when I realised the true depth of my actions. And I knew then that I had made the wrong decision. I should have run away when I had the chance. Because I had just let myself be led to my own death.

A death Trice now had no choice but to have a hand in, as he was forced to drag me away screaming, being the one ordered to take me to the prison. One where I was to wait until my sentence could be carried out.

Because Gryph had been right.

Now when Trice finally got his soul back, it would be tainted with my blood.

For now, I faced my fate because of him.

Now, I was to be executed.

CHAPTER THIRTY

PRISONER

After this point everything became a blur as I was dragged out of the throne room with Trice having no choice but to take on the role of my jailor. He tried to calm me down, but this became an impossible task as I kicked and screamed my way through the castle. Then, just before the escort of guards could intervene, Trice had clearly had enough and pinned me against the nearest wall to shout at me,

"Fur fck sake, calm yersel', woman!" Then as I screamed in his face,

"SCREW YOU!" he then decided the best way of dealing with me was throwing me over his shoulder and forcefully carrying me to the prison. And I didn't give up, not one little bit! Not now I couldn't help but see my death being by the end of a rope, unable to stop the image as this was all my mind would focus on.

To die how he had died the first time.

The only difference being that it wasn't a death I was going to be coming back from. So, all I had left was my desperate need to fight, and I did. I hit him and kicked until he pinned my legs. I also didn't once listen to a single word he said, as in my rage and fury, in my mind he had become the enemy. He had become the whole reason for me being here and what would soon be my death. And I wanted him to know it. To know what this was doing to me! Because why should I make it easy for him. Trice was about to get everything he wanted. His brother back, his soul, his freedom, meanwhile the cost of that would be my life.

But more importantly to me, the life of people I cared about!

I didn't know where Gryph was, but if I had seen him then I would have shouted for him to help me, knowing how he felt about making this exchange.

It would taint their souls.

This was why, the second I felt myself being lowered to my feet, my reactions kicked in and I came up swinging. I punched Trice in the face so hard, it hurt my knuckles. I connected with his face and it was clear that he really hadn't been expecting it. And it certainly did what it was intended to do, which was of course, for it to cause damage. He staggered back a step and looked so shocked, it would have been almost comical had the moment warranted it.

Then he raised his hand slowly to his now bloody lip and dabbed it before looking down at his own bloody fingers as if he couldn't believe it. Meanwhile, I was just left to watch this whilst panting through my rage, and not getting very far away from it. Then he shook his head to himself, as if he was still trying to make sense of what just happened.

"I guess ah deserved that," he admitted rubbing his jaw and I snapped,

"That and a lot fucking more!" He swallowed hard and closed his eyes a second before telling me,

"I won't let them kill ye." I scoffed at this and said,

"Why, do you have an army you're not telling me about?!" He frowned before telling me,

"I had no choice, Lass, he is me brother."

"And if they didn't have Vern, what then, huh?" I questioned and his face said it all, making me raise a hand and say,

"Yeah, yeah…and you're blood bound, so I guess that's a stupid question…well great, now you can just go and collect your souls and be on your merry way… I am glad it worked out for you and was worth it! Now you can just fuck off and leave me to face whatever execution they fancy…in a place like this, I can't imagine they ever run out of ways to kill someone!" I threw at him making him angry, and he turned quick and hit out at the metal wall behind him, reminding me in that moment of Lucius.

"Damn it, Lass, twas never like that!" he roared making me snap back,

"No? Funny then, seeing as Gryph thought it would be, but hey, I was only ever a job to you, huh? Nothing more, I think were your exact words!" I lashed out at him making him flinch as he knew I was right.

"Lassie," he said making me shake my head, knowing I couldn't look at him anymore, so told him,

"Just leave."

"Amelia…"

"LEAVE!" I screamed, this time because I couldn't stand the sound of my name coming from his lips. It was Lucius' right to call me that and his alone, so right now, it hit a nerve! And he knew it had, because his reaction was to turn away from me, as if he couldn't stand the guilt. Which meant when I did finally look up at him, it was to find his back to me, tensed by the cell door as if he was torn. His hand gripped tight onto the metal frame like he was ready to crush it but holding himself back.

"I promise ye, I will try everything in me power tae prevent yer death...I will make an appeal fur yer life wi' th' King, I will git him tae see..."

"Don't make promises you can't keep, Trice...I am pretty tired of trusting people right now," I snapped making him release a sigh before he walked through the door and I flinched when I heard the click of the door closing. Then he turned back to face me and told me softly,

"I will come back whin yer are ready tae listen, fur I can see that yer tae angry right now."

"Yeah, an impending death and being thrown to the wolves by who you considered a friend usually does that to you," I replied in a hateful tone, making him wince against the verbal assault, one I would no doubt feel some guilt over at some point. But as for right now, well, all I saw was every plan I'd made to save Lucius, come crashing down around me. But he didn't understand that. He didn't know how many lives I had counting on me.

He only had one, that of his... *brother*.

Speaking of which, the guards who had escorted us down here were now bringing the limp body in between them down the hallway and I cried out when I realised it was Vern!

I lost all my anger and ran to the cell door. This was a wall that consisted of thick strips of metal and reached out with my hand through the diamond shaped gaps, before uttering a devastated,

"Gods, no!" Trice looked furious and pushed aside the guards so he could take hold of his brother.

"Vern, Gods in Hell, tell me yer alright, Lad," Trice asked making his brother seem to come awake and move to grip on to him with bloody knuckles as if he had gone down fighting.

"Trice?" Vern asked as if he was seeing things.

"Aye Lad, I am here…I'm here with ye" But then this fact must have meant something to him, as he quickly looked up and his head searched around until finding me. It was also a sight that made me hiss through my teeth, as his bloodied face looked to have received a good beating. Then, with one eye swollen shut, his other widened at the sight of me in a cell.

"Och, no, no brother…please tell me that you didn't…"

"Ssshh, now, we can discuss it later," Trice said in a hard tone.

"Then it was all for nothing," Vern said sadly, now letting his head hang once more, as if he couldn't stand to witness what it had taken to get him back.

The sacrifice his brother had made with my life.

It was in that moment that Gryph turned up and his quick steps stopped dead when he took in the scene in front of him.

"Oh Lad, 'ere, give him tae me, Trice. I brought ye this tae bribe th' jailor with." Then Gryph nodded to me making me frown in question.

"Och lad, where did yer bonnie looks go?" Gryph asked as he took his brother in his arms.

"Still prettier than ye be, ye ugly bastard." Gryph laughed making Vern moan as he held his ribs, as if they had been broken.

"Are ye alright, Lad?"

"Apart from getting me head kicked in fur sounding lik' a posh twat…Aye, then things be just pure barry," Vern said on a laugh that ended in a groan of pain, as Gryph walked away with him in tow. Then I looked to Trice who was watching me the whole time, making me finally release some of my anger.

"At least it wasn't all for nothing…I am glad your brother is alright, Trice." I said, letting my hand fall from the iron wall of my cell and going to sit down in the corner, one of the only places that didn't look covered in someone else's excrement. Then I let myself slide down the wall and slump in this shithole, swiping angrily at the frustrated tears that fell, no matter how much I loathed to let them.

"I am going tae at least git ye out of this fcking cell," Trice promised making me shrug my shoulders, before resting the back of my head on the wall as I looked up at the stone ceiling. Now not exactly thinking that the wrought iron hooks and draped chains looked like a fun sign of things to come. Oh well, maybe I would be dead by then.

Here's hoping, eh.

But it was after this point I had no more to say to Trice and it became clear that standing there talking to me was pointless.

I was too numb.

In fact, I didn't know how long it was before I looked up again and found I was alone. In fact, I lost all track of time and didn't know how many hours I had been sitting there, only that it was long enough for me to feel the ache of moving. I knew this as the next time I looked up, it was the sight of who was obviously my real jailor.

He had a big ring of funky looking keys, that looked more like demonic toothpicks for some snarling beast. As for the being that had come to unlock my cell door, he was a demon with light grey skin. One that looked more like it was made of rock than of flesh as any scars there looked more like cracks. And like most in Hell, he was another big bastard, that didn't own a damn shirt!

Which meant I could see the rounded, defined shoulders pebbled with bumps under his skin and up the muscles of his neck that gave him a large hump of muscle at the top of his spine. Two horns started at his brow line, making his eyes set so deep that they were barely seen. White hair flowed down his back and looked like it was covered in dust clinging to the strands. Crudely sewn trousers looked like he himself had made them from the skin of others, as they were patched in no particular way or pattern. At the front of his legs was a strip of material with a plaited edge cut in a T shape and was enough to hide the very male part of his anatomy, as it became clear when he moved by the slither of pale thigh that could be seen that his trousers didn't do the job for him.

His nose was cut square and his top lip naturally curled up creating an S shape. I also didn't like the way he looked at me.

"Well, get your ass up human, those three stupid bastards paid me well enough to put you somewhere nicer than this Gorgon shit pit." I looked around at the three walls of stone and shit on the floor and not much else, which was why I didn't need to be told twice. Because if I only had a short amount of time left in this hellhole, then if I could spend it somewhere even remotely nicer, then I was taking it.

I also still held out hope that I could get Trice to reach out to my Grandfather, as in my anger I had forgotten to ask him. So as my jailor banged open the door, he stepped aside and snapped,

"I don't have a fucking age, get that sweet ass moving!" I frowned, not liking the comment but then looking at the size of the guy, I didn't think throwing sass his way was going to get me anywhere. So, I walked out and then followed him until we reached the bottom of the corridor. One that looked like your typical prison in Hell, being that it was all stone walls and flaming torches. These were held in rings at the pillars that seemed to separate the cells, offering a hellish glow in the dark and ominous place.

But then came actual doors, instead of being on show to the world and he unlocked the door with one of the shards pushed into the hole without even having to twist the strange key. Then he kicked open the door and grabbed my arm to push me inside, making me stumble into what was now, in its most basic form, a bedroom. Because it held a few pieces of plain furniture, one of which was a bed that at least looked clean.

In fact, I was just looking around the room when I heard the door close behind me, releasing a new sigh of relief, before muttering to myself,

"Well, at least this is...*oh shit!*" This ended on a gasp of horror as I realised that the jailer hadn't just locked the door, leaving me inside alone, before pissing off.

Oh, but he had locked the door alright, but as for the pissing off part, that was where he had failed. As he now turned to face me, swinging the ring of keys around his meaty finger, grinning in that knowing way.

Then he yanked away the flap of material covering his crotch and rubbed his hand up and down a huge erect grey cock, that looked as if it was only ever intended for splitting girls in two, as there was no way a human girl would survive that thing!

But then again, I suppose that down here, in Hell and on death row...

I wasn't meant to survive anything.

CHAPTER THIRTY-ONE

FOR THE LOVE OF A BITEY

He took a step towards me and rubbed his cock harder.

"You look like you have all the right places for me to put my cock in, little girl," the demon said making me grimace before telling him,

"Oh, you think? Well, you obviously have never met a demon like me." He frowned making his horns dip lower slightly before he snarled,

"You're human."

"Yes, that's what we Biteys want you to believe," I said, admittedly losing slightly more confidence after I had named my made up demon Bitey. I swear if it hadn't been too obvious to do so, then I would have rolled my eyes at myself and slapped my forehead.

"Biteys? What the fuck is a Bitey?" he shouted.

"Well, I am you grey hunk you, so sure, you wanna go a round then we can play, but just so you know, we are called Biteys for a reason."

"And why is that, little mouth?" Little mouth? Err yeah, sure okay, weirdo demon.

"Because our mouths aren't the only places we have teeth," I told him, snapping my jaw and nodding at his still naked and erect grey cock. I nearly smiled when I saw him recoil his hips back, but then it totally started to backfire as he lunged for me and said,

"I want to see this for myself!" Thankfully, due to his big size, he wasn't that fast and I managed to dodge him, *at least this time*. He snarled at me as I put the bed in between us, wishing it had been more than just a few shitty pallets put together. But then, with a side table at my back, I reached behind me for anything I could get my hands on.

"I don't believe you!" he snarled, making me say,

"It's true, I mean they don't call me the pussy meat chomper for nothing!" I said knowing that even Pip would have been proud at that one.

"I don't think so, but after I am done with you, they will call you something else!"

"Yeah, what's that? Bleach Girl, 'cause that is what it will take to get your stench off me!" He growled low before charging again and I grabbed whatever it was behind me and smashed him across the face with...

"Oh great, a fucking piss pot...perfect," I said after holding the dented metal bowl up to look at it. This, of course, was when he grabbed me, doing so by the neck and ending the beginning of a shout by cutting off my air supply. I started kicking out at him, but this was about as effective as if I had been tickling him with feathers.

Damn, but I swear this guy was made of fucking rocks!

I started to see black spots cloud my vision which I knew wasn't a good sign, which was when I suddenly remembered what Nero had given me! So, I reached inside my pocket quickly before he could just snap my neck and it was game over. Then I dumped the whole contents of the pouch in my hand and before I passed out, I used the last of my strength to lift my fist to his face. Then I opened my fingers and blew that shit in his face, making him howl in pain and drop me.

I fell to my knees and was just smart enough to roll out of the way before he too dropped to his knees and landed hard on his face. This naturally made me wonder what the hell Nero had given me to put in my own eyes. Well, with that reaction rate, I didn't see Specsavers investing any time soon.

I coughed through the new pain at my neck and the second I saw him start to move, I grabbed a chair and hit him over the head with it, making it split on impact. Yet this still wasn't enough as the big bastard still kept moving thus giving way to the new game to play, mainly one named…

'What else I could find to hit the demon in the head with!?'

So, I then grabbed something bigger which was a side table and hammered that down, again making it break on impact. That didn't work either, so the next thing to go was a full shelving unit that I had to tiptoe towards him, it was that heavy! It actually reminded me of Caspian, and it made me mutter under the physical strain,

"Oh yeah, now I need that vow to save my ass, you're nowhere to be seen, huh." Then when I got it close enough, I let it go whilst shouting,

"TIMBER!" Again, it crashed into him, and the shelves broke free, with the frame now twisted. Then I kicked the broken pieces off him and when he moved again, I shouted,

"Aww come on! Gods, what the hell are you made off, fucking granite!" Then I picked up a shelf and smacked him with it over and over again!

"JUST DIE ALREADY!"

Again, he moved and I slumped back exhausted, panting

against the bed, asking myself where was Arnold Schwarzenegger and his Terminator ass when you needed him! But then the second he started to try and get up I knew that I had to do something, as I couldn't just continue hitting him with shit. Besides, I was running out of furniture.

But then I looked at the bedding and had an idea.

Which meant that by the time the three brothers showed up and they kicked in the cell door as if they were there ready to save the day, what they found was me sat on the back of a demon currently hogtying him with long strips of torn bedding and hitting him with the metal chamber pot every time he moved, so I could finish the job.

Of course, when they had all burst into the room, I had just hit him, meaning their dramatic entrance ended with a ding sound and made for a comedy moment. All three faces were pretty much the same, as let's just say, it wasn't a sight they expected to see.

"Next time when a lady says no, I think he will listen," I told them as a way of explaining the situation. Which made all three of them reply,

"Aye," Trice said.

"That he wull, Lass," Gryph said.

"I bet my fcking arse he wull," Vern said then he turned to Trice, patted him on the back and said,

"Good luck, cowboy, th' lass be tae wild fur me." Then he limped back out of the cell and nodded for Gryph to join him.

"Are yer alright?" Trice asked the second we were alone, well, all except the groaner beneath me.

"I will be when you get me out of here," I said gathering now that was why they had burst in here, but then as I was getting up, I noticed his tense expression making me say in a questioning way,

"That is why you're here, right…to bust me out?" At this

Trice took a deep breath and his pained face gave me my answer,

"Oh, I see."

"Lass."

"Then why did you come?" I snapped and he nodded to Mr grey shit stain, hogtied on the floor.

"We git wind of th' jailor bein' one who liked tae rape th' prisoners," he told me with a tensed jaw, obviously thinking what could have happened had I not been able to fend him off like I done.

"Oh, well I don't think he will be doing that again, not until it heals anyway," I said making Trice wince and I laughed once, telling him,

"Joking… he got to keep it…besides, I didn't have anything to cut it off with." Then I winked at him, making him mutter,

"Remind me never tae piss ye off, Lass." I opened my arms out wide and said,

"Really?"

"Good point," he said getting my sarcasm, seeing as I was currently in this situation because of him and him pissing me off was an understatement of the bloody year!

"Are ye sure yer alright?" he said coming to me and I backed up until I had nowhere else to go, meaning he was touching me in seconds, checking that my sore neck was okay.

"I'm fine, Trice," I said in a gentle way, as his concern for me counted enough for me to let go of my anger.

"Gods, Lass, when I think about what could have happened!" he snapped, clearly angry with himself.

"Yeah, well it didn't and besides, I am harder than I look."

"Aye, clearly," he said making me release a sigh before slipping out from beneath his gentle touch, needing the space.

"Well, thanks for coming to my rescue and all, but as you

can see, I am fine and well... I guess I will live for another day at least," I said making him say my name softly,

"Amelia." Gods, but I hated that the way he said it with his accent, as he made it sound so beautiful, almost like a purr. Which was why I tensed before telling him,

"Don't, Trice,"

"I wish I could break ye out of 'ere, bit it just wouldn't be possible, aye, nae 'til we were strong enough tae face that type of army," he said and I released a deep breath, knowing that I couldn't expect them to risk their lives for me, and despite him being the reason I was here now. I knew I didn't have it in me to hate him.

"And I shouldn't ask you to," I admitted making him growl angrily,

"Bullshit! Yer me woman 'n' I should..."

"What?" I asked interrupting him and he shot me a look before straightening and stating boldly,

"Yer mine." I released a sigh and told him,

"No, Trice... I am sorry, but I can't be yours."

"Why the fuck not?!" he snapped folding his arms and looking pissed.

"Well, apart from the obvious, 'about to be executed' reason."

"I won't let them..." I cut him off,

"And how will you ever stop them, Trice, you said it yourself, you're not strong enough yet and I don't know..." This was when he decided he'd had enough and was the one to interrupt me this time.

"Stop. Just stop, okay. I wull find a wey and if nae, then I wull tell th' King that I have claimed ye as my own, that way he is bound by law tae accept it and..." I held up a hand to stop him and said in a sad tone,

"I can't let you do that, Trice." Gods, the man was breaking my heart. I couldn't believe the lengths he was willing to go, and I felt terrible knowing that I had done this. I had caused this amount of guilt for him to feel.

"Why the fck not!" he demanded.

"Because you don't need to. I am not your responsibility and you shouldn't be letting guilt guide your actions."

"That is not why I am doing it 'n' ye fcking know it. Now answer me wi' th' truth!" he snapped, which is when he needed to know the reason why. So, I took a deep breath and said,

"Because I am already claimed." At this he jerked back and said,

"How? Yer human 'n' it's against th' law in yer world," he said, telling me without saying the words that it obviously wasn't the case down here. Which is when I admitted,

"I am not who you think I am."

"Aye ye are."

"No, I'm…" I started to tell him but he cut me off,

"A princess, aye, I know." Hearing this shocked me, and I was about to ask how when he said,

"I can smell royal blood when I know it, besides I know nae all this fuss would be over just a human girl who woke up one day in Hell 'cause a witch has a grudge…I know I may look lik' a have thick scales bit I kin easily piece together th' truth… besides, yer be a shite liar."

"You've known all this time?"

"I suspected aye, but then I met ye, saw how fearless ye were 'n' knew ye had grown up aroond demons. Now we maybe in Hell bit even gossip travels down 'ere 'n' when th' King of King's Chosen One gives birth tae a human baby, then aye, we have heard of ye. Besides, I knew when I tested yer name that 'twas ye, as ye didn't deny it," Trice said, telling me all the things I knew I had done wrong.

"So, you know that I am claimed then."

"No." he stated surprising me again, which is why I questioned,

"No?"

"No news of you being claimed has ever reached down here," he told me and I guess that made sense, seeing as I had been the one that wanted Lucius to keep it quiet for the time being. Back when I thought my dad would pop a vein and snap.

"Well, I did tell you I had a boyfriend," I said, defending my actions.

"And?"

"And what? It means I am claimed," I told him after shaking my head in question.

"No, it means ye fooling aroond wi' some poncey lad, when yer need a man tae claim ye. I am that man," he stated making my mouth drop.

"No, you're not!"

"Why? I know ye lik' me, Lass," he said arrogantly.

"Well, I…err, well of course I like you but as a friend, in the same way I like Vern and Gryph." At this he laughed and said,

"No, ye dinnae."

"Dinnae?"

"Do. Not." he stated firmly when I questioned his accent.

"Yes I…" At this his actions cut me off as he stepped up to me, pressed me against the wall and pinned me there with his big body.

"No. You. Don't." he said again, more clearly this time.

"And how would you know, huh!?" I threw at him.

"Because yer heart dinnae quicken fur them, bit only when I am near ye. Yer breath dinnae shudder fur them, Lass, only fur me. 'N' when I kiss ye, ye may nae realise this, *bit ye moan fur me,*" he said making me suck in a shuddered breath just like he said, and I already knew my heart rate was up! Damn him! And as for the last one, well, I was sure I didn't moan...*did I?* Oh Gods, but now I was doubting myself!

"Well, whether you think that or not, I can't be yours, Trice," I stated more firmly this time.

"Why nae, tis because yer a princess, as that's nae a problem, seeing I am of royal blood 'n' considered a prince."

"Well, no it's not that...wait a minute...you are?!" I screeched, obviously getting sidetracked here. At this he grinned big and said,

"Aye, Lass, that I be." I released a sigh and said,

"It doesn't matter, Trice." He then swapped his confident grin for a frown and said,

"I told ye I will get ye out of here."

"Yeah and you also said that I was just a job to you, remember that?"

"Och, I was talking shite then!" was his defense, making me say his name softly,

"Trice."

"Aye, alright, I did say that, 'n' I was angry when I did, thinking I'd just lost me brother. Have ye never lost anyone before? Never had anything make yer so angry ye said shit ye didn't mean?" he asked giving me the space I wanted, as he stepped away and dragged a hand through his loose hair before looking back at me.

"That isn't the reason I can't let you claim me, Trice, it's just one of many," I said in a pained tone, hating that I had no choice but to hurt him.

"Ye dinnae mean that," he said in a hard tone.

"I wish I didn't," I admitted on a whisper he heard, hating that it was true. Not because I wanted to be with him in that way but hating that I had so many reasons to say this to him, when I cared about him as a friend.

"Then ye wish tae..." I put a hand up and said,

"Don't say it. Don't cling on to false hope, as now is not one of those times." He growled at this and then said,

"I know how I feel fur ye."

"No, you don't," I argued.

"I will nae stop fighting fur th' right tae claim ye," he told me, but this was when I had enough.

"Trice, you brought me here. You bargained for your soul and your brother and I don't blame you, I really don't…not anymore, but it still doesn't change the fact that you did that, even when you knew what could happen to me."

"No," he said shaking his head.

"Yes, *you did.*" He growled and told me,

"I promise ye… I will try everything in me power tae prevent yer death…even if it means walking into me own…" This was when I stepped up to him, put a hand over his mouth and said,

"Don't say it…please Gods, just don't say it, Trice," I begged then rested my forehead on his chest with my hands framed either side on his shoulders, knowing that I would never forgive myself if he did something foolish, like dying trying to save me.

"Fine, then I will say something else instead…" he told me and the second I looked up at him, he took me by surprise as he framed my face in his large hands and just before either of us could make another mistake, I said,

"Trice, don't…" but then, just before his lips were crushed to mine, he told me…

"I love ye."

CHAPTER THIRTY-TWO

PLAY ALONG

The second I gasped he used it as an opportunity to deepen the kiss. And this time, I lost the fight in me. Because I felt in that moment I was going to die and whilst I kissed this man, all I could think about was one being in all the world I would never get to kiss again.

And it should have been him. It should have been Lucius' kiss.

But it wasn't.

It was Trice's.

This should have been Lucius' goodbye kiss on the edge of my death, one that felt like no-one had the power to stop. As a ruthless King wanted to see me executed and I had no idea why. And the man I loved was imprisoned with no clue as to what was going on. But then the man who had just claimed to love me, was the one kissing me now and I just let him.

And by doing so, I was being unfaithful.

I couldn't die that way!

I just couldn't!

Lucius deserved more than that! Suddenly my senses came back to me and I tore myself from his lips and out of his arms. Then whilst looking at the wall I told him,

"That was your kiss goodbye."

"No, it wasn't," he stated firmly.

"Yes, it was, for even if I survive this, that is the last kiss you are going to give me," I told him and then had to end it when he asked me,

"Why?" So I took a deep breath and told him something I should have from the very beginning but had wanted to spare him the pain. Because he was right, I did care about him. But it wasn't love and he needed to know that.

The cruel way.

So, I turned back to face him, because he deserved that and told him,

"Because I am in love with someone else." At this he jerked back a little as if I had struck him and the pain on his face soon turned to one of anger. But then, as he looked off to one side, he snarled,

"Who is he?"

"It doesn't matter now," I said, not knowing what problems I would cause should I tell him, seeing as Lucius was currently imprisoned and obviously vulnerable.

"I want a name," he demanded.

"Trice, it doesn't…"

"I want a fucking name!" he roared and just then the door opened, and a few demon servant girls walked in. Ones that looked like they were also dressed for a personal Harem, in see-through dresses with more slits in than what made the dress seem worth it. Behind them were a few guards who quickly took in the sight.

Yet Trice hadn't moved a muscle and looked beyond furious

with me. So angry in fact that I found myself taking a step forward and wanting to comfort him. So, I raised my hand to his cheek, but it was enough to snap him out of it as he snarled down at me making me drop my hand. Then he turned and demanded,

"What is all this?!" He was referring to the basket of food in one of the girl's hands and the flowing material over the arms of another. But the servants, obviously not permitted to speak, lowered their heads and moved either side to let a man inside. One I now recognised after first removing his helmet,

"Carn'reau, I might have known," Trice growled angrily, instantly creating a fist with his hand.

"Nothing personal, shifter, as you know I was under orders…just as you were," he said nodding towards me then, once catching my eyes, he said as way of hello,

"Human." I rolled my eyes and commented dryly,

"If I went by that name, I think quite a few people would turn their heads, don't you?" This made him smirk and remind me,

"Not down here they wouldn't."

"Good point," I admitted.

"But of course," was his arrogant reply making me roll my eyes, but meanwhile Trice had clearly had enough,

"What th' fck are they doing 'ere?"

"Well, our King heard of what happened here…" Carn'reau said pausing so he could gesture for his men to come and pull out my hogtied buddy before he carried on,

"…And well, naturally, he was not pleased. Besides it's time she gets presented…*properly,*" he said nodding to the servants who were actually looking more like beautiful slaves, with shackles on their wrists as if they had been claimed by a master. Most likely the King.

"Oh goodie, he wants me to look nice whist I entertain him

with my death," I said sarcastically, making Carn'reau raise a perfectly shaped black brow in question.

"M'laird, ordered her to be executed," Trice told him making Carn'reau looked surprised before tapping two fingers on his lips in thought before he said,

"Um, is that so...we shall see then won't we?" I frowned at that, not exactly loving the easy manner of my death been spoken about like it was the Gods be damned weather! A death which this dark elf looking dude didn't look too bothered by, not that there was any reason for him to but still, it irked me all the same.

"Now as for you Trice McBain, I believe your presence is requested by the King, for don't you have a payment to retrieve?" At this he growled low as if being reminded of this in front of me pissed him off. He turned to me and looked as though he was about to say something but stopped himself and said something else instead,

"Eat something, Lass, yer stomach has bin growling at me fur two turns of th' sky." Then he nodded down at the food briefly before storming out of the cell looking pissed off.

Then Carn'reau looked down at my stomach and said,

"Curious little being." Then he ordered his men to stand guard outside and left.

"Wow, well isn't he just the smooth operator, eh?" I said looking to the two slave girls and seeing them each looking at the other in that questioning way, making me mutter...

"Wow...tough crowd."

A little time later I found myself sat on the bed of my cell because it was the only piece of furniture that I hadn't broken over Mr 'once was cock proud before beaten by a girl'. Okay so granted, as far as made up names went, admittedly it was a little long. But then here I was, now waiting to be escorted to the King once more and wondering what my fate held this time. Was he just feeling impatient and wanted to get the job done quicker?

Not only that, but I was also wondering why I was now wearing a sexy white and red toga style dress? It was a sheer material but thankfully one with so many layers, that it wasn't see through in the places you wanted to keep decently hidden. The skirt was full and trailed long behind me, with a revealing slit up to the top of my thigh exposing one leg completely.

The top part was a wide length of the same material as the skirt and twisted through the tie at the back where the skirt was knotted like a belt. These two lengths were then brought to the front, before being crossed over my breasts and over my shoulders. Then the remaining length was twisted and tied to the waist of the skirt. This style meant that it exposed an upside-down V shape from the valley of my breast, down to most of my stomach, making me look like some sacrificial virgin that I didn't think boded well for me. Not considering the edge of the skirt that touched the floor looked as if it had been dip dyed in blood.

As for my hair, this had been brushed to a high shine, (by the slave girls who weren't exactly big on talking, in the sense that they didn't…as in, *at all),* then it was coiled up in twists at the sides allowing the length to flow down my back. Blood red lips were painted on, and a dusting of gold was brushed around my eyes, as makeup around here came in the form of an artist's palette, and your face was the canvas.

Well, at least I am gonna die pretty I thought with a roll of my eyes. Then I spotted the dried fruit and flat bread and also thought, well there is no sense dying hungry either. So, I picked up the bread and started tearing little mouthfuls off, so as not to smudge my painted lips when something suddenly floated to the ground.

It was a note.

I remembered what Trice had said about me eating and wondered if this was why? So, I reached down, picked it up and read the single line.

It said…

'Play along, Princess'

Now, what this meant I had no clue, but I gathered it meant that Trice had figured out a way to get me out of here and help me escape. I quickly screwed up the paper and stuffed it under a pillow the second I heard someone coming. Then I quickly stood as the door opened and Trice was walking back inside looking bleak,

"I have been asked to…" He started to say but tailed off the second he raised his head and saw me, making me blush as his heated gaze ran the length of me. His eyes even started to glow and a rumbling sound he made from the back of his throat almost made it sound as if the beast inside of him was now purring.

"Erm…Hey, Trice," I said in a shy and unsure way, suddenly feeling very vulnerable dressed like this. He opened his mouth once and after thinking better of what he was about to say, closed it again. Then he opened it and this time, he committed to what he wanted to say,

"You nae be just a bonnie Lass, yer be fcking beautiful." I smiled at this and had to say, even without knowing what he was about to say first, I preferred this best, as it was all Trice.

"Thank you," I said before he reached for my hand and said,

"Come on, Lass, I have been asked to escort you to the King," he said making me nod and put my hand in his. Then we left my broken cell and made our way through the castle together. We were back to being on the upper levels again and nearing the throne room when he noticed,

"They took off yer bandages," Trice commented after looking down at my practically bare back and I nodded, telling him,

"I guess they didn't think it went with the dress." He scoffed at this in an irritated way that seemed as if he wasn't happy that the wound was nearly exposed.

"I wull have tae slow th' Hex again soon."

"Well, I guess we will have plenty of time for that, *once we get out of here,*" I whispered this last part just as I was being escorted by the royal guard inside the throne room with Trice by my side. But now he looked down at me and frowned before asking me,

"What dae yer mean?" I gave him a questioning look back and reminded him,

"I got your note." Then I heard the sound of lots of people all shifting and now, unlike before, there was a sea of people all in the grand throne room that had been transformed from once plain to luxurious.

But then I noticed the King was now stood next to his throne as if waiting for something and I had to wonder if it was me? We seemed to be standing off to one side as if waiting to be called forward by the King, but the whole thing seemed off for some reason. But then something Trice had said started to creep in,

"What did you say?"

"I said I dinnae give ye any note, Lass." At this I frowned at him and tried to piece together what was going on here. If he hadn't given me the note, then who had? I was about to ask him this when another question replaced it. Something that was nagging at me more.

"Why does the King stand to the side like that, what is he waiting for." I looked up at Trice who was now frowning down at me as if he couldn't understand where this question had come from. Which was when things finally started to fall into place and it did this at two things, the first when Trice informed me,

"Because that nae be th' King, Lass." I sucked in a quick breath and with wide eyes, turned back to him and hissed in shock,

"Then who is?!" Then the moment the wave of people all lowered themselves to their knees, I looked back to the front just as a very obvious looking King came to stand in front of his throne. He looked exactly like the demonic King you would have expected everyone to fear, all covered in hellish armour with his face covered in a matching helmet.

This was also when Trice whispered down at me, in what seemed obvious at this point…

"That is the King."

And this was when he removed his helmet and I swear my world suddenly felt as if it had been turned upside down. As it was a King…and a King I knew well.

It was of course…

Lucius.

To be continued in…
Transfusion Book 8
Release date 28th June 2020
Pre-Order Now!

About the Author

Stephanie Hudson has dreamed of being a writer ever since her obsession with reading books at an early age. What first became a quest to overcome the boundaries set against her in the form of dyslexia has turned into a life's dream. She first started writing in the form of poetry and soon found a taste for horror and romance. Afterlife is her first book in the series of twelve, with the story of Keira and Draven becoming ever more complicated in a world that sets them miles apart.

When not writing, Stephanie enjoys spending time with her loving family and friends, chatting for hours with her biggest fan, her sister Cathy who is utterly obsessed with one gorgeous Dominic Draven. And of course, spending as much time with her supportive partner and personal muse, Blake who is there for her no matter what.

Author's words.

My love and devotion is to all my wonderful fans that keep me going into the wee hours of the night but foremost to my wonderful daughter Ava...who yes, is named after a cool, kickass, Demonic bird and my sons, Jack, who is a little hero and Baby Halen, who yes, keeps me up at night but it's okay because he is named after a Guitar legend!

Keep updated with all new release news & more on my website

www.afterlifesaga.com
Never miss out, sign up to the
mailing list at the website.

Also, please feel free to join myself and other Dravenites on my Facebook group
Afterlife Saga Official Fan
Interact with me and other fans. Can't wait to see you there!

facebook.com/AfterlifeSaga
twitter.com/afterlifesaga
instagram.com/theafterlifesaga

Acknowledgements

Well first and foremost my love goes out to all the people who deserve the most thanks and are the wonderful people that keep me going day to day. But most importantly they are the ones that allow me to continue living out my dreams and keep writing my stories for the world to hopefully enjoy… These people are of course YOU! Words will never be able to express the full amount of love I have for you guys. Your support is never ending. Your trust in me and the story is never failing. But more than that, your love for me and all who you consider your 'Afterlife family' is to be commended, treasured and admired. Thank you just doesn't seem enough, so one day I hope to meet you all and buy you all a drink! ;)

To my family… To my amazing mother, who has believed in me from the very beginning and doesn't believe that something great should be hidden from the world. I would like to thank you for all the hard work you put into my books and the endless hours spent caring about my words and making sure it is the best it can be for everyone to enjoy. You make Afterlife shine. To my wonderful crazy father who is and always has been my hero in life. Your strength astonishes me, even to this day and the love and care you hold for your family is a gift you give to the Hudson name. And last but not least, to the man that I consider my soul mate. The man who taught me about real love and makes me not only want to be a better person but makes me feel I am too. The amount of support you have given me since we met has been incredible and the greatest feeling was finding out you wanted to spend the rest of your life with me when you asked me to marry you.

All my love to my dear husband and my own personal Draven… Mr Blake Hudson.

Another personal thank you goes to my dear friend Caroline Fairbairn and her wonderful family that have embraced my brand of crazy into their lives and given it a hug when most needed.

For their friendship I will forever be eternally grateful.

I would also like to mention Claire Boyle my wonderful PA, who without a doubt, keeps me sane and constantly smiling through all the chaos which is my life ;) And a loving mention goes to Lisa Jane for always giving me a giggle and scaring me to death with all her count down pictures lol ;)

Thank you for all your hard work and devotion to the saga and myself. And always going that extra mile, pushing Afterlife into the spotlight you think it deserves. Basically helping me achieve my secret goal of world domination one day…evil laugh time… Mwahaha! Joking of course ;)

As before, a big shout has to go to all my wonderful fans who make it their mission to spread the Afterlife word and always go the extra mile. I love you all x

Also By Stephanie Hudson

Afterlife Saga

A Brooding King, A Girl running from her past. What happens when the two collide?

Book 1 - Afterlife

Book 2 - The Two Kings

Book 3 - The Triple Goddess

Book 4 - The Quarter Moon

Book 5 - The Pentagram Child /Part 1

Book 6 - The Pentagram Child /Part 2

Book 7 - The Cult of the Hexad

Book 8 - Sacrifice of the Septimus /Part 1

Book 9 - Sacrifice of the Septimus /Part 2

Book 10 - Blood of the Infinity War

Book 11 - Happy Ever Afterlife /Part 1

Book 12 - Happy Ever Afterlife / Part 2

Transfusion Saga

What happens when an ordinary human girl comes face to face with the cruel Vampire King who dismissed her seven years ago?

Transfusion - Book 1

Venom of God - Book 2

Blood of Kings - Book 3

Rise of Ashes - Book 4

Map of Sorrows - Book 5

Tree of Souls - Book 6

Kingdoms of Hell – Book 7

Eyes of Crimson - Book 8

Afterlife Chronicles: (Young Adult Series)

The Glass Dagger – Book 1

The Hells Ring – Book 2

Stephanie Hudson and Blake Hudson

The Devil in Me

OTHER WORKS BY HUDSON INDIE INK

Paranormal Romance/Urban Fantasy

Sloane Murphy

Xen Randell

C. L. Monaghan

Sci-fi/Fantasy

Brandon Ellis

Devin Hanson

Crime/Action

Blake Hudson

Mike Gomes

Contemporary Romance

Gemma Weir

Elodie Colt

Ann B. Harrison